To Tabby

EMERALD GREENE

AND THE WITCH STONES

Daniel Blythe

Daniel Blythe

ACORN BOOKS
WWW.ACORNBOOKS.CO.UK

This edition published in 2014 by
Acorn Books
www.acornbooks.co.uk

Acorn Books is an imprint of
Andrews UK Limited
www.andrewsuk.com

Contents

To Elinor Sarah Madeleine and Samuel James William
For past, present and future.

EMERALD GREENE
AND THE WITCH STONES

Part One

A Door is Opened

1

New Girl in Town

'She's a bit weird,' said Jessica Mathieson, over the noise of the end-of-school bell.

Richie Fanshawe looked up from his *Fortean Times* and blinked at Jess over his ham sandwich. 'Have you spoken to her?' he asked.

'Just seen her.' Jess indicated the upper floor of the school with a toss of her long brown hair. 'She's sitting upstairs. I think she starts tomorrow.'

'Well, weird is relative,' Richie said. He tapped his magazine. 'Corn circles in Devon, now *they're* weird.'

'Really?' Jess frowned, leaning on her locker. 'I thought corn circles were, like, so last century?'

'Not in the middle of football pitches.'

'Oh. Right... Well, do you want to see her or not?'

Richie folded the magazine shut and stretched up to his full height - which was still only level with Jess's shoulder. They were both in Year Eight, but he was lagging behind her in the growth stakes. 'Okay, show me, then.'

Pupils were pouring out of all the exits, anxious to get home, so they had to battle against a blue-blazered tide of children to get back upstairs. When they got to Classroom 12, Jess and Richie peered in at the door.

There she was - the Newbie. She was sitting on her own, feet up on the desk, reading a volume of the *Encyclopaedia Britannica*.

Her shiny, tomato-red hair was tucked behind one ear, and she had a hawkish nose on which rested a pair of blue-tinted glasses. Her pale, high-cheekboned face tapered to a pointed chin. The Newbie's blazer and skirt looked new, neatly-pressed. And she was thin. Not scrawny, Jess decided, and not waifish - it was a lean, lithe look, one which hinted at hidden strength. She was wearing school uniform, but with striped black-and-white socks - like the Wicked Witch of the West in *The Wizard Of Oz*, Jess thought. And in contravention of all school rules on jewellery, the girl wore a silver omega-chain around her neck on which a smooth green stone, set into silver, sparkled like a Christmas light.

'Let's go in,' said Jess.

Richie grabbed her arm, held her back. 'Are you sure?'

'Richard Fanshawe, are you a man or a mouse?' Jess opened the door to the musty room, strode up to the Newbie and offered her hand. 'Hi. I'm Jess.'

The girl smiled, looked up as she closed the book. Her green eyes gleamed behind the blue lenses, burning with intelligence. For a second, Jess felt her mouth go dry and almost took a step backwards - as if those eyes were scanning her deeply, reading her every thought.

'Emerald,' said the girl, shaking Jess's hand firmly. Her skin felt marble-cold. 'Emerald Greene. Pleased to meet you.'

She spoke precisely, Jess thought, as if IN CAPITAL LETTERS. This was the kind of thing that usually got you teased.

'So where have they sent you from, then?' Jess asked, perching herself on the desk.

'Nobody sent me,' said the Newbie - Emerald - in her rounded voice. 'I came willingly.'

'Which school were you at before?' Richie asked.

'I have never been to school before,' said Emerald, eyes wide. 'At least, not what you would call school.'

Jessica was good at telling if people were lying or winding her up. The Newbie, frustratingly, appeared to be doing neither. It was perplexing.

It was a year since St Agnes' High School, Meresbury, had unofficially gone mixed. The boys' school two miles down the road, King George VI High, had been burned down one night in an act of sabotage, and its six hundred pupils had been redistributed throughout the county. The girls had quickly assimilated their fifty-three newcomers. Emerald, though, was the first new girl to arrive in their year, and it seemed she would take some getting used to.

'Where do you live?' asked Jess.

'Live?' The girl frowned for a second. 'Oh, I see. Yes, I live at Rubicon House.'

'Where's that?' asked Jessica.

'It is a large house, near Beeches Point. At the edge of the Darkwater.' She pushed back a stray lock of red hair and smiled placidly up at them, as if to say that this was all the information she was giving for now. 'Would you excuse me?' she added, swinging her feet down. 'I have some more information to catch up on.' She hefted the encyclopaedia. 'There is rather a lot of it, and this would appear to be only Volume One.'

'You're reading it,' said Jess, and immediately felt stupid.

Emerald gave them a dazzling smile. 'Of course! I find this the best way to acquire information.' She thrust the encyclopaedia into her satchel. 'Now I know about everything from Aardvarks to Bohemia. Time to get my next volume.' She gave them a wave, and strode past them out of the classroom.

Jess and Richie remained rooted to the spot for a moment.

'Okay,' Richie said, tapping his glasses nervously. 'That beats corn circles any day.'

Jess grabbed him by the wrist. 'Come on.'

'Where are we going?'

'Following her, of course!'

Richie looked at his watch. 'My mum thinks I'm at Astronomy Club,' he said reluctantly. 'She's expecting me home for tea at five.'

'Oh, *Richard*! Where's your sense of adventure? Does James Bond go home for tea?'

'But won't your aunt be wondering where you are?'

'She can wonder. Come *on*!'

Afternoon shoppers filled the Old Town - elderly couples, students gossiping, children trailing unwillingly to supermarkets with parents. Outside the gate of Meresbury Cathedral, a juggler on a unicycle had drawn a small crowd.

Jess and Richie didn't have time to stop. Dodging between shop-fronts, they tailed Emerald Greene at a discreet distance, Jess leading the way and Richie hiding behind her. They crossed the Cathedral Close, passing through the jagged shadow of the

Cathedral itself. A couple of times, Emerald seemed about to turn around and they ducked back into the shadows.

They followed her across the open garden at the side of the Cathedral, which led to a gap in the old city walls and some stone steps down to the main road. They were just in time to see Emerald disappearing down the steps.

Jess jumped the chain and cut across the lawns, leaving Richie to trail in her wake. They got to the ringroad in time to look down and see Emerald boarding a Number 32 bus, which closed its doors with a swish and started to pull out.

Richie caught her up, panting for breath. 'We can't chase a bus,' he pointed out.

'Taxi!' exclaimed Jess with a glint in her eye, looking up and down the streets.

'What?'

'Well, it's what people do in movies. They leap into a taxi and say, "Follow that car!" And the driver says "I've been waiting all my life for someone to say that!"'

Richie scanned the busy ringroad. 'I can't see any taxis,' he pointed out. 'I doubt we could afford one, anyway.'

Jess shrugged, and slumped dejectedly on the bus-shelter seat. 'I suppose "follow that bus" doesn't have the same ring to it.' She sighed, chin in her hand.

'So this is where we fall down,' said Richie despondently. 'James Bond can *drive*.'

'Where does the 32 bus go?' Jess wondered aloud. She jumped up, ran her finger down the list of destinations on the wall. 'Beeches Point... That's out near the Darkwater.' Jessica shivered, and for a minute it was as if the passing cars and buses zooming around the Meresbury ringroad belonged to another world. 'But that's where she said she lived... *Rubicon House at Beeches Point...*'

'My mum said you'd get me into trouble,' Richie muttered.

'Oh, for goodness' sake, Rich. Don't be a wet blanket.' Jess's eyes narrowed in determination. 'Look, we can catch a number 54 round to the other side... Come on!'

On the escarpment, the land was steep, studded with boulders, ugly and menacing. The dip slope rolled more gently, bracken giving way to a forest of conifers about a hundred metres away. A few farm buildings were scattered across the moors, but otherwise it was an empty landscape, quiet and still in the setting sun.

'I'm really late for tea, now,' said Richie awkwardly, scrambling through the bracken behind Jess and trying to polish his glasses on his handkerchief.

At the edge of the pine forest, they ducked for cover. Jess liked the pungent, comforting Christmas-smell of the trees, which made her think of oranges and wrapping paper and melting candles in jars. The sun was low over the glittering Darkwater, shards of orange dancing in the glassy blue-black.

'There!' said Richie suddenly, and pointed.

Up ahead, they saw Emerald Greene approach a large, empty clearing. Jess nudged Richie and, heads down, they slipped between the pine-trees, keeping the Newbie in sight. Emerald appeared to be in no hurry, strolling round the clearing with her hands in her pockets and whistling.

To their right, the sun peeped though the forest and pulled long shadows across the earth.

Hardly daring to breathe, they crept along the pine-needle-covered earth. They watched as Emerald stepped into the clearing.

They saw her stroll across it, apparently checking something on her watch, then they saw her stop and stretch out her arms as if feeling for something, palms flat like a mime artist.

What happened next was completely impossible.

The afternoon sunlight was painfully bright in Jess's eyes and for a second she had to shut them. And when she opened her eyes, the clearing was completely empty.

Jess looked at Richie, open-mouthed. His eyes were wide.

'I blinked,' he said. 'Where did she go?'

Jess rubbed her eyes. 'I blinked as well. She was there a second ago, right?'

'Right,' said Richie, but he didn't sound too confident.

'It must be a trick of the light,' said Jess firmly. She ran forward, pushing thorns and branches out of her way, and emerged into the clearing, feeling the sun on her skin. There was a slight breeze, which hissed in the rustling aspens and tugged at her hair.

'Emerald!' she called out loud. 'Emerald!'

There was no sign of Emerald Greene.

It was unnaturally silent apart from the breeze - no birdsong, nor any woodland creatures. Also, there was an odd taste in Jessica's mouth - a cold and bitter tang.

'Can you taste that?' she asked Richie, who had followed her into the clearing.

He nodded. 'Like metal.' Suddenly Richie was shivering and pulling his blazer tightly around him. 'Look, um, Jess - I don't want to go on about it, but I should be getting home.'

'Yeah,' she said abstractedly. She squatted down, scooped handfuls of pine-needles and ran them between her fingers. 'It's got to be some kind of illusion,' she murmured to herself.

Richie wasn't listening, though. 'Um... you see, the thing is...' He cleared his throat and took his glasses off to polish them again. 'I'm not terribly brave, really. Sorry and all that.'

'It's okay,' said Jess with a sigh. 'I prefer honest people to brave people.'

Richie smiled awkwardly and put his glasses back on.

Jessica straightened up and took one last look around the clearing. 'I'm going to come back here. I'm going to solve this if it's the last thing I do.' She nudged the pale Richie in the ribs. 'C'mon, let's get back.'

The clearing remained silent, still and empty. Sunlight - the heavy, treacly light of early evening - dripped through the leaves on to the forest floor.

For a second, there was a brief, faint rustling, as if something had been disturbed - it could have been the sound of an animal, or maybe the swish of a girl's skirt as she moved. But there was still nothing to be seen.

2

The Investigation Begins

Jess slammed the front door shut and hurried down the steps to the road, shoving schoolbooks into the last few spaces left in her bag.

'Eight forty-two,' she muttered, glancing at her watch. 'Well, I might just do it.'

Jessica Mathieson and her Aunt Gabi lived at 38, Chadwick Road, a handsome Victorian terrace on the outskirts of Meresbury. It sported a trim front garden with geraniums, thorn-bushes and a hydrangea. It looked pleasant this morning, dappled with sunlight, but Jess - late for school, her mind buzzing from the previous day - was in no mood to appreciate its charms.

Late, she thought. *Going to be late again.*

The air was chilly in her lungs as she began her descent, and a listless sun was peeping out from behind the clouds. Below her in the valley, the Cathedral gleamed, jutting above the city on its hill, its golden spire reaching up into the morning haze. Beyond the city, greenish moorland rolled away into the blue-white distance. As she rounded the corner into Montrose Avenue, she saw a cat perched on the street-sign, its tail trailing over the A. It wore a plain collar with something shiny inlaid into it. The cat was making the most of the sunlight and its sharp, green eyes seemed to follow her as she hurried along.

Jessica frowned, shaking off the sense of unease again. They'd never had pets in the house. Aunt Gabi had allergies, and most animals made her eyes water or set her off sneezing for a good half-hour. So Jess wasn't used to cats, and she found them unsettling.

Creepy. Just like the feeling in the forest clearing yesterday.

She hurried on. A cloud passed across the sun, flooding the street with shadow and making Jessica shiver slightly.

'You're going to be late, you know,' said a smooth voice from behind her. 'No point letting it worry you.'

She whirled around, almost dropping her school-bag. Heart thumping, she looked up and down the road, searching for the origin of the voice.

The street behind her was empty. Just suburban houses with neat lawns, all in a line, stretching uphill towards the recreation ground. The road in front of her was also quiet and still. A distant lorry thundered on the main road, and somewhere across town a police-siren wailed.

The black cat sprang off the road-sign, landed nimbly and trotted across the street on its own private mission.

Jess blinked. 'Must've imagined it,' she told herself firmly.

And yet, she knew she *had* heard the voice, rich and velvety-smooth like chocolate.

Jess shook her head. This was silly. She hoisted her bag on her shoulder, narrowed her eyes and headed on her walk to school, quickening her pace.

'Well,' she said to herself, 'so I may be late today. There's got to be a first time.'

As Jessica rounded the corner and disappeared out of sight, the cat, which was curled up on the pavement on the far side of Montrose Avenue, watched her go. It lifted its head and its eyes seemed to sparkle a glittering green.

Or it could just have been the reflection of the sun, passing for a second outside its filmy cover of cloud.

'Sorry I'm late, sir.'

Mr Stone raised his eyebrows as Jess scurried into her form room, out of breath, just after the bell, but then just nodded. Leeann Brooks and one or two other girls turned, giving triumphant looks - Jess Mathieson, the golden girl, was never late.

Jess scanned the room. Yes, there she was, sitting at the front of the class, looking perky and attentive. The Newbie. Emerald Greene. And the only seat available was right next to her.

Jess sat down gingerly, as if afraid the seat might be hot. Emerald turned her head and gave her what would, from anyone else, have been a welcoming smile.

'Rrright!'

Mr Stone always rolled his Rs. Aunt Gabi described him as having a 'nice Scots burr', which had made Jessica think of the little green things which clung to your clothes in the garden.

'Now, then,' said Mr Stone, and raised an eyebrow in the direction of Leeann Brooks, who had her feet on the desk. Leeann swung her legs down with a token show of resistance. Mr Stone put his palms flat on the desk and leaned forward. 'Good morning, 8A. Firrst things firrst. I'd like to welcome a new student to the class today.' He gestured towards the Newbie.

'Yeah, and she's weird,' muttered Leeann.

There was a ripple of laughter. Jess, feeling guilty, bit her lip and glanced at the Newbie, but Emerald did not seem in the least bothered - in fact, she smiled knowingly, as if being weird was something she was perfectly happy about.

'Don't be so rrrude, Leeann Brooks,' said Mr Stone in a dark, serious voice. 'We welcome everrry-one in this school.' He paused. 'Besides, some people would find you quite unnaturally terrrr-ifying if they met you on a storr-my night.' There was a ripple of laughter, and Leeann blushed.

Mr Stone moved to stand behind the Newbie.

'This is Emerald Greene. She'll be joining 8A from this week, and I want you to make her feel welcome.' He smiled, then gestured towards Jess. 'I'm going to put you in Jessica's capable hands, Emerald. She will be your guide, companion and men-torrr.'

Everyone turned to stare at Jessica. She looked up in alarm, feeling as if the bottom had dropped out of her stomach.

'That is, someone who acts in an advisorrr-y capacity. Someone who is there to convey their experrr-ience and their knowledge when needed.' He wiggled his eyebrows. 'It's usually someone devastatingly charrr-ming and intelligent, such as myself. But as I'm, ah, kind of tied up with teaching a few classes, I thought I'd delegate.'

'I see,' said Jess, biting her lip. She wasn't sure she was up to being a mentor, as it was not something she had ever done before. 'I'll try, sir,' she offered.

Mr Stone started the register, and the twenty-eight girls and four boys answered with varying degrees of boredom.

Jess felt something dig into her side. She gasped, looked down. It was a bony elbow. Emerald Greene had nudged Jess sharply in the ribs.

'I would not worry,' whispered Emerald Greene in a calm, serious tone. 'I am sure we will manage to get on very well.'

'I hope so,' replied Jess politely, and she managed a weak smile.

Underneath it, though, she had the most tremendous sense of unease and foreboding. Everything she'd seen so far made her think that Emerald Greene spelt trouble - and trouble of a very odd kind indeed.

Aunt Gabi had managed to lose her keys again, and she had to run some errands before she started at the shop today. It wasn't a good time to be dealing with a pushy suitor.

'No, Miguel, look,' she was saying patiently, the phone cradled under her chin as she frantically unpacked her college bag. 'I keep telling you, evenings are *no good...*'

There was an unhappy babble on the other end of the line. Gabi upturned her bag on to the dining-room table and inspected the contents under her reading-lamp.

'No - no, I'm sorry, but I have a hungry teenager to support, precious... I'm working God-forsaken hours down at the Spar and doing my college course, darling, and I really can't - '

There was more babbling. She sighed with relief as she found her keys wedged into her folder of notes.

'Relationship?' Gabi exclaimed. 'Miguel, I hardly think we can call it a relationship. We've had two cups of coffee. And one of them was decaf. Look, we'll do lunch sometime, okay? Gotta go. Ciao, darling. *Mmwah.*' She clicked the phone off with an audible sigh of relief and threw it into the waste-paper basket. '*Hasta la vista,* baby,' she muttered, and bit into an apple.

The reading-lamp flickered. Gabi tutted, told herself to make sure she got the bulb fixed. There was never time for all the little things like that. Young Jess, she thought, was remarkably tolerant of the house falling apart. Armed with purse and keys, Gabi strode towards the front door, apple jammed in her mouth, just as the phone started ringing again. Insistently.

Gabi sighed in exasperation. She retrieved the phone and thumbed Talk, forgetting to take the apple out of her mouth first. 'Mmm-hmmff?' she said.

First of all, there seemed to be no sound but a wash of static, or possibly heavy breathing.

Aunt Gabi grimaced. *That's all I need*, she thought - *a crank caller*. She removed the apple and said calmly, 'Listen, you creep, I can hear you. Don't think you're freaking me out, because you're not. Got it?'

Another sound was growing in the background, though. A slow crescendo of *singing*. At first she thought the prankster had switched on a CD or something, but there was a fullness to the sound, a richness, as if the women's voices were wrapping themselves around her head. The singing was beautiful, melancholy, yet somehow rough-edged, not like anything one normally heard. And Gabi found herself rooted to the spot, half in fear and half in fascination.

The reading-lamp flickered again and dimmed.

The women's voices were growing louder, and she now seemed to hear them *inside* her head. And she found her eyes fixed on the reading-lamp, which now appeared to be filled with a crackly, blue light -

Bang bang bang, went the front door.

And in a split second, Aunt Gabi was back in her dining-kitchen, holding the phone. The lamp was just an old reading-lamp and there was no sound from the telephone at all. She stared into the receiver, holding it at arm's length as if she expected it to bite her.

Bang bang bang. Someone was knocking persistently.

Gabi threw the receiver aside, paused in the hallway to smooth her dishevelled hair and went to the front door. She took a moment to compose herself and opened the door.

Two men stood there, long dark coats framed in the early-evening light. One was about fifty, burly, with a pink complexion and a thick grey moustache. The other was black, young, with a bald head, a square goatee beard and trendy glasses. Good-looking, she thought. She smiled winsomely at the younger man.

They flipped ID cards at her. 'Good afternoon, ma'am,' growled the older man. 'Courtney, Special Measures Division. This is my colleague, Mr Odell.'

Gabi gave them the same suspicious, head-to-toe appraisal which all her doorstep callers got, from brush salesmen to the Jehovah's Witnesses.

'What's the "Special Measures Division" when it's at home?' she demanded.

'We're never at home.' This time, it was the young Mr Odell who spoke, giving her a brief smile. 'Too busy, you see.'

'You're Miss LaForge, the home-owner?' Mr Courtney asked.

'Nope. I'm Ms LaForge, the home-owner. Close, but no cigar.'

'Fine. Have it your way, *Ms* LaForge.' Mr Courtney nodded politely. 'Have you noticed anything... unusual happening in this neighbourhood in the last few days? Anything, shall we say, out of the ordinary?'

Gabi drew breath, raised her eyebrows and leaned against the door. 'Oooh, well, depends what you mean,' she said. She decided to keep her distance from these two, because she wasn't getting good vibes from them at all. 'Debbie Graham at number 27 - divorced, you know - she had two pints of milk on Thursday. And that Liam Johnson over the road, he's been getting in with the wrong sort at school. Mind you...' Gabi lowered her voice. The two men leaned nearer, Mr Odell with his pencil poised over his notebook. 'I always had my doubts. Eyebrows too close together, if you know what I mean.' She gave a knowing nod, leaned back and folded her arms.

The two men exchanged glances.

Mr Courtney held up an A3 poster. It featured the grinning face of a man in his fifties or sixties, super-imposed over a picture of a stone circle. Underneath, in big black letters, it read:

PROFESSOR EDWIN ULVERSTON, MA (Oxon), PhD, FBA, MIFA

invites the citizens of Meresbury to witness a historic event!
The opening of an **ancient Viking tomb**
within the Ten Sisters Stones at Scratchcombe Edge
Monday 14th September, from 7.30pm at the Plateau

ADMISSION: FREE.

'Have you seen this before?' Mr Courtney asked.

Gabi shrugged. 'Of course. They're all over the place. My niece is going with a group from school, in fact.' She narrowed her eyes. 'Why? What's up?'

'Classified information,' snarled Mr Courtney. He nodded at Mr Odell, who snapped his notebook shut. 'If you experience anything unusual, anything at all... *unearthly*, in the next few days, ma'am,' said Mr Courtney sternly, 'I'd be much obliged if you could call this number.' He gave her a silver business-card. 'Understood?'

'Oh, absolutely.' Gabi gave him a brief, scrappy salute. 'I'll be straight on that blower, never you fear.'

'Right,' said Mr Courtney, frowning sternly. 'I'll bid you good day, then.'

They turned to go, but just as Gabi was closing the door in relief, Mr Odell turned back. 'Oh, one other thing, Ms LaForge,' he said, index finger raised.

'Yes?' said Gabi.

'Lock the door at night. There are some funny people around.' He nodded politely to her, and turned to follow his superior down the steps.

Gabi, frowning at this last comment, found herself scurrying into the lounge to watch where the men went. She twitched her net curtains open and peered out - just in time to see them getting into a sleek, black car with tinted windows, which was parked at the end of the street. It moved off, smoothly and swiftly.

Gabi went back into the dining kitchen and, treading very carefully, approached the reading-lamp. It seemed to be back to normal again.

All the same...

She shivered, and switched off the lamp at the mains.

Richie Fanshawe dreamed of going into space.

It had been Richie's dream since he was little, when he'd watched the NASA Space Shuttle taking off on the TV news. It had not deterred him when his older brother Tom told him that one of them had blown up once and that everyone on board had been killed. Richie had later written a poem about the *Challenger* and its crew, these distant voyagers who had died years before he was born, and it had won a national competition.

When Richie wasn't scouring the astronomical news, he listened to short-wave radio, trying to pick out a pattern in the bleeps and crackles. His prize possession was an illuminated globe of the Moon - a present from Tom, who had turned out all right now that he was grown-up and working.

Ever since he could remember, Richie had been drawing pictures of himself as a spaceman, either planting the Union Flag on the moon's surface, or re-entering Earth's atmosphere in a capsule, or battling multi-headed alien invaders. He wasn't sure about the last bit - he liked to think that if he ever met any alien life-forms he'd sit down and chat to them rather than zap their tentacles - but at the end of the day, they might be bad guys and someone would have to defeat them.

People laughed at him, of course. Partly because he didn't look much like an astronaut. People always laughed at you if you loved something, Richie realised. Love was weak, love was poncy, love was for girls. Except football. You could love a football team and nobody would call you names. Richie wasn't much good at football, though, and he didn't have a favourite team or player. In PE lessons, he'd be the last to be picked. He would spend the game shivering on the wing, not able to see much without his glasses, hoping that the ball wouldn't hit him. If he didn't get muddy and the game came nowhere near him, then it was a good result.

Jess seemed to understand him, or at least tolerate him. She treated him a bit like a younger brother.

Luckily, Richie's talents meant that he wasn't often bullied - he was in demand as a resident boffin. Barely a week went by without a pupil asking him to help write a computer program or mend their iPod. He was thinking of charging for his services.

Today, at lunchtime in the deserted IT room, he had another mission - only this time, it was one of his own.

He typed 'Rubicon House' into the search engine, and clicked on the first website he found. Text flowed on to the screen, alongside a picture of an imposing Georgian mansion.

Richie blinked. 'She lives *there*? You're kidding!'

He kept reading - and after about the second paragraph, he blinked again, sat back in his chair and felt a shiver run through his body.

Well, *that* couldn't be right. Could it?

And then he found he had another problem.

'Where's *that* coming from?' he said out loud.

There was an odd noise coming from the speakers. *Singing.* It echoed in the room, and now it was bouncing round the inside of his head as if in a giant cavern. A great, echoing cavern of stone and a glittering lake of sheer, black water.

Where did that appear from? The image, as clear as a picture on the screen, was right inside his head.

The songs seemed almost tangible. Richie blinked as it tickled his nostrils: a musty, damp, vegetable odour. The hot smells of computer and carpet were permeated with it, a cold, underground *wetness* which -

He had to reach out and touch the coldness. Taste it. And the only way to do that was to reach for the bright lights of the pixels, to reach into the harsh voices of the song, to step forward from the darkness and *walk right in* -

The screen was suffused with a cold, hard light, shining brighter than computer screens were ever meant to. The angry singing was now at an incredible pitch, strong and urgent, the same discordant song over and over.

And then - a bone-shaking *bang!* like a car backfiring. Richie leapt to the floor, hid under a desk and covered his head. Smoke was pouring out of the back of the computer, and the screen was flashing like a strobe light.

Richie could feel the floor vibrating.

A second later, a whirling mass of flame shot through the air - right through the spot where Richie had been sitting - and hit the back wall with a *whoomph* and a noise like sizzling sausages.

There was a horribly pungent smell of burning. In its wake, a great billow of choking, rubbery smoke rolled through the room.

Cautiously, he looked up, coughing and wafting the smoke away.

The shattered screen yawned open, resembling a toothed predator, while thousands of globules of molten plastic and metal were dotted across the back wall of the IT Room. The liquefied fragments of computer dribbled down the walls like something out of an unpleasant cookery accident.

'Wow,' said Richie unsteadily, lifting his head. 'Now that's what I *call* a bug.'

Looking after Emerald Greene proved to be an eye-opening experience for Jessica, in more ways than one. In General Science, Mr Gretton was explaining the theory behind the acceleration due to gravity. He dropped a tennis-ball and a lead weight through a laser beam to demonstrate it, and was about to put the equation up on the whiteboard when Emerald's hand shot up.

'Sir,' she said crossly, 'the acceleration due to gravity is not ten metres per second squared. It is nine point eight one.'

There were a few groans from the back of the room, derisive laughs, and a not-quite-under-the-breath catcall of, 'Girly swot!'

Mr Gretton beamed. 'Well, that's absolutely right, er...' He peered at her, obviously unable to remember her name.

'Emerald Greene, sir.'

'Well, Emerald, I think you can have a house point for knowing that. However - '

'I was not seeking any kind of reward, sir,' said Emerald, causing Mr Gretton to blink in astonishment. 'I just wanted to point it out. If you are always rounding up to ten in your calculations, then I expect science will be put back several centuries by imprecision.'

Lesson two was French. Halfway through a practice of simple likes and dislikes, Emerald put her hand up and asked Miss Bridie a question in completely fluent, colloquial French - at least, this was how it sounded to Jess. Miss Bridie, taken aback, sat down heavily and answered Emerald with her usual precision, before sending her away for a solo chat with Yves, the Assistant. Jess, despite making protestations, couldn't go with her.

And then double Maths in lessons three and four. Emerald slammed down her pen in frustration, making Jessica jump and causing Ms James to swing round instantly.

'Is something wrong?' asked Ms James quietly, her brow creasing under her spiky blonde hair.

'These algebraic equations, Ms James,' said Emerald, narrowing her eyes and folding her arms. 'They are rather pointless, are they not?'

Ms James smiled indulgently, like someone who had heard it all before. 'Well, Emerald, it depends what you mean by pointless. Yes, they're not actually applied, but they're examples. They're to help you understand the concepts of algebra - one of the keystones of modern mathematics.'

Emerald put her fingers to her temples and made a growling sound, so unexpected that it made both Jess and Ms James recoil. 'Oh, you do not *understand*! What about the chaos coefficient? Mm?' Emerald opened her palms flat and held them out to Ms James. 'How,' she demanded, 'can we *begin* to calculate variables without the quantum factor?'

Ms James, to her credit, was thrown only for a moment. 'Well, Emerald,' she began, and smiled. 'You do have a point... but sub-atomic physics does fall a *little* way outside the requirements of Key Stage Three. If you like, I can lend you a book?'

Next came Geography, and with it another shock.

Mrs Morris was talking about population growth in cities. 'Now,' she said, pointing to a map of Europe, 'if we take the capital of France, which is - ' She looked round expectantly, and her gaze alighted on Emerald. 'Yes, you, the new girl. With the, ah, *hair*.'

'Emerald Greene, Miss,' said Jess helpfully.

'Yeah, like that's her real *name*,' came a muttered comment from the back.

'Settle down!' snapped Mrs Morris. 'Hand up to speak, if you wouldn't mind, Leeann Brooks. And keep your comments relevant.'

Mrs Morris was a no-nonsense, old-fashioned teacher who didn't hold with modern ideas like girls wearing trousers and boys doing cookery, and she considered the Internet and mobile phones to be part of a vast conspiracy to addle children's brains. What, Jessica wondered, would she make of the bizarre Newbie?

Next to Jess, Emerald sighed and laid down her pen. 'Yes, Miss?'

'The capital of France, girl! Come on, don't hang around!'

'I'm afraid I have no idea,' said Emerald, as if the question were of no consequence. 'Please ask someone else.'

A murmur of unease went around the room. Mrs Morris laid down her pointer on the overhead projector and folded her arms.

'I - beg - your - pardon?' said Mrs Morris, in that slow, measured tone which always meant You Have Said Something Dangerous.

Jessica stared open-mouthed at Emerald, who just shrugged. *It's impossible, thought Jess. She must know. She's just acting up for the sake of it. Only this morning she was rattling away in French like a native. Why is she pretending not to know where Paris is?*

'I have no idea,' said Emerald again, in a bright, perky voice. 'My apologies.' There was a beat of silence, in which things could have gone either way. 'Please do not ask me again,' added Emerald.

Jessica jumped in, for Miss Morris was evidently about to explode. 'It's just her... sense of humour, Miss,' she said quickly, and said the first thing which came into her head. 'She went to an alternative hippy school. In...' (*Somewhere that sounded bohemian... what was that place Gabi was often going on about? Yes...*) 'In Goa. She knows it's Paris really. Don't you, Emerald?'

'No,' said Emerald, her green eyes glittering and her face a picture of innocence. 'I had no idea... Why did you just kick me?' she added.

It was the end of the day, and chattering, blue-blazered hordes streamed towards the gates.

'Look,' Jess said awkwardly, hurrying after Emerald. 'You've got to try and fit in here. Otherwise people will think you're... odd.'

Did Emerald have something wrong with her eyes? They certainly seemed unnaturally bright and piercing. From behind the blue lenses, the Newbie fixed an unblinking, unyielding gaze on Jess.

'Odd?' She seemed amused by the idea.

'Well, yeah. All that stuff you were coming out with in Maths... And don't cheek old Doris Morris - you won't get away with that next time. I saved your neck there. What did you think you were *doing*?'

Emerald nodded as if it was all suddenly clear to her, and gave Jess a broad, friendly smile, full of dazzling, perfect teeth. 'I have embarrassed you. My apologies.'

'No, no...' Jess thumped her school-bag in frustration. 'You didn't embarrass me, Emerald. It's just that you seem... not like everyone else.'

Emerald's smile did not waver. 'Excellent,' she said. 'Why be like everyone else? If you are like everyone else, you may as well not be you, Jessica Mathieson. You may as well cease being an individual.'

It sounded like such a logical answer that Jess, for a moment, was completely thrown. 'I'd... not really thought about it like that,' admitted Jess.

She opened her mouth to ask another question, but Emerald had disappeared. Jess gulped and looked around the playground. A second later she backed into Emerald, who was down on her hands and knees with a magnifying glass.

'Definite traces,' Emerald was muttering. 'Here, of all...' She looked up, appearing to notice Jess looming over her. 'Oh, I see. This is embarrassing again, is it not?'

Jess shook her head. 'What are you playing at?'

Emerald concealed the magnifying-glass in one of the capacious pockets of her duffel-coat. 'I am not at liberty to disclose that for now,' she whispered. 'I shall see you tomorrow?'

'Yes,' said Jessica faintly. 'I expect so.'

Emerald Greene strode off, tomato-red hair bouncing in the sunlight. She didn't turn to look back.

Suddenly, Jessica felt a momentary chill pass over her, as if she'd passed by a grave with a familiar name, or seen a frightening shadow in the bushes at the bottom of the garden. She had a strange, deep sense of something beyond the everyday, but something that she couldn't place or give a name to.

It was just a feeling.

And then, she was sure she could make out, just at the very edge of her hearing, almost round the back of her head like wraparound stereo sound - *singing*.

Choir practice?

Nope. Couldn't be. She was too far from the Hall, and besides, it wasn't a Tuesday.

No, this was the sound of ethereal women's voices, deep in a cavernous room somewhere... a beautiful sound, yet harsh as briars and cold as stone...

She shook her head, and the odd sensation began to pass.

The noise faded from her head and warm sunlight flooded over her again, painting her golden as she stood there, and the world tuned itself back in - car doors slamming, children laughing and squabbling.

As Jess walked home, she was unnaturally nervous, and kept glancing over her shoulder at the sunlit streets, the gleaming cars, the washing billowing in the breeze. She couldn't shake the feeling that she had brushed against something much bigger, deeper and darker than most people ever sensed in their lives.

She had an inkling, too, that there was something dangerous about Emerald Greene, and that if she hung around with her long enough, she'd find out what it was.

And even though the feeling frightened her somewhat, it made her a little bit excited.

At home, she called Richie while she made herself a cup of tea.

'Weird stuff alert,' she said. 'Need to talk about it.'

'You too?' he answered, not sounding surprised.

'You promise not to laugh?'

'Course. Look, Jess, we don't take the mickey out of each other. Scouts' honour.'

'Richie, you're not *in* the Scouts.'

'Okay, well, Astronomy Club honour, then. Just tell me.'

'All right, then.' She took a deep breath. 'I saw this cat on the way to school, right, and I think... well, I think it spoke to me.'

'The cat *spoke* to you? What did it say? Eight out of ten of us prefer CattoBix?'

'You said you'd take me seriously,' she reprimanded him.

'Sorry. So where did it speak to you, then?'

'It was sitting on a street sign, right? Corner of Montrose Avenue. And it told me I was going to be late. Richie, I am deadly serious about this. There was *nobody* else in the road. The cat spoke to me.'

'So this cat not only speaks, it tells the future too.' Richie whistled quietly. 'It could set itself up in business. It could appear on telly.'

'That's just silly, Richie.'

'Sorry.'

'So, come on... what's happened to you?' she asked crossly.

'Okay. I was on the Net this lunch-hour and I got a really nasty virus... Blew the front out of the computer and would have frazzled me if I'd not ducked.'

'Phew...what did you do?' she asked.

'Told Mr Watson. He got the engineers in. He didn't really seem bothered. He says the machines are too old and are always blowing a fuse somewhere.'

'Which is true.'

'Which is true, but this was a bit more than that. I got this... sensation. Like I could smell something damp, and... there was this *singing*.'

Jess's fingertips tingled. 'Like a choir stuck at the bottom of a well?'

'You heard it too?'

'Uh-huh. In the playground. Just after *she* walked off.'

'Blimey, Jess. Is someone having a laugh, do you think?'

'If they are, it's not funny. I tell you, Rich, whatever is going on in our school is somehow connected with *her* - and we've got to find out what she's up to before it's too late!'

'Something else, too,' he said. 'What I was looking up, when the computer blew a fuse.'

Jess listened as Richie told her what he'd discovered from the website about Rubicon House. It was a splendid, old building, one of the best-known and best-loved stately homes in the county. Or at least, it had been - until it had burnt down in an unexplained fire in 1912. Nothing remained of Rubicon House, not even a shell - the authorities had stripped away its blackened beams and its burnt stones, and now the forest had grown up around it, trees which were nearly a hundred years old obscuring the place where the house had once stood.

'I don't get it,' said Jess, when Richie had finished. 'Why would she pretend to live somewhere that doesn't exist?'

'You know what?' Richie said. 'It's a flipping good thing Emerald Greene wasn't around a few hundred years ago. The people round here would have burnt her as a witch.'

'I think you're right, Rich... I think you're right.'

That weekend, it was warm for September. The residents of Meresbury found themselves in shirt-sleeves and summer dresses again. On Sunday morning, the pungent smells of fresh grass and car-wax drifted over the suburbs, while the snip-snip-snip of secateurs and the whirr of lawnmowers punctuated the glorious pealing of the Cathedral bells.

At sunset, though, things changed rapidly. The temperature dropped and black clouds began massing above the Mere Valley. People scurried outside to bring their washing in and stack their tools away in their sheds, just as the first ominous roll of thunder boomed across the moors.

In the darkening streets of the old town, fringed with their neat Tudor gables, lamps had begun to glow early. Umbrellas sprouted above the waitresses, the barmen and the late-night shop assistants who were hurrying to work. The Cathedral floodlights came on, bathing the stonework in a soft honey-gold glow.

And then the rain began. First with a pit and a pat, edgy and nervous on the awnings of shops, as if it were feeling its way.

The pitter and the patter grew by the second into a loud rushing as the drops formed bars of rain, striking the pavements and the Cathedral Close, making little silver sparkles; then the bars massed into torrents, filling the air with brackish water. The torrents formed great, foaming puddles. Grey pavements were sheened like glass and umbrellas sagged under the weight of the water. Young couples pulled jackets over their heads as they hurried for the shelter of pubs and restaurants. In just a few minutes, the whole of the City of Meresbury was cold, grey and awash.

In Chadwick Road, the rain gurgled into drains and hammered on slate roofs. The occasional car sloshed its way home, its headlamps picking out the dancing raindrops in cones of light.

Aunt Gabi pulled the curtains tightly to, shivering a little, and switched on the television for the local news on County TV.

A pinstripe-suited man in his fifties was the studio guest, holding forth about something important. His hair was white, with a hint of curls, and he had a proud Roman nose, white teeth and bright blue eyes. A caption gave his name as Professor Edwin Ulverston.

Gabi suddenly realised she had seen the name before.

'Hey, Jess,' she called, 'it's that mad professor bloke. The one Cameron's - er, Mr Stone's taking you to see.'

Jessica, coming in from the kitchen, noticed the correction, but she smiled and didn't say anything.

'It's a hugely important find,' Professor Ulverston was saying in a mellow voice which commanded authority. 'I think it could be the first really big archaeological event of this century.' He sat back, and treated the audience to a toothy grin.

'Now, Professor,' said the smooth presenter, Mike Devenish, 'the local and national media will be there, of course - but you've chosen to make this a very special day in another way for the people of Meresbury, haven't you?'

Professor Ulverston seemed to be enjoying the interview immensely, to the point where he appeared to be trying not to laugh out loud. 'Yes, absolutely!' he boomed, and his eyes bulged.

'I feel it's *vital* to show the young people of the area some of the important work we do, so I've invited several schools and colleges to bring groups along.' He leaned forward, grinning conspiratorially, and lowered his voice to a whisper. 'It'll be a tremendous *hoot!*'

Jess, sipping a Diet Coke, watched with detached interest. She knew all about Professor Ulverston's project - they'd been doing it in their Local Studies module for weeks, in preparation for their visit to his dig. The Professor had made a wide-ranging study of the Ten Sisters stone circle on a desolate part of the moors known as Scratchcombe Edge. The stones were ancient, that much was certain, but they had never been the subject of a proper survey before. So, armed with the latest equipment, the Professor's team had spent weeks measuring and logging every last detail of the circle.

In the last few weeks, however, Ulverston had thrown the academic world into disarray with an astounding discovery. He claimed to have evidence that the tomb of a Viking warrior had been placed beneath the stones - in fact, that the western keystone had been displaced for the very purpose of a full ritual burial. Ulverston, ambitious like all academics, had used all his connections to allow an excavation of the ground beneath the circle. Ulverston would not reveal what he had discovered so far - rather, he had set a date for what he promised would be a spectacular revelation, and had sat back to let the media do its business.

The Professor waggled a finger at the camera. 'Believe me, they'll be fascinated. After all,' he added with satisfaction, 'I am the country's leading expert on megalithic structures.'

'Yes, Professor - so we've established.' Mike Devenish gave a slightly weary smile. 'But tell me, isn't an excavation of this kind fraught with hazards?'

Professor Ulverston gave a snort of disapproval and leaned forward, his face flushing a deeper shade of pink under the studio lights. 'Absolute rubbish!' he exclaimed, waggling a finger. His big blue eyes opened wide again, fixing Devenish with a look of authority. 'The opening of this tomb has been planned like a military operation! I assure you that we have done everything to ensure that the stones are *completely* unharmed.'

'Now,' said Mike Devenish, his smile intact, 'throughout history, the Ten Sisters have been associated with numerous myths and legends, haven't they, Professor?'

'Of course they have,' grumbled the Professor, waving a dismissive hand and scowling. 'Come on, Mr Davenant. Every site attracts its fair share of gullible nincompoops and moon-worshippers.'

'So, Professor, your message to the viewers on *Mike's Open Mike* is that you don't have any time for these people?' persisted Devenish.

'Weeeeell, come on. They eat too many lentils, you know. It can addle the brain, hmmmm? Believe that claptrap if you want.' And the Professor beamed again, his teeth shining like beacons in the studio.

'One of the legends you may choose to believe,' Mike Devenish went on, to the camera, 'is the story of the Ten Sisters, the young girls who went dancing on the moors one night. The story goes that they were lured by the Devil to dance on the Sabbath day rather than going to church, and were turned to stone in the morning sun. Any thoughts on that story, Professor?'

The Professor's eyes twinkled. 'A great many people have a vivid imagination,' he said solemnly. 'They should be encouraged to go into television. Fortunately, Mr Dervish, science is about *facts*, not fairy stories.'

Mike was unfazed. 'Well, we shall be there, Devil or not, to cover the historic event - live, with me, Mike *Devenish*. Professor Ulverston, thank you very much... Now, let's see what the weekend weather has in store. Jan, it's been a bit changeable these past few days, hasn't it?...'

'How's your new friend getting on?' Aunt Gabi asked Jessica over their hurried, informal supper.

Jessica looked up. 'Um... she does... odd things,' she said eventually, with a shrug.

In truth, Jessica was getting pretty hacked-off with Emerald Greene. For one thing, she appeared to live in her own little world and only acknowledged other people - even Jess, her supposed mentor - when she felt like it.

At break-times, Emerald appeared to be conducting her own little survey of the school buildings. Out would come the blue glasses and she would stroll back and forth, tapping the bricks and making notes on what looked like a palm-top computer (which always vanished into a pocket if anyone came close). Once, Jess and Richie watched her in fascination as she unrolled a lead weight on a piece of string and swung it like a pendulum over the bottom step. 'Major *weird* points,' was Jess's comment.

Furthermore, Emerald seemed to find most classwork insultingly easy. She would fling down her pen after a minute or so and lean back in her chair, hands behind her head, looking bored and humming quietly. A disbelieving teacher would usually come over, glance at her work and do a double take, before picking up and reading what turned out to be a 100% accurate set of maths questions, or a cross-section of an escarpment with all the strata correctly labelled.

On the other hand, she found some things impossible. She would gnaw her pen to shreds, pick angrily at the paper of the worksheet and sit there sulkily, her arms folded. If the teacher asked her what was wrong, she would argue that the problem was too basic. 'There *must* be information you are withholding!' she would exclaim, or, 'The parameters are *not* correctly defined!'

It drove the teachers to distraction - and if Jess was honest, she felt a lot of sympathy with them.

It was also difficult to have a conversation with Emerald Greene. Jessica couldn't put her finger on what precisely disturbed her about the Newbie's manner, but after a couple of days she had realised - Emerald couldn't *chat*. She didn't do the reassuring, meaningless conversations of friendship. If you asked her something, she would give a precise and rounded answer, or none at all, and then she would look at you with her sharp green eyes. And keep looking at you. And still keep looking at you. Until you felt so uncomfortable that you had to blow your nose, or hide behind your cup, or start babbling just to fill the silence.

'But look,' said Aunt Gabi, waggling her glass of wine, 'everyone interesting is odd in some way, darling. Including me,' she added. 'What exactly does she do, then?'

Jessica took another brave forkful of Gabi's vegemince dumpling and tried to chew and swallow without actually tasting it. 'Well,' she began indistinctly, 'I'm supposed to be looking after her and showing her round, but she always seems happier just going off on her own. She doesn't seem to need looking after. And she doesn't like talking. Not properly.'

'Mmmm.... it could be that you aren't talking about the right things,' Aunt Gabi suggested with a smile, her bangles rattling as she served herself a large helping of organic potatoes. 'What's she interested in? Not fashion and boy bands, I take it.'

Jess narrowed her eyes, but Gabi's smile gave away that she was teasing. 'Well... experiments,' said Jess thoughtfully.

'Ah, there you are, then. She's a boffin. She's probably full of fascinating information, if you just give her a chance.' Gabi topped up her wine-glass. 'Want some?'

'No, thanks,' Jess said quickly, covering her glass with her hand.

'There were girls at my school, you know,' said Gabi, 'who didn't fit in. They were the ones who sat in the corner looking serious and reading books. Those "weird" girls might have had the mick taken a bit, but when they got out into the real world they were probably more interesting.' Gabi smiled, gazing into the distance. 'Took me a bit longer, till university. I was a late developer.'

At that moment there was a telephone call.

'Darling, hellooooo,' exclaimed Gabi in delight, putting her feet up and settling down in her long-call pose, phone against her earring-less left ear.

Has to be Gabi's latest admirer, Jess thought. So she covered the remains of the vegemince dumpling in HP Sauce, which made it altogether more palatable, and almost managed to finish it.

When she'd had enough, she scraped the burnt remains into the nearby newspaper, crumpled the paper up tightly and jammed it into the outside dustbin.

'They're *saying* it was an electrical fault,' Richie muttered darkly the next day as he ate his sandwiches on the wall by the sports hall. 'I think it was a bit more than that.'

Jess nodded, idly watching the children running round the playground in their various games. She didn't feel like joining in with anything - there was too much to think about.

'The weather is pleasant today, do you not think?' said a familiar voice. An unmistakable bob of tomato-red hair had appeared beside them.

Emerald sat down beside Richie. She was wearing her duffel-coat again, and was smiling as if she'd just found the secret of eternal youth.

Richie did a double take. 'Um, do you mind?' he said. 'We're, kind of, having a conversation here?'

Emerald held up her finger and narrowed her eyes. 'Oddness,' she said. 'Strangeness. Something in the air. I have been observing you two, and I know you have seen it too.'

'And I suppose,' said Richie with heavy sarcasm, 'that you're as baffled by it all as we are?'

Emerald Greene seemed to give the question serious thought. 'Possibly,' she said, 'but then I do have the advantage of being a little ahead of you... May I see that?' she added politely, pointing to Richie's phone.

Jessica suddenly had a strange feeling that something was going to happen. And a second later, she was proved right.

One minute the small, black phone was sitting in Richie's hand. The next, it seemed to flip over in a somersault and land neatly with a *thwack* in Emerald Greene's palm, as if someone had smacked his hand from underneath.

Jess and Richie gasped.

Emerald Greene, seemingly oblivious to the amazement she had caused, gave the mobile phone a perfunctory examination. 'Hmm,' she said. 'Fairly primitive device. Hand-held, operated by simple rechargeable energy cells... Linked to some kind of transmitter network, I would imagine.' She beamed and held the mobile out for Richie. 'Very interesting. Thank you.'

He took the phone back gingerly, as if expecting it to be hot, and tucked it very carefully into his blazer pocket. 'Yeah,' he said. 'Right,' he added.

Emerald Greene stood up, hands in pockets, and strolled off, whistling an indefinable tune. In her own little world. Her own universe.

'Weird,' said Jess, shaking her head.

'*Well* weird,' Richie agreed.

They both stared after the retreating figure of Emerald Greene for a few moments.

'You know,' Jess said thoughtfully, 'I had two all-chocolate Kit-Kats in a row last week.'

His eyes widened. 'The ones with no biscuit in? You... I *love* it when you get those!' He frowned. 'Two in a row? Chances of that happening?'

'Oh, infinite,' she said. 'Like winning the lottery twice. There are *definite* weird vibes in this school now, Rich. You can feel it in the air.'

'So, um... what are we going to do about it?' Richie asked nervously, straightening his tie. 'If anything?' he added hastily.

'I think you ought to take a closer look at that exploded computer,' Jess murmured.

'What about you?' he asked.

'Me?' Jess lowered two index fingers like pistols in Emerald's direction. 'I'm gonna keep tabs on Madam there.'

Small and slight, Richie often went unnoticed. Now, he was hoping this would work to his advantage. He crouched behind a large rubber-plant and peered between the leaves.

The top of the stairs leading to the IT Room had been screened off with what appeared to be a sheet of white plastic and there were some people talking in front of it. He recognised the Head, Miss Pinsley, and the head of IT, Mr Watson. The other two were men in long, dark coats. The older man, who had grey hair and a bushy moustache, seemed to be doing most of the talking. Every so often the men would exchange a nod and the younger one would write something in a notebook.

Richie, straining to hear, caught odd snatches of the mumbled conversation:

'...pupils in the building?'

'...never expected it would...'

'...but if it's replicated...'

'...surely a simple parameter adjustment...'

While Richie was watching and trying to listen, something very odd happened which made his stomach do a backward flip and his fingertips tingle with excitement.

A black, green-eyed cat appeared to emerge from the plastic barrier and trotted past the group on the stairs.

Not one of the adults turned to look at it.

As if it wasn't really there - or as if they couldn't see it.

The cat padded down the steps, eyes seemingly scanning the route ahead. And suddenly, some instinct made Richie duck behind his plant-pot and try to curl himself up very, very tightly.

Richie could hear his own breathing, amplified horribly. Distantly, from outside, the usual playground sounds echoed - shouts, squeals and bouncing footballs. He could also hear the cat making quiet, thoughtful *skerrowling* noises to itself as it walked softly in a slow circle around the Plaza.

It seemed to be looking for something.

Sniffing.

Hunting.

Richie, biting his knuckles, pressed himself between the wall and the plant-pot. The next few seconds seemed like an eternity.

He could *smell* it. That damp, feral, cat-litter smell... it was that close to him.

He wondered if the cat was looking for a mouse, and almost giggled. Somehow, this cat didn't seem like the sort to be hunting mice - it gave the impression of being after bigger prey. And yet Richie had absolutely no idea why he should be thinking this, nor why he should be trembling with irrational fear.

He risked a glimpse. It was still there, furry feet padding on the varnished floor of the school corridor, the shiny green jewel in its collar catching the reflection of the strip-lights above. He bit down hard on his knuckles and screwed his eyes up tightly.

And then, to his relief, he heard the pitter-patter of feline footsteps receding. He glanced out from his leafy hideaway, just in time to see the cat's tail disappearing between the swing doors.

Only now, as he relaxed, did he realise how hard his heart had been thump-thump-thumping against his ribcage.

He let out a long, deep breath and uncurled himself from behind the plant-pot, straightening up.

'Blimey,' he muttered under his breath. 'If this kind of thing carries on, I'm going to need nine lives myself.'

'Emerald!' Jessica called. 'Emerald, wait!'

Pushing her way past a squabbling group of Year 7 boys, she caught up with Emerald Greene by the lockers.

'Ah, Jessica. You are passing a pleasant day, I trust.' Emerald Greene looked through her in that mesmerising, unearthly way of hers. She gave Jess her fixed, switched-on smile, all gloss and radiance with nothing behind it.

'Um, yeah. Not bad... You know, Emerald, you talk like a book.'

'Thank you.'

'Um... no problem. So... how's the encyclopaedia-reading going?'

'Very well, thank you,' said Emerald Greene politely. 'I have informed myself on everything from Cataracts to Devolution this lunchtime.'

'Are you... swotting up for something?' Jess wondered, furrowing her brow.

'Swotting... up?' Emerald repeated the unfamiliar phrase, shook her head.

'Revising? You know, like, for a quiz or something? *Schools Challenge*? *Junior Mastermind*?' Jess pulled a face. 'You're not telling me this is just for fun?'

'For enlightenment,' said Emerald, and smiled.

'Okaaaaay...' Jess decided it was best to move on. 'Listen, Aunt Gabi said I could have someone home for tea on Tuesday. D'you want to come round?'

'No, thank you,' said Emerald Greene, her smile unwavering, and she left Jess standing open-mouthed as she headed off down the corridor.

What kind of answer was that? Okay, so it wasn't *rude* exactly, but it was a bit more abrupt than it needed to be. She could have said she was washing her hair, or shopping, or that she'd set Tuesday aside to learn about everything from Eggplants to Fiji.

Something was *definitely* up with that girl. Emerald's smile wasn't natural, and her eyes were always so big and staring. Jess shivered. Could Emerald, she thought, be like the girls in those bad Channel 5 movies? Kids who always turned out to have awful things happening at home, or a mysterious, unrecognised illness?

Anything was possible.

The Friday end-of-school bell always seemed more triumphant, more shatteringly beautiful than any other. It brought with it a heady rush, a feeling of energy in the limbs, of freedom and power. A liberation. Pupils poured downstairs, chattering and shouting and giggling and whirling bags over their heads.

Jess Mathieson and Richie Fanshawe, oblivious to the conversations of their classmates, were ticking things off on their fingers.

'So we've got an exploding computer,' said Jess, as they hurried along with the tide. 'And a house that doesn't exist.'

'A girl who wanders home into the middle of the woods and disappears,' added Richie indistinctly, chewing on a Mars bar.

'She seems to know everything,' Jess said, 'and nothing.'

They stopped at the bottom of the stairs and faced each other, arms folded.

'Don't forget the singing,' said Richie, gesturing with his Mars bar. 'The weirdo chanting.'

Jess gently pushed the chocolate bar away from her face where he was waving it. 'And the fact that she reads the flipping *Encyclopaedia Britannica* for *fun*.'

'Not even Wikipedia.'

'I know. Crazy.'

'And the cat,' he said, finishing the last mouthful of Mars bar and shoving the wrapper into his pocket. 'The cat who walks through walls... and nobody sees it.'

Jess sighed. 'This is *so* doing my head in.'

'Mine too... Hey, only a few hours till the Mad Professor's dig, by the way. Don't want to miss that. It's not every day someone discovers a Viking tomb, is it?'

'Yeah, I know.' She looked at her watch. 'Better get home. Aunt Gabi's doing that well-known recipe, sandwiches. Want to come?'

'Sure. Thanks.'

Jess hoisted her bag on her shoulder. 'I dunno,' she said as they followed the hordes out into the playground. 'Don't you miss those days when the most complicated thing in life was SATs?'

The Darkwater. That was the only name it was called now, although it had been known by other names, long ago. Silent and imposing, the great lake nestled in the moorland above Meresbury.

That evening, mist drifted across its smooth surface, wraithlike fingers of vapour trailing on the water. The surface rippled slightly in the breeze, and the reflection of the setting sun dissolved in the lake into sparkling orange shards.

Out in the centre, where the lake was at its deepest, a bubble broke the surface. Then another. Then another. After a few seconds, a patch of water about three metres across was bubbling like a pan of soup.

With a low sploshing noise, a shadowy shape was heading out across the water from the shore. It emerged from the mist and revealed itself as a small rowing-boat, steered by a figure in a coat, its face hidden under a cowled hood.

The figure manoeuvred the oars expertly, guiding the boat to the edge of the bubbles. It fished out something from its pocket - a heavy lead weight, attached to a roll of twine on a wooden bobbin. The figure threw the weight into the water and watched it sink, allowing the twine to unroll from the bobbin as the weight went deeper and deeper. A good half-minute passed before the twine went taut over the edge of the boat, and the hooded figure nodded, apparently satisfied.

It took a small calculator out of its inside pocket, tapped in a few figures and nodded again.

The bubbling appeared to become more agitated, as if something had been disturbed. The mist, too, seemed to have grown thicker around the little boat. The figure, after looking over its shoulder one way and the other, hurriedly began to wind up the twine into a ball again. When it had finished, it grabbed the oars once more and rowed back into the thickening mist, heading for the shore.

For now, its job was done.

3

Moonlight Shadow

'Why,' said Aunt Gabi, slicing bread, 'does this guy want to open an ancient burial chamber anyway? The dead should stay buried, if you ask me.'

Jess looked at Richie and raised her eyebrows. They were sitting on the sofa, sharing a huge plate of cheese-and-pickle sandwiches. They had half an hour before catching the school minibus to see Professor Ulverston's unveiling of his wondrous discovery.

'It's history, Ms LaForge,' said Richie in his Serious Voice. 'Bringing the past to life.'

'Believe me, I wouldn't want any of my past bringing to life,' said Aunt Gabi with raised eyebrows. 'It'd be most unedifying. And please, it's Gabi, okay?' She tutted. 'I don't know, kids today are so *proper*. When I was your age I was out on the town drinking pina coladas with unsuitable boys and getting tattoos.'

'Have you got one?' Richie asked, wide-eyed and pausing in mid-chomp.

Jess groaned in mock despair. 'Don't encourage her, Rich!' she exclaimed, and flicked the TV on. On the screen, bronzed Australians bickered in a brightly-lit lounge.

Gabi grinned. She sashayed over, bread-knife still in her hand, and plonked a foot on the coffee-table. With a jangle of bangles, she pulled down the left shoulder of her top. 'There,' she said proudly.

Richie peered at the artwork etched into her skin. It was a clenched fist, about the size of a coin, and underneath it there was an inscription, made to look like ill-matched letters cut from a newspaper.

'PrettyVac,' Richie read, and frowned. '*PrettyVac*? What's that, some kind of hoover?'

Gabi blushed and pulled her top back over her shoulder. 'It's meant to say *Pretty Vacant*,' she said. 'Punk rock, you know?'

They stared blankly. 'Well, anyway, I passed out in the middle. Never plucked up the courage to have it finished off.' She waggled a finger at them. 'So let that be a lesson to you, kids - tattoos are not big or clever. There, that's my responsible parenting done for the day. Now get those sarnies down you.'

Jess just tutted, scowled and pretended to be interested in the antics of the Aussie actors. Sometimes, Gabi just embarrassed her.

Her name was Xanthë. She hovered between life and death.

She had died long before this world of hot, angry engines and tar-black roads cutting through the countryside. She had died in a place which was already cursed, and now she was cursed again, for although she was meant to be dead, she had not passed over. Not like others in the Craft, others who had gone on to new existences up or down the timeline, or whose souls had passed into their familiars. Those who had completed the cycle.

Her name was Xanthë and she was a witch-ghost. A witch hanging between life and death. A witch, like others, slipping between the timelines, never wholly present nor wholly absent.

In this form, her body was hideous. It had been beautiful and lissom before, so slender, her hair like spun gold as they danced around the stones. Now, she dared not look at herself. The Timelines had taken a hideous toll. They were all the same, all nine of the group; twisted, ragged-haired, their skin like parchment and liver-blotched. They hid from the light beneath cowled hoods, hunched and shuffling.

They seemed lost in different sectors of the totality. Sometimes they would glimpse one another, passing through a village or across a moor, and they would exchange the latest intelligence from their travels; but mostly, they passed in and out of phase, flickering like candles in a cold church.

But now, the news was astonishing. There had been a fragmentation at one of the points of energy, a discharge which had rippled through the timelines like a storm, causing huge breakers to crash against rocks. Pure psychic power converting itself into something which could be channelled - something called *electricity*.

There had been a partially successful breakthrough already, but the portal had not been stabilised.

However, a major disturbance in the equilibrium had just happened, at one of the strongest points - the standing stones.

And now, it seemed - if they could, together, muster the power - they could once more cross over into the land of the living. Through a door waiting to be opened by a foolish man.

At last, after centuries of waiting, there could be a way out.

By the time the school party got to Scratchcombe Edge, crowds had been gathering for four or five hours.

Jess guessed that some five hundred people were already assembled on the plateau, chattering in the twilight. A rope kept them at a distance from the standing stones, and from the two big silver tents which housed much of Professor Ulverston's scientific equipment. In the centre of the circle a round metal opening, from which various cables trailed, led to the tunnel which the Professor had so far excavated. Two flat video screens on scaffolding were set up to the east and west of the circle, she saw, so that the audience would have a clear view.

The Professor himself was giving a radio interview in the shadow of the stones, his booming voice carrying through the chilly air: 'And so they told me it was impossible. Weeeellll, I said, nothing's impossible if you set your mind to it...'

Mr Stone was there in the crowd, and Aunt Gabi was there too, in thick leggings and a biker jacket, laughing and gossiping with a group of other parents-and-guardians. She was passing round a small metal flask, which Jess suspected contained something stronger than tea.

Jess and Richie slipped away as soon as they could and managed to elbow their way to the front of the crowd. Nobody seemed to mind. Richie nudged Jess and pointed to a dark-haired, tanned man a little way off, tucked away in his own small enclosure of monitors and microphones, who was smoothing his hair and checking his cuffs. Jess grinned as she recognised Mike Devenish, the local TV presenter.

'Shall we go and listen to him?' Richie said.

They squeezed through the tall bodies around them to move a bit closer to the Outside Broadcast unit. Mike Devenish, while having his face powdered by a bored-looking make-up girl, was rehearsing his script to camera.

'The Vikings,' he was saying, 'were pagan Scandinavians, and acknowledged a huge range of gods. The dead were often buried with objects they might need for life in the afterworld. A poor man might be buried with just a single knife - a rich man, however, would share his tomb with many luxury items.... *Many luxury items*? Blimey, Dave, who wrote this rubbish? Sounds like the Shopping Channel!'

Someone babbled into Mike Devenish's earphone for a few seconds. He shrugged.

'Okay, okay. If you say so...' He waved the make-up girl away, cleared his throat and returned to the script. 'However, this Viking tomb is a little special - if a Viking tomb is indeed what the Professor has discovered. It's been found beneath an ancient stone circle - the famous Ten Sisters, here,' Mike Devenish gestured behind him, 'on Scratchcombe Edge, high on the moors above Meresbury. For some reason - we don't know what - the relatives of this Norseman, a man who would have lived about a thousand years ago, chose to make his final resting place beneath a stone circle from the Bronze Age. A stone circle which, as we know, would have already been here for nearly *three thousand years* by the time the first Viking warships arrived on the coastline of England.' Mike paused, grinned. 'OK, Dave,' he said, 'is that a bit too melodramatic?'

Jess nudged Richie. 'Come on, we could head further up on the rocks. We'll get a good view from there.'

Richie looked dubious. 'I don't really *do* climbing up rocks,' he said.

'Well, you do now,' said Jess, and she grabbed him by his scarf. 'Come on.'

From a flat-topped boulder a little way up behind the plateau, they had a magnificent view of the proceedings. The nine stones dominated the panorama, lit like a stage-set. Striding up and down within the circle, tall and imposing in his pinstripe suit, was Professor Edwin Ulverston, MA (Oxon), PhD, Fellow of the British Academy, Member of the International Fellowship of Archaeologists. He was checking details on a clipboard, occasionally barking orders at his assistants and the TV people.

The heads of the massed spectators bobbed in the gathering gloom, and from among them there came the occasional flicker of a camera flashlight, or the flare of matches as people lit candles. A murmur of excited voices carried up to the rocks, and it made Jess's fingertips tingle. The air, Jess thought, smelt of - what? Petrol, certainly, and also matches and hot wax. There was no doubt that something big was happening here tonight.

Jess narrowed her eyes and leaned forward, peering down at the crowd. 'I might have known it,' she breathed. 'What's *she* doing here?'

Moving swiftly and silently around the back of the crowd, dressed in her duffel-coat and with her hands thrust casually into her pockets, was the Newbie - Emerald Greene.

'She's at Aggie's too, you know,' said Richie mildly. 'She's allowed.'

'But she wasn't on the list!' Jess snapped.

Emerald Greene appeared to be checking something on her wristwatch - only Jess suspected that it probably wasn't a wristwatch at all, but rather one of those gadgets which Emerald toted around with her and hid whenever anyone came to look at them.

'I'm going to find out what she's doing,' muttered Jess, clambering over their little flat-topped rock and hopping back on to the grass. 'I don't trust her. You stay here and watch.'

'Hey,' Richie called. 'Don't get lost!'

As Jessica scrambled down the slippery path, her footing not always as sure as she would like it to be, a great roar went up from the crowd. She drew a sharp breath of excitement. The two enormous TV screens, she saw, were displaying a close-up of Professor Ulverston's commanding smile.

Jess, reaching the foot of the slope, mingled with the tail-end of the crowd. She could feel the quickening in her body, that strange sixth sense which told her Emerald Greene was somewhere near. Well, she was going to find her.

The TV image pulled back to reveal Mike Devenish standing next to Ulverston, and delightedly pointing his microphone into the Professor's jowly face.

'So,' Devenish's amplified voice was saying, 'you join us here live at Scratchcombe Edge. It's nearly eight-thirty, and we have just half an hour to go before Professor Ulverston reveals his major find to us!'

A digital clock appeared on the screen and began counting down from 30 minutes in lurid green figures.

'The Professor is accessing the tomb,' Devenish went on, 'through a carefully-excavated tunnel beneath the stones. Of course, archaeology is a very precise science. One cannot simply go racing in with a hammer and pickaxe - the Professor is using the very latest in computer-controlled equipment. The countdown you can see represents the time to the point at which the excavation drill will penetrate the central chamber of this thousand-year-old Viking tomb.' Devenish paused for effect. 'Now, I have the man himself here with me! Professor, how does it feel to see all these people here?'

'Oh, splendid, absolutely splendid!' The Professor's smile was dazzling. 'I can't tell you how wonderful it is to see all these super people taking an interest in my work.' Ulverston, again, seemed at home on television. He turned to look into the camera and pulled a face of mock seriousness. 'You *are* taking an interest in my work, aren't you? Of course you are!'

Jessica slipped through the crowds, dodging past them all - families with sparklers and hot-dogs, young fathers bouncing toddlers on their shoulders, pensioners, students with cameras and notepads. Lots of people held the candles which someone had been giving out in the car-park - their waxy scent drifted across the plateau, mingling with the pungent odour of onion from the hot-dog stands.

And Jess cursed the growing crowds of onlookers, for now she had managed to lose Emerald Greene.

Professor Ulverston opened his big eyes wide, held his hands up, palms outward, and beamed out at the crowd - just like a dodgy TV evangelist, thought Jess. The two pixellated images of his teeth lit up the plateau almost as brightly as the floodlights above the Ten Sisters.

The countdown clicked on to 18 minutes.

'Dangerous. Very dangerous,' said a soft voice at Jess's ear.

She whirled around and found herself looking into the pale, impish face of Emerald Greene. She was wearing her duffel-coat like a cape, with the hood over her face like a cowl, and just a few strands of hair trailed like blood against the ivory skin of her face. Even tonight, her eyes were shaded with her cobalt-blue glasses.

'Where did you pop from?' said Jess with a shiver.

'Just over there,' said Emerald innocently, nodding over her shoulder. 'I am finding this a most interesting public event. Although it is being transmitted live on the television, hundreds of people have made the journey to be here in person - only to find themselves watching it on television.' She smiled, seemingly directing her words at a point just beyond Jessica's left ear. 'Ironic, no?'

'Emerald,' Jess hissed, moving closer to her, 'what d'you mean, dangerous?'

Emerald Greene turned to face Jessica and stared at her as if the answer were obvious. 'What this *Professor* is about to do will cause chaos beyond the imaginings of his limited mind,' she said scornfully. 'Do you not understand, Jessica Mathieson?'

'No,' said Jess faintly, 'not really. But then there's been a lot recently that I've not understood.' Suddenly, she broke off and stared hard at Emerald. 'Why aren't you trying to stop him, then? Ulverston, I mean?'

Emerald tutted and shook her head. 'You see the security,' she answered patiently. 'One cannot get near the Professor or his scientific equipment without... drawing attention.' She began to move smoothly through the crowd, making her way towards the front.

Jess, dodging a small child with a sparkler, hurried after her. 'Drawing attention? Yeah, I know what you mean,' she said angrily. 'Flipping it over like you did with Rich's phone, maybe? That was a cool stunt, wasn't it?'

'It was not intended to be a *stunt*,' said Emerald coldly.

'Oh, right. How about vanishing into thin air, then?' Jess folded her arms and heard her voice sounding full of bravado - which she didn't feel at all. 'You pulled it off pretty well, didn't you? Who taught you that one? David Blaine?'

Emerald stopped. She turned round and stared hard at Jessica, eyes bright like tiny jewels, and for a moment Jess felt a chill in her heart, something so cold and powerful and frightening that she took an involuntary step backwards.

'You - *followed* me,' said Emerald, with cold deliberation.

'Yeah.' Jess tried to hold her chin up and meet Emerald's gaze, but those green eyes seemed to hold a terrible, vivid light which she just couldn't look at. Around her on the plateau, the night seemed to have grown darker and colder. 'Me and Richie. We followed you across town, that first day we met you.'

Jess licked her lips, shivering. Emerald Greene was circling her, now, watching her interestedly with her head tilted strangely on one side. The boom of Mike Devenish's commentary and the excited hubbub of the crowd seemed to shrink to no more than a soft background murmur.

'Only Rubicon House isn't there, is it?' Jess went on, coolly meeting Emerald's gaze. 'Not any more.'

'All right. Continue,' said Emerald quietly.

Jess caught a glimpse of the countdown - 15:39. Just a quarter of an hour to go. 'And - and we saw you down by the lake and we followed you.' She was hugging herself, now, arms tightly round her body as if for protection. 'Back to the forest. You didn't see us, but we saw you walk into the middle of the clearing.'

'And?' said Emerald threateningly.

'And... you disappeared,' Jess concluded. She swallowed hard, nervously fingering the velvet choker which Aunt Gabi had given her for Christmas.

Emerald gave a thin-lipped smile. 'I did not disappear,' she whispered. 'I am here.'

'Yes,' Jess said with a frown, 'but - '

'What you saw,' Emerald murmured, 'was the simple effect of a piece of technology. A keyed chronostatic barrier.'

'Excuse me?'

'You know how some cats have an electronic device on their collars which enables them to enter a cat-flap, so that only the right cat with the correct key can pass in and out? The barrier is like that. You need the right chronometric alignment.'

'Chronometric?' Jess frowned, thinking about the word. 'You mean something to do with *Time*?'

'Yes,' said Emerald wearily, 'I mean something to do with Time.' She held her hands out, cupping them. 'The clearing houses a bubble, if you like. An artificial space of stability, which...' She sighed. 'Look, I do not have time for this.' Emerald glanced at her watch, then up at the video-screen.

Jess saw that the countdown now read 11:55 - less than twelve minutes before the moment of breakthrough. The screen was showing a computer graphic image of Ulverston's electronic probe, burrowing through the peaty earth on its steady way to its target.

'What are you going to do?' Jess asked, panic in her voice.

Emerald sighed and folded her arms. 'If I cannot stop the fool,' she said, narrowing her eyes, 'then I must intercept his damage.' She made as if to move off, then stopped, remembering something. She looked Jess in the eye. 'Coming?'

Jess was taken aback. 'Right. Okay.'

'Right,' said Emerald, and smiled at the unfamiliar word. 'We need to be near the front. Follow in my footsteps.'

Jess hurried after her. She had no idea whose side Emerald Greene was on - nor what she intended to do - but she wasn't going to let her out of her sight.

Richie shivered.

His mum wouldn't be pleased now, he thought, to find that Jess had deserted him and that he was stuck up here on his own. Even the stars, the bright constellations whose names he knew and loved, didn't bring him much pleasure at the moment.

Richie rummaged in his pocket and found the chocolate snack he'd been going to share with Jess. 'Well,' he said, 'I'm going to have it all myself now.' He took a bite. It was chewy, smooth and comforting.

He could see one of the video screens clearly. Now, Mike Devenish's amplified voice echoed up towards him. He strained to hear.

'So, Professor, just seven minutes on the clock! Are we on schedule?'

'Yes, yes. Really rather exciting, isn't it?... I must say, tonight will be featuring prominently in my memoirs - did I mention that I'm writing my memoirs? I did. Of course. One does forget things, you know. So much to remember. Life is so... short, isn't it, Mr Cavendish?'

'Yes, it's *Devenish*, actually.'

'I expect so,' said Ulverston, his smile not wavering.

For a second, his booming voice made the microphones sing with feedback. It bounced off each of the stones in the circle, and Richie thought that he heard it echoing also on the rocky tor behind him. He shuddered because - just for an instant - it sounded like the plaintive wail of a woman's voice, singing the last notes of an old lament. But then it was gone.

The audience below him was clapping, cheering.

The moon, a bright crescent, was high in the sky now.

Less than five minutes remained on the digital clock.

Aunt Gabi was enjoying herself. She cracked open a can of lager from the back of the minibus, took a deep and much-needed sip from it and passed the can to Jess's form teacher, Cameron Stone.

'Ah, beturrr not, Gabs,' he said. 'The kids are around.'

She grinned. 'Suit yourself,' she said, and took another gulp.

'Y'know - I didn't rrealise old Ulverrr-ston was such an egotist,' Mr Stone offered with a wry smile.

Gabi shrugged. 'These academic types usually are, aren't they?...' She realised she had lost sight of Jessica and the others a while ago. 'Hey, is Jess up the front somewhere?'

'Yeah, she and that boy, er, Fanshawe went up togetherrr... How long to go?'

Gabi squinted at the screen. 'Three minutes?... Listen, Cameron, I've been meaning to tell you something.'

'What's that?'

'The other day, right, these two really weird guys came round to the house. They were like policemen, only, well, they weren't. They were asking about - '

Just then, a great cheer went up, and they all turned to look towards the stones. The clock had clicked down to a minute, and the audience started to chant the numbers in unison as they clicked off.

'*Fifty-nine! Fifty-eight! Fifty-seven!*'

Mike Devenish was in full flow.

'*...for nearly three thousand years by the time the first Viking warships arrived on the coastline of England. Yes - we're live at Scratchcombe Edge again, and now, as you can hear, the crowd are getting louder, the atmosphere is wonderful, and we are, indeed, on the verge of a historic discovery here. Professor Edwin Ulverston is a name to go down in history - a name, indeed, which may even rewrite history as we know it!*

'*On this clear, beautiful September evening, the Professor's probe has now almost reached the outer wall of the chamber beneath the stones. In less than a minute's time, history will be made - and you're watching it here, live on County TV, with me, Mike Devenish.*'

Emerald grabbed Jess's arm, steering her past the last two rows of spectators until they were right up against the rope barrier. Jess, worried about what Emerald might do if she let her go, allowed herself to be led.

'*Thirty-eight! Thirty-seven! Thirty-six!*'

And then Emerald said, 'Come on,' ducked down, and slipped under the barrier.

Horrified, Jess scrambled after her, scurrying round the edge of the stone circle. Luckily, they were in the shadowed zone at the edge of the floodlights, and nobody appeared to have seen them.

The girls took cover behind the nearest of the stones. Jess, certain that they were about to get caught at any moment, could hear her own ragged breath and could feel her heart pounding against her ribcage.

The stone felt cold and rough, even through her jeans.

Professor Ulverston stood, arms folded, before the opening to the tunnel, laughing delightedly to himself. Monitors next to him gave readouts which Jess couldn't make out, and which she knew she wouldn't have been able to understand anyway.

'*Thirty! Twenty-nine! Twenty-eight!*'

Jess was about to move again, but Emerald's hand was on her shoulder. Emerald shook her head firmly, and pointed.

Something was flitting among the stones. It was small, black, agile. Jess's eyes widened and she felt her spine tingling as she recognised the cat. The one which had spoken to her. It trotted towards them, eyes shining, and the jewel inset on its collar gleaming a bright green.

The green jewel. Something clicked in Jess's mind.

'*Twenty-one! Twenty! Nineteen!*'

The cat suddenly bolted across the stone circle and leapt into Emerald Greene's outstretched arms.

'Calm, Anoushka,' said Emerald Greene in a soft, soothing voice, stroking its dark fur. 'Calm.'

'*Eighteen! Seventeen! Sixteen!*'

Jessica stared. Her mind boggled. 'It's yours,' she said in astonishment, looking from Emerald to the purring cat and back to Emerald again. '*Yours!*' she exclaimed again.

The cat lifted its head and stared at Jess, its eyes shining with the reflection of the stone circle.

And then it spoke again.

'Of course she's *mine*,' the cat drawled haughtily. 'What other possible explanation did you think there was, hmmm?'

Professor Edwin Ulverston clasped his hands together and gazed upon the pitted surface of the western keystone. The Ten Sisters were silent like ghosts, seeming to watch the elated crowd as they counted down the final seconds on the TV screen.

'*Ten!*'
'*Nine!*'
'*Eight!*'

There was, suddenly, a helicopter flying overhead. It appeared swiftly, like a bolt of living darkness, clattering out of the sky above the distant city. Most of the people watching assumed it was somehow connected with the television broadcast, and waved their candles in the air.

'My life's work,' said Ulverston softly, but just loud enough for the microphone clipped to his lapel to pick it up for the viewers. 'My life's achievement!'

'*Seven!*'

'*Six!*'

The helicopter, getting nearer and louder, zoomed across the moorland and came to hover directly above the Ten Sisters.

'*Five!*'

'*Four!*'

Jess, down behind the stone, suddenly found herself pulled away by Emerald Greene. She lost her footing and went rolling over and over, everything becoming a blur of faces and grass and sky.

The smell of mud filled her nostrils and then she slammed up hard against something which knocked the breath from her.

Ulverston was lifting his arms, looking up into the sky.

'*Three!*'

'*Two!*'

Ulverston appeared for the first time to see the helicopter hovering there. For a second, he wavered. He looked uncertain.

But it was too late now.

'*One!*'

'*Zero!*'

For a moment, nothing happened. The audience held its breath. A second later, there was a cavernous BOOM from beneath the ground.

A sky-shaking cheer went up from the crowd. And then, out of the tunnel-mouth flashed what could have been a bolt of lightning - only its colour was an angry crimson.

The TV cameras caught it all.

The horrified crowd, shrinking back, watched on the big screens as it happened.

The bolt of fire struck the keystone, turning it bright red in an instant like a burning coal. There was a *whoomph* like a gigantic flame being lit - and then the stone *screamed*.

The sound, ancient and terrifying, echoed across the moors. People clamped their hands to their ears.

Glowing within a column of light, the stone flickered with tendrils of lightning. They spread across the circle in a filigree web, smashing into each of the stones in turn and suffusing them with radiance. There was a harsh, crackling noise like a raging bonfire, and then one by one, the stones began to glow - cherry-red, then vermilion, then a bright orange.

The tall figure of Professor Edwin Ulverston stood for a second in defiance, his arms held aloft. His big eyes opened wide and his toothy smile, fixed across his face, seemed to turn into a grimace of sheer panic.

The light blazed, and the filigree web crackled upwards, encircling Ulverston like ivy round a tree. Ulverston struggled helplessly, but the light seemed alive, snaking upwards and entwining itself around his body.

It flared up like a Chinese firework - and when the flame guttered and fell, the Professor had completely vanished.

Part Two

A Gathering of Shadows

4

Rubicon House

Jess awoke.

Her head hurt, and she could hear a sound, like an engine. It was throbbing through her, making her shake.

Rubbing her eyes, she sat up, aware now that a tartan blanket covered her. She was lying on the back seat of an old camper-van, and as she slowly came to, she could see familiar countryside rolling past - trees, hills, farmland. It was before dawn, to judge by the grey light and the dark blue sky. The van smelt of petrol and pear-drops, and up at the front - at the wheel, a big, old-fashioned steering-wheel emblazoned with a VW symbol - was Emerald Greene.

Jess sat bolt upright. '*Stop!* Let me out!' she shouted angrily. 'Where are you taking me?' She pummelled the back of the driver's seat in anger.

Emerald, unflustered, changed gear, with a horrible crunching sound which seemed to shake every panel of the camper-van.

'Well,' she called over her shoulder, 'so this is how you express your gratitude to me for saving your life, Jessica Mathieson? And *please* stop that thumping, or you will cause me to crash.'

'But where are we going?' Jess asked miserably, rubbing the sleep from her eyes. She was cold and tired, her body was sore in every limb, and she was suddenly aware that her stomach ached with hunger.

'To a place of safety,' Emerald said, and the van lurched as it cut through a swathe of mud and started to rumble up a dirt track.

Jess looked up, taking in Emerald's earlier comment. 'Just a minute. Saving my *life*?'

'That is correct.' Emerald glanced in the rear-view mirror. 'We were in a very dangerous place beside the stones. I should have realised it.'

Everything came rushing back.

Professor Ulverston.

The countdown.

The red lightning dancing round the stones, and the sudden panic as she rolled away, away -

'What happened back there?' Jess asked in astonishment.

'Severe temporal disturbance,' said Emerald casually. 'That, I am afraid, is what happens if you go poking into old places that are best left alone.'

'And what about me? I was out cold!'

'No, you were just in shock, that is all. A little dazed. Luckily, I had my Dormobile nearby, so I was able to get us both out of there before the authorities arrived.'

'And... is everybody all right? Gabi, Richie?'

'Do not concern yourself. Everybody is unharmed.'

Jess frowned, shaking her head. 'But Professor Ulverston! It absorbed him! It was horrible, like... black magic, or something.'

Emerald clicked her tongue and shook her head. 'No, no, no. Think about it. Magic is just science by another name.'

'It is?' Jess asked dubiously, struggling to clear her dull head.

'Of course! If a 14th-Century peasant saw a car, a computer or a television, he would have no rational explanation for it, would he? He would call it devil's work. Sorcery, or *magic*. Any sufficiently advanced technology will, to the untrained eye, be indistinguishable from magic.'

'The untrained eye being mine, I suppose?' she said sarcastically. 'Thanks. So kind of you to compare me to a medieval peasant, Emerald.'

'*Merely a parallel*,' said a clipped voice from floor-level.

Jessica jumped.

A dark, furry head popped up from under the back seat. It was the cat.

'It's perfectly all right,' said the cat. Emerald had called it Anoushka, Jess remembered - a girl's name, although the languid, actorish voice sounded neither male nor female. The cat arched its back and sternly fixed her with its unblinking gaze. 'Come, now, don't be so touchy,' it said. 'Anyone would think I wanted to bite you, or something.' It tutted in disapproval, trotted to the front of the Dormobile and hopped on the passenger seat.

'Sorry,' said Jess. Then she added in her head: *I can't believe I just said that.*

Well, she thought, either she was going crazy or she had to start accepting all this. Several hours ago, at a guess, she had seen the world's leading Professor of Archaeology disappear in a pillar of flame. Now she was stuck in a rattling Dormobile with a girl of her own age who somehow knew how to drive. Her fellow passenger was a talking cat, and the girl was apparently able to pass at will through something called a - what was it - *chronostatic barrier*?

There was weird, and there was really weird, and then there was *too* weird.

'Take the phenomena you call *ghosts*, for example,' said Emerald, as the Dormobile emerged from the track onto an even bumpier woodland path. 'Are you aware that the city is teeming with traces of their activity?'

'Ghosts?' Jess felt her skin crawl.

'Or more accurately, intrusions of temporal-psychic instability.'

'Intrusions of whatty-what?'

'Listen. The fabric of Time is like a patchwork quilt. Every so often, something pokes itself through that quilt and starts to unravel the threads.' Jess saw Emerald smile briefly in the rear-view mirror. 'It is my job to put them back together.'

'Your job... Is that why you're always poking around in the tarmac, and playing with pendulums?'

'Precisely. I have been tracing the temporal fields in those areas. You would not notice, because you are not sensitive to these phenomena, but in any space where there has been a break, local time slows down fractionally... The best way to see it is by checking the density of the surfaces, or testing the Earth's gravity in that space.'

Suddenly, Jess realised the van was slowing, and that they were back in the woods on the shore of the Darkwater - in the same clearing where she and Richie had seen Emerald disappear.

'So,' Jess said, 'am I about to get some answers?'

'Oh, how tedious,' said Anoushka the cat, glancing out of the window and then settling down to lick his paws. 'Have we got to explain?' He flipped his tail back and forth and bared his teeth at Emerald. 'I *really* find that part rather tiresome.'

Jess looked down at the cat, then back up at Emerald. 'Actually, yes, some explanations would be good. You say you've never been to school, but you seem to know an awful lot of complicated science. So? Where *are* you from?'

'Not now,' said Emerald Greene. 'Another time.' The Dormobile had come to a halt in the centre of the clearing, and Emerald turned round in her seat. 'How do you feel?' she asked.

'Hungry. Confused. Frightened,' admitted Jess.

'Good!' said Emerald with a firm smile. 'Now, what happened to Professor Ulverston is the key to the whole thing. I believe, now, that I know what we are dealing with.'

'You do?' Jess was astonished. 'How did you work that out?'

Emerald ignored her question. 'And if I am right, it worries me greatly. I am going to find out, Jessica Mathieson, because it is my business to find out things like this.'

'She *makes* it her business,' interjected the cat. 'Personally, I'd give anything for a bowl of cream and a quiet life, but there you are.' He carried on licking his paws.

'I may need your help,' Emerald went on. 'Do you think you will be able to help me?'

'I... don't know,' said Jess uncertainly. 'Right now I'm cold and hungry, and I want to go home.'

'Worry not - I have some culinary ability. I shall organise you a cooked breakfast.'

Wrinkling her nose, Jess looked around the cramped interior of the VW Dormobile. 'Right... You've got a Primus stove tucked away somewhere, have you?'

Jess could have sworn that the cat sniggered. She turned and gave it a hard stare - or at least she tried to. Anoushka met her gaze, his eyes unblinking, and after a second or two Jess's eyes were stinging so much she had to blink and look away.

'Better than that.' Emerald turned to face forwards again, revved the engine. 'I suggest you hold on to something. Oh, and - my apologies - you may feel slightly sick for a second or two.'

Jess was about to ask why, but she didn't get a chance.

Emerald revved the engine.

She lifted the clutch.

A second later, the Dormobile shot off, the engine roaring, every part of the vehicle shaking like an old washing-machine on its spin-cycle. Jess gasped, just managing to grab hold of the foldaway table beside the back seat, and she caught sight of the speedometer climbing beyond sixty in just a few seconds.

One moment they were rocketing forward - and the next, they smacked full-tilt into something soft.

It sounded *fluid*.

Globules of blue light washed over the windscreen and enveloped the van, rippling its surface, making it seem as if they were inside a giant lava-lamp. Jessica had the sudden, unpleasant sensation of leaving her stomach behind - *worse than the Nemesis at Alton Towers*, she thought briefly. Then, she tasted something familiar in the air - something cold and metallic - and she remembered it from before, from the time when she and Richie had seen Emerald disappear right here.

The sound of the engine seemed to slow and wobble as if on a mangled tape, then zipped back up to speed again. The blue wall snapped shut behind them with a loud, echoing *schloooooop-pop!* and the van landed on the ground with a jolt that slammed the suspension and shook every bone in Jess's body.

The Dormobile slowly stopped vibrating. Jess's mouth was dry and tasted horribly metallic. Her body was trembling, and she didn't dare open her eyes.

'You may as well look,' said Emerald.

So she did.

And she couldn't believe it.

Swallowing hard and blinking, Jess saw that they were no longer in a forest clearing at dawn. The Dormobile, its engine purring quietly, sat in the sunlight of early afternoon. Before them stretched rich green privet hedges, a line of creamy-white Greek statues and green lawns lined with beds of carnations and yellow roses. Beyond the grass was a stone fountain set into a gravel forecourt, sparkling with silvery jets of water. And further back still, Jess could see a beautiful Georgian house, its walls festooned with scarlet creeper and its windows glittering with honey-gold sunlight.

'Welcome to my home,' said Emerald. 'Welcome to Rubicon House.'

The indigo sky in the east beyond the Darkwater was painted with a stripe of sunlight, and birds were cautiously beginning to twitter. Richie Fanshawe stood in the forest clearing and remembered.

He was shading his eyes, as the stone circle crackled with red light...

A grandstand view of the hordes, a human tide streaming away from the stones...

Spectators shrieking, running as fast as their legs could carry them back towards their cars and coaches and buses...

Mike Devenish, standing amid the chaos with his microphone, looking in vain for a functioning camera.

When Jessica hadn't turned up after two hours, and policemen in yellow jerkins were efficiently finishing off clearing the area, Gabi had, in a panic, collared the nearest police officers and asked them if they'd seen her. The two nodded sympathetically, took some brief notes, and told her to go home and get some sleep. One of them asked how old the young lady was - and when Gabi said thirteen, the two policemen had exchanged a knowing look before giving her a reassuring smile. 'Nine times out of ten, kids just turn up the next day. You go home and wait, miss.'

Richie thought he knew better.

He could hear rooks cawing overhead and scuttling of woodland creatures in the undergrowth. He glanced around nervously.

'Okay,' he said. 'Nothing ventured...'

He tried to flex his hands and crack his knuckles, like his older brother Tom could. It just hurt. He winced and rubbed his hand, thinking that he wouldn't try that again. He positioned himself centrally, then put his hands out in front of him, palms flat, as if feeling his way in the dark.

Nothing at first. He moved forward a few centimetres.

Still nothing.

Richie had an idea. He rummaged through his pockets until he found something he didn't particularly want - a packet of

Extra Strong Mints which had been there about three weeks. He peeled the paper back and took off the top sweet, holding it between thumb and forefinger.

With his best overarm, he hurled the sweet forward into the clearing.

A second later, with a sound like a firecracker, the peppermint hit an invisible wall and came bouncing back at him, skimming past his ear with the force of a flying bullet.

'Wow!' Richie ducked as the sweet shattered against a nearby beech-tree, white fragments scattering in the undergrowth.

More impressed than frightened, he straightened up and re-positioned his crooked glasses. Right. So that was good. He knew where it was, now. He moved forward, palms flat again, and - *there*. It felt like a solid, invisible brick wall.

He pressed his palms against the barrier.

Yes - *there*. He felt a tingle on his skin, like he was touching cold water. And no, it did not feel like brick now. It was softer than that - somehow tough but yielding. Like... yes, like *canvas*. It felt just like the taut, thin, strong wall of the tent his mum and dad had bought, the one they'd used last year on that camping trip to Devon.

Richie pressed hard with both hands, feeling the tingling in his palms growing stronger. The barrier pushed against him, but he got the sense that he was winning.

He closed his eyes. His tongue tingled, and began to taste of metal.

She walked through this. We saw her. So I ought to be able to as well. So just ignore it. Ignore the fact that there's even a barrier there and walk forward.

Something whooshed past his body, like a warm summer breeze washing over him. He wobbled, steadied himself.

The sound of the cawing rooks grew quieter, as if someone had turned down their volume. Now, there was an oddly fresh smell around him, like newly-cut grass, and he could hear the splashing of fountains, tuning itself in like a radio station on short-wave. He felt warm sunlight on his face and something crunchy beneath his feet. He could hear a breeze rustling in leaves somewhere nearby, too. Not daring to open his eyes and look yet, Richie lowered his hands.

'Okay. Don't get freaked out by this,' he said out loud to himself. Then he added,

'You're talking to yourself again.'

And then, 'I know,' and, 'Well, stop it, I don't like it,' and, 'Okay, then.'

He opened his eyes.

He was standing on a long gravel drive lined with splashing fountains, neatly-trimmed hedges and statues. About fifty yards in front of him sat a house - large, golden and welcoming, with scarlet creeper on its walls and its sunlight glinting from its windows.

He whirled around. The gardens stretched away in the other direction, towards high hedges and open parkland. No sign of the woodland clearing at all.

'Oh, yes! *Result!*' Richie waved a fist in the air.

As magic goes, he thought cheerfully, *that pretty much takes the chocolate cream bourbon.*

He started to hurry up the crunching gravel drive towards the front door. After a second, he staggered, as an overwhelming dizziness took hold of him, like someone shoving him hard to one side, and he almost lost his balance.

'Come on,' he said, steadying himself. 'None of that.'

He blinked, focused on the front door of the house and marched forward determinedly.

'*This* is what we need!'

Emerald Greene thumped a thick volume down on the Library table. Clouds of dust billowed up towards the vaulted ceiling, and Jessica stared worriedly at the book.

If she was honest, Jess was still in a state of shock. In the last half-hour, she felt she had just wandered into the middle of someone else's dream.

Emerald had parked the Dormobile - olive-green, Jess noted - and they had disembarked, Anoushka hopping down after the girls. Breathing fresh and summery air, a dizzy Jess had allowed herself to be frogmarched up the front steps into the house. And with Anoushka trotting at their heels, Emerald had shown her around her impossible home.

Emerald, quite casually, flung open one door after another and let Jess look in. First there was a yellow lounge with a chaise-longue and a huge chandelier, then a big drawing-room with comfortable sofas, then a massive, oak-panelled library with rows and rows of ancient books stretching off in all directions.

'I don't get it,' Jess had said at last, staring around her. 'How is this house here, hidden in the middle of the woods? It shouldn't exist any more!'

'The chronostatic field allows a bubble of Time to exist one millisecond ahead of what you call reality,' Emerald Greene explained. Her eyes glinted, as green as the pendant she wore around her neck. 'We are within the bubble. A fold in Time, if you like.'

So casual, she could be describing the Number 32 bus, Jess thought.

'So much to take in, isn't it?' drawled Anoushka, who was circling round at Jess's feet. 'Let me know if your unfeasibly tiny mind gets overloaded, won't you?'

Jess gave the cat a strained smile.

'This,' Emerald said, 'is Rubicon House *before* it was destroyed by fire - only without it actually *being* in the past. And with a few minor adjustments of my own.'

In a big, tile-floored kitchen, Emerald had cooked Jess the best English breakfast she had ever had: fresh orange juice and crunchy, buttery toast, then a plate of crumbly bacon, smooth poached eggs and organic mushrooms which popped inside her mouth with a juicy taste explosion. She had also brewed a gloriously strong pot of Darjeeling tea.

'Salt, sugar, proteins,' explained Emerald Greene. 'Passing through the Barrier has odd effects on your body the first few times. You need to restore these to your body.'

Then they had headed down an oak-panelled corridor, past some suits of armour, and had come out on the far side of the Library. Emerald had climbed a huge, rickety stepladder; Jess, gawping upwards with a crick in her neck, had been convinced it wasn't going to stay upright.

The Library seemed to stretch upwards for ever. Surely it was taller than the house? While Jess was puzzling that one over, she thought she saw something - a shadow? - flitting among the highest shelves. She couldn't be certain, though, and dismissed the idea.

Finally, Emerald had descended with the dusty, leather-bound book.

'Witches,' whispered Emerald now, leafing through the book.

Jess frowned. 'Which is what?'

'No - *witches*.'

Jess paused, blinked. 'You're joking, right?'

'I am joking, *wrong*,' said Emerald, looking up coldly. 'It is what we are dealing with.' She had taken off her blue sunglasses and her green eyes seemed to shine with that compelling inner light again.

'But - *witches*?' Jess repeated. 'Warty old biddies with big noses and bad teeth who ride broomsticks? And have cats?' she added pointedly.

Anoushka peered out from behind a bookshelf, where he was scrabbling suspiciously. 'Mythology has a lot to answer for,' the cat purred, his green eyes flashing, and then he slunk back behind the books.

Then Emerald seemed to stop for a minute, leaning back and pricking up her ears like a cat. 'Who is there?' she asked. 'Come out!'

Jess swallowed hard. Her heart pounded as a shadow appeared from behind one of the bookcases.

And then she breathed a sigh of relief.

'Sorry,' said Richie, awkwardly, and polished his glasses. 'I... wanted to make sure Jess was all right,' he explained to Emerald.

'How did you get in?' Jess asked admiringly.

Richie shrugged. 'Same way you did.'

Emerald sighed. 'I can see I will have to do some work on the chronostatic alignments... Well, now you are here...'

Jess smiled gratefully at Richie. 'Welcome to the madhouse,' she whispered.

'I'd never have believed it,' he whispered in awe, gazing up at the vast ranks of the Library shelves. 'Good job I came to see for myself.' He rubbed his eyes. 'I feel a bit weird. I think I need a cup of tea.'

Emerald folded her arms. 'Later. Now, look, both of you - forget folk legends and children's tales.' She leaned forward over the table, red hair falling across her face. In the dusty gloom of the library, her eyes seemed to shine like her emerald pendant. 'Witches are dangerous creatures who should never be crossed. Sometimes their own powers are...' Emerald shuddered. 'Too monstrous for them to contain.'

Richie pulled a sceptical face. 'But they only come out at Hallowe'en, right? The rest of the time they hide away in forests, chucking eye of whatsit and tongue of doo-dah into big casseroles... Don't they?' he added, slight doubt creeping into his voice.

'I've been there already,' said Jess, holding up a hand. 'Trust me, she didn't like it.'

Behind them, there was a squeal and a slither as Anoushka pounced on an unfortunate mouse.

'You are not taking this seriously, are you, Richard?' Emerald shook her head in despair. 'Believe me, witches are no laughing matter. They are real, they exist. They can take many forms. And they can be truly *evil*.' She thumped the book to emphasise the last word.

Jess looked down at the book. According to the gold embossing on its cover, it was called *Lore of Albion Guiding the Fullest History, Taming and Containment of Witches*. Despite herself, she felt a little shiver. 'Evil...' she repeated softly, and her fingers traced the golden letters on the front of the book.

Emerald nodded eagerly. 'And, what is more, I think we may be facing something more dangerous still. These are not just witches. *They are the ghosts of witches*. Wraiths.'

'The ghosts of witches?' Jess looked up sharply. 'You mean, intrusions of temporo-whatsit? Like you said before?'

Emerald nodded.

'This is all a bit beyond me,' said Richie, slumping into an armchair.

'So... you've been *sent* here to deal with the... *witches*?' Jess asked.

She didn't like saying the word, now. It didn't sound as comical and childish as it had done. It sounded a scratchy, scraping, spine-tingling word, a word of shadows and dark laughter.

'Yes,' said Emerald.

'But how - how did you end up getting here, living here? And being a pupil at Aggie's?'

'Where are your mum and dad?' Richie asked suddenly.

Jess realised that they had seen nobody else since entering the house. 'Yeah, do you have a mum and dad, Em?'

For the first time, Emerald looked away, as if Jess had touched upon something which she ought not to have mentioned.

'Well?' Richie asked.

There was a hushed stillness in the Library. An ancient silence, but for the creaking of the old shelves and the skittering, somewhere deep within them, of Anoushka's paws.

'I am Displaced,' said Emerald Greene. 'It is my shame.'

'Shame? What - '

'I cannot discuss it,' said Emerald sharply.

'Why not?' said Jess, who was beginning to feel a little aggrieved.

Emerald looked up, and her eyes were strangely piercing for a moment. '*Because I would rather not!*' she snapped.

'That's not an answer.'

'All right - then try this. I have seen your aunt. Why does she only wear one gold earring when it is obviously part of a pair? Is she absent-minded? I think not.'

Jess felt her face reddening, both in embarrassment and anger. She knew the answer to this, of course, but she wasn't about to tell Emerald Greene. Not yet. Richie looked from one girl to the other in concern.

'There,' said Emerald, with a note of triumph in her voice. 'Some things you do not discuss, some things I do not discuss. You see?' She opened the heavy book and started riffling through the gold-leafed pages. 'Now,' she said, 'it is here somewhere...'

'What... what are you looking for?' Jess asked, folding her arms somewhat defensively now.

'The answer to some of your questions. Aha!' she said, stabbing a finger down at a page.

Jess and Richie, their qualms forgotten in their excitement, peered over Emerald's shoulder. The yellowing page showed an old map of Meresbury and the district; Jess guessed it had to be at least a hundred years old.

'Here is the Ten Sisters circle.' Emerald pointed to the symbol, north-east of the city on Scratchcombe Edge. 'And here is the Cathedral.' She indicated the cross in the city centre. 'And here...' Her finger ran along the page to the east. 'Here is the Darkwater.' She looked up at them, expectant. 'What do you notice?'

'A triangle!' said Richie.

'Exactly. Some people might call it a conjunction of ley-lines. *Look.*' Emerald fished a school exercise-book from her pocket, and with a red felt-tip, she marked three dots on the page.

'Not just a triangle,' said Jess. 'Almost a *perfect* triangle.'

'Equilateral,' said Richie.

Emerald nodded. 'These old superstitions have some basis in fact. And that idiot Ulverston, so dismissive of the old ways, has opened up a channel.'

'For... what?' Jess asked, and she felt a cold shiver throughout her body.

Emerald held her hands out as if cupping an invisible globe. 'Meresbury,' she said, 'stands on what you might call a *chronomutic fissure* where the ley-lines meet. A... *crack*, if you like, in normal space and Time.' Emerald splayed her fingers out.

'A crack?' exclaimed Jess, alarmed.

'Yes, yes, do not worry. They are found all over Albion. All over Britain, I mean... They are perfectly harmless if you do not go poking about in them.'

'But... if you do?' Richie ventured.

'Well, you saw. Ulverston could see no further than his own ambition. And he may unwittingly have provided an entry point back into this world for...' Emerald turned slowly to look at them each in turn, and her eyes were open wide, unblinking. 'Something which should have left it behind, a long, long time ago.'

'Right. You're scaring me now,' Jess admitted.

'You'd be scaring me, too,' agreed Richie, 'if I had any idea what you were on about.'

Emerald, hands in her pockets, started pacing up and down and muttering to herself. 'It would be just a question of getting the temporal resonance right... Of course, of course!' She flicked rapidly through several pages of the book, finally jabbing her finger on to another page. 'Here we are. Listen to this. *When a Witch loses her Life by Force - whether this has been by the Burning or the Drowning - she may enter the State of Wraithdom, a perpetual and wretched Existence where the Knowledge of Eternity is combined with the Absence of Magical Powers. The Witch exists in Limbo, unable to enter Death or to re-enter Life, unless a Channel shall be provided from the Otherworld into either of the Regions beyond.*'

'A channel,' said Jess. 'That's what Ulverston's made?'

Emerald looked up, nodding, and there was a lustre like starlight in her eyes. 'Either of the regions beyond...' she repeated. 'Ulverston is a fool. He may have put the entire fabric of the continuum in danger!'

'Hang on,' said Jess. 'Wasn't the Prof excavating the tomb of a Viking? Where does that fit into all this?'

Emerald ignored her and carried on reading.

'*To contain a Wraith when she has begun to take corporeal Form, a Barrier in the physical World may be set down, such as a Circle of Chalk or a Ring of Salt. Alternatively, a Challenge may be made, whereby the Strength of the Observer's Belief banishes the Wraith back to the Otherworld.*'

'Faith moves mountains?' said Richie nervously.

Emerald turned to him and gave him a broad, dazzling grin. 'If you like. Yes. That is not such an unusual concept.'

'Okay, look.' Jess held out her hands in a 'slow down' gesture. 'So you're saying that the Prof, without meaning to, disturbed the ley lines when he opened the tomb? And that this is going to let witches return from a state of... limbo?'

Emerald looked at them both very intently, with a wise and serious expression beyond her apparent years.

'This triangle of land,' she said, 'this channel of energy between the stones, the Cathedral and the Darkwater, has been - *charging* itself with psychic energy for months. I have been monitoring the levels myself!' She lowered her voice to a whisper. 'The darkest, oldest powers are gathering in the shadow of Meresbury. Restless spirits... Already they have tried to make themselves manifest.'

'The computer?' said Richie, remembering.

'Yes,' Emerald flashed him a broad grin. 'The computer. Luckily, the channel they chose could not carry the energy, and it blew a fuse. But it tells us something else very important.'

'What's that?' Jess asked.

Again, Emerald seemed to ignore the question. She flicked through several pages of the book, then, which a cry of triumph, stabbed her finger down on a page. 'It is all here! I doubt the libraries used by the Professor had a copy of this text. Emerald slammed the book shut. 'We must borrow this! Excuse me, I need to call the Librarian.'

She opened the book at the flyleaf, then put her fingers in her mouth and let out the most piercing, echoing whistle Richie had ever heard. It made his ears sing with pain.

There was a fluttering noise from high up in the vaulted ceiling. Richie, heart pounding, looked up and saw an enormous, winged shadow descending from the uppermost shelves.

There was a great rush of chilly air - and then, with wings outstretched and talons flashing, *something* began to descend silently from the ceiling.

Normally, the Ten Sisters would have been silent and still in the pale morning sunlight, watching over the dewy grass - but today the stone circle, sectioned off by striped plastic tape, bustled with activity. Figures stood guard, two at each stone; men and women in black uniforms, black caps and sunglasses, carrying ugly, snub-nosed weapons. A helicopter, blades gently turning, squatted beside the circle like a fat, watchful black raven.

The burly man with the moustache and the young black man with the glasses and the goatee beard were squatting in the centre of the circle. They were picking through the wreckage of Ulverston's instruments and the tattered rags of his two equipment tents.

'The Ten Sisters, Mr Odell,' said the older man pensively, hefting a twisted piece of metal in his hand. He sniffed the air, looked up and around.

'That's what they call them, Mr Courtney.'

'Yes,' said Mr Courtney thoughtfully. 'Funny, that.'

Behind them yawned the tunnel to the Viking tomb, also guarded by two of the sentries. The entrance to the tomb was ragged and charred, tatters of burnt grass fluttering in the wind like bunting. It looked as if it had been blasted open by high explosive.

'You know the story of this place? The legend?'

'It's fairly well-known, sir. The girls used to come up here and dance in the moonlight. Got themselves a reputation for carrying out pagan rituals and the like. Some people even said they were witches.'

Mr Courtney nodded. 'Excellent, Mr Odell. We appear to have been reading the same websites.' Mr Courtney straightened up and smoothed down his coat. 'The legend goes,' he said, staring thoughtfully at the nearest stone, 'that the girls were dancing, their long hair flowing in the silvery moonlight, their bodies garlanded with flowers and woodland herbs.' His commanding voice had dropped almost to a whisper. 'They danced and danced into the night, accompanied by the bewitching music of an old fiddle-player. His music worked them into a frenzy beneath the intoxicating light of the full moon. But they forgot it was past midnight, and so it was the Sabbath day - and they didn't know they were being led astray by the fiddler, who was the Devil in disguise... And when the daylight came, and they were still dancing, the first rays of the morning sun turned them all into stone.'

Mr Odell shot him an admiring look. 'Poetry, sir. Sheer poetry.'

'Sheer *poppycock*, more like!' Mr Courtney clicked his tongue and shook his head. 'Typical demonising of the old religions by the new. A common propaganda tool.'

'If you say so, sir.'

'I do.' Mr Courtney patted the nearest stone affectionately. 'So, to get back to reality, Odell, what we have here would appear to be a big old discharge of raw electrical energy which, somehow, didn't reach beyond these stones. Must be a good reason, eh, lad?'

Mr Odell nodded. 'The TV people's camera-lenses melted, but nobody in the audience even had their eyebrows singed!'

'And yet,' said Mr Courtney, 'our feller Ulverston appears to have been... whadyoucall... vaporised.'

'Forensics are doing tests, sir,' Mr Odell said.

Mr Courtney nodded, and pulled on a pair of black gloves as he and Mr Odell stood at the head of the tunnel. 'All right,' he said gruffly, 'let us in, then, lads.' The sentries moved smartly aside.

Inside, Mr Odell switched on a powerful flashlight. The chamber was small, with just enough room to stand up in. The walls were rough-hewn, shored up with powerful hydraulic props made of metal.

'Damn cheeky fellow,' said Mr Courtney, folding his hands and nodding as he looked around. 'He'd actually done it!'

'The Professor's equipment did cut through the main entry wall,' Mr Odell confirmed.

'So,' said Mr Courtney quietly, 'where's old George, then?'

'George?' Mr Odell didn't understand.

'The occupant, man. The *corpus horribilis*!... Our venerable Viking?'

'Ah,' said Mr Odell, swinging the flashlight down to the level of the earth floor. 'I think you may be standing on him, sir.'

Mr Courtney took a hurried step back as the flashlight's beam tracked slowly across the floor. There were some fragments of pottery lying in the dirt, and what might have been the rusty handle of a knife. Mr Odell adjusted a button on the flashlight and the beam became broader and more intense.

Then they saw, half-buried in the ground, towards the back of the cavern, something which could have been a yellowish jug or vase. But as they moved closer and Mr Odell brought the flashlight in to bear on it, the object's shape became clear. Mr Courtney and Mr Odell turned to look at one another, then turned back towards the object buried in the earth. It was undeniably a small, cracked and discoloured human skull.

'Well, saints preserve us,' chuckled Mr Courtney. 'Or in this case, high-quality peaty soil preserve us, eh, Mr Odell?'

'Yes, sir,' said Mr Odell, sighing indulgently.

'Right,' said Mr Courtney, 'Get everything cryo-sealed and then double the guard. I want a full analysis by lunchtime.'

'Yes, sir... Do you not want it taking back to the labs, sir?'

'No, Mr Odell - I've no idea how fragile this all is. Let's keep it here for now.

And tell them not to bash the chap about too much, eh?'

'Very good, sir.' Mr Odell nodded and hurried out of the tunnel.

Jess and Richie gazed up in astonishment.

The golden eagle, its feathers beautifully plumed and shining with a soft light, flew down between the shelves and landed beside them. Its talons came to rest around the silver globe on a nearby desk. With its beak lowered, the bird tucked its wings back and flicked its stern gaze from Emerald to Jess and Richie and back to Emerald again.

Richie, who was quaking, was not that surprised when the eagle opened its beak and started croaking poetry at them :

'Who calls the guardian of the books
Down from the eyrie high,
Where on the ancient words he looks,
With never-faltering eye?'

'That's a *terrible* poem,' said Richie crossly, and his hand flew to his mouth. 'Sorry!' he said frantically. 'I didn't mean to be rude!'

The Librarian tilted his head on one side and looked him up and down.

'No, no,' he said, 'you're right, young sir, hmm. Been trying to write a better one for three centuries, but it's so difficult, hmm? Surrounded by Milton, Shakespeare, Auden... all masters, you see, hmm? Cramps the style. Fellow can't really compete.'

Emerald Greene smiled indulgently.

'It was... a much better poem than I could have written,' said Jess, and glowered at Richie. He shrugged helplessly.

'Gets quite lonely up in the eyrie,' the eagle confessed, nodding up towards where the bookcases vanished out of sight. 'Up there next to Quartos and Apocrypha. Frosty, you know, on those top shelves. Poetry books covered with it. Rhymes covered in rime! Ha-ha!... Hmm, yes, well. You know,' the Librarian went on, fixing them with his beady eyes, 'tried limericks for a while. Any idea how difficult 'tis to find rhyme for *library*, hmm?' He tut-tutted and flapped his wings.

'It must be very hard,' said Jess politely. 'I can't think of one myself.'

'*Bribery*,' said Emerald, and produced a banknote from an inside pocket. Richie frowned - it looked to him like old-fashioned money. 'I'm sorry, Librarian, but I think I was late bringing back that Shakespeare First Folio last week. Ten shillings, I believe?'

'Thank you, hmm, yes,' said the eagle, pouncing on the ten-shilling note and secreting it among his golden feathers. 'Now then, what you want this time, hmm?'

Emerald held up *Lore of Albion Guiding the Fullest History, Taming and Containment of Witches.*

The effect on the Librarian was startling. The great bird lowered his head, flapped his wings in agitation and made a strange, tortured hissing noise from his beak. 'No, no. That is, um, restricted loan, yes... Can't have it.'

'Why not?' said Emerald, one hand on her hip and the other holding the book open at the flyleaf. 'Come on - your stamp, please. We are in a hurry.'

The eagle shook his proud head once more. 'No, hmm, sorry. That book is dangerous in the wrong hands. Book has, mm, unusual energy fields. Restricted loan.'

Emerald sighed. 'Look, Librarian - I live here now. I am the owner of Rubicon House. You should make an exception for me.'

'You live here, yes. The owner, no,' croaked the eagle. The eagle shook his head, made a disapproving clicking noise in his beak and began muttering to himself. 'Dangerous, hmm. Time fractures, spells and incantations. Leads to chaos. No, can't have that, no, hmm. Order, what we need, mmm. Order, perfection, yeeessss... The Dewey Decimal system! No talking! No eating! Loans returned by the date stamped, yes.'

Jessica and Richie exchanged glances.

'It's no good arguing with librarians,' said Richie knowledgeably. 'They always know best.'

'It is an emergency,' said Emerald firmly. 'Can I not make a special request?'

'Hmmm,' said the eagle thoughtfully, gazing up into the shelves as if it had spotted something to eat. 'Must fill in a special request form, yes. Will be considered.' With his beak, he rummaged in his feathers for a moment and produced a rolled-up piece of parchment. He stamped his claw on it, making a mark, and pushed it towards Emerald Greene. 'Sign there,' he ordered.

Emerald took an old quill pen from the desk, dipped it in ink and scrawled an illegible signature. 'Is that it?' she asked with a sigh.

'It will be processed. Must leave the book here, yes, mmm.'

Emerald reluctantly put the book back down on the table. 'All right. Good day.'

'Good day,' said the eagle, and swivelled away with a flourish of his golden plumage.

Emerald steered them back through the dusty bookshelves to the door. The Librarian, spreading his wings, rose high into the reaches of the bookshelves, the leather-bound tome grasped firmly in his talons.

Half an hour later, Emerald Greene, Richie and Jessica stood on the glittering lawn in the impossible summer sunlight. Jess could still not quite believe that the house and gardens were real, and kept expecting them to vanish in a puff of smoke. Anoushka lazed on the lawn, preening himself.

'You know,' Jess began hesitantly, 'there are a lot of things about this I still don't understand.'

Emerald sighed, folded her arms. 'Just focus on what I have told you already.' Jess began to speak again, but Emerald held up a hand. 'Trust me.'

'All right,' said Jessica bravely. 'Rich?'

He scowled. 'I suppose so. For now.'

Jessica leaned down to stroke Anoushka's fur, but the cat gave a threatening hiss and she withdrew her hand sharply. 'Sorry,' she said. 'Look, um, I don't mean to be... uneasy around you. It's just that I've, er, never had a cat actually *speak* to me before.'

'I should think not,' drawled Anoushka, turning away from her. 'We don't converse with any old riff-raff, you know.'

Emerald was checking her watch. 'It is only about... eight-thirty out there. You should be fine.'

'Gabi's ready to send out the search parties,' said Richie apologetically. 'I tried to cover as best I could, but...'

Jess turned towards the end of the garden. Beyond the clipped hedges, the sky shimmered in a heat-haze. 'What do we do?' she asked. 'Say the magic word?'

'Just walk through. Walk through, and *believe* it is there.'

'It's that simple?'

Emerald nodded.

Jess took a deep breath and rubbed her hands together. She started to walk, and did not look back.

'Richie?' she said, looking over her shoulder.

'All right, all right.' He glowered at Emerald again. 'I've no idea what you're up to,' he said, 'but it had better be good.' He ran over to Jess and grabbed hold of her sleeve.

They shut their eyes, swung their arms, kept walking.

There was a noise like slurping mud, a flash of blue light, and then they fell -

But like in a dream, Jess thought, when you fall into your bed but you've been there all the time -

And they were sprawled face-down on the dewy grass of the forest clearing. The warmth of the sunlight had gone, and the light was newer, greyer.

Jess rolled over one elbow, shivering. At the edge of her vision, there was a flash of blue and a slurping noise as the barrier closed. Then, silence.

They scrambled to their feet, suddenly fearful.

'You okay?' Richie asked, brushing leaves off himself.

She nodded. 'You?'

'Think so.'

And then they turned and ran, ran, ran through the trees towards the morning sunlight, until they emerged from the woods and found the little lane, canopied with chestnut trees, which led back down to the main Meresbury road. Fallen conkers split and squashed under their feet as they hit the lane running.

They did not look back.

Luckily.

Fifty metres down the winding lane, still and silent in the dawnlight, a grey figure stood, watching the retreating pair.

The figure was hunched, quivering, pale as a smudge against the woodland. It was leaning on a long, slender staff and it seemed to shimmer as if not quite there.

As it saw the girl and boy running down the lane, heading for the great road with its noise and clamour of early morning, the figure nodded, perhaps at something understood.

Then it swung abruptly round, as if to head back into the trees.

As it turned, its hunched body seemed to twist in on itself.

There was a buzzing, fizzing noise like an electrical discharge, and then the cowled figure shrank to a pale vertical line as if an invisible door had closed on it. The line shrank to a dot, which popped out of sight as if it had never been there.

A second later, the birds in the clearing began to sing again.

5

Manifestations and Ruminations

'*Good evening - this is County TV, and I'm Mike Devenish, bringing you sixty minutes of news, weather and features.*

'*Investigations are continuing into the tragic death of the eminent archaeologist Professor Edwin Ulverston at the Ten Sisters stone circle, near Meresbury. Experts are now saying the Professor's death was caused by a freak emission of ball lightning.*

'*It is understood that Professor Ulverston - who was 56 and divorced - absorbed the full impact of the multi-volt discharge of lightning and was killed instantly, although investigators at the site have yet to confirm the recovery of his body.*

'*The tomb which the Professor and his assistants uncovered appears to be that of a Viking warrior from approximately 800 A.D. The archaeological world, while mourning Professor Ulverston, is marvelling at his exciting discovery. The tomb is strikingly unusual, not only for being located within a Neolithic circle, but also for containing what seems to be a well-preserved skeleton - Viking burial custom was normally to cremate the dead and bury the ashes, usually in a clay pot, with a variety of different utensils. You'll find more on this story at our website, and you can follow me on Twitter...*'

The black Mercedes carrying Mr Courtney and Mr Odell churned its way along a muddy track.

The car stereo was blasting Verdi's *Nabucco* at a volume which made Mr Odell's teeth vibrate as he drove. He wondered whether his boss realised quite how loud it was - but, as Mr Courtney was happily singing along to the opera, he supposed he liked it at that volume.

'Is that, ah, a new stereo system, sir?' Mr Odell asked.

'Fantastic, isn't it, lad? Enhanced digital octophonic sound. Just like being there, eh?'

'Marvellous, sir,' said Mr Odell drily.

He should be grateful his boss wasn't into techno or gangsta rap, he reflected as they locked the car and walked over to the barrier around the stones. At least opera wouldn't put a strain on the car's suspension.

They showed their passes at the roadblock, and were waved on.

The car stopped on Scratchcombe Edge. Here, black-capped Special Measures operatives still surrounded the stone circle, looking tense and alert. Parked beside the stones now was a Transit van, sporting a large dish-shaped aerial, and several white-coated technicians were deep in conversation outside it.

'By the way,' Mr Courtney said as they got out of the car, 'top-notch work on the cover story. The media chaps seem to have swallowed the "ball lightning" nonsense like a bunch of kids. Well done.'

'Thank you, sir,' murmured Mr Odell with a modest smile. 'I got my best spin-doctors on the job.'

The tomb entrance had been draped with white plastic, but the guard pulled it aside when he saw them coming.

Inside, it looked very different. The walls were covered with plastic, while spotlights illuminated every crevice with a gentle blood-red glow. Against the rugged walls, several probes had been set up, pointing down at the cracked skull. Its eye-sockets stared vacantly upwards.

Despite himself, Mr Odell felt a slight shiver.

'Therein lies the answer, Mr Odell,' said Mr Courtney. 'Damn sure of it, I am... Well, Strickland?' he barked at the white-coated, bespectacled lackey who had hurried up behind them, clipboard in hand. 'Any luck?'

'Several energy surges while you were away, sir. All pinpointed and fully logged.'

Mr Courtney nodded to the scientist. 'Jolly good. That all?'

'The analysis team have run all those tests you requested, sir,' said Strickland. He handed Mr Courtney the clipboard and hovered nervously.

Mr Courtney waved him away and flicked through the pages, his moustache bristling. He raised his bushy eyebrows at one point and made a 'Hmmm' noise, but otherwise he betrayed no emotion. Mr Odell stood with his hands behind his back, awaiting his superior's verdict.

'Well, Mr Odell,' muttered the older man, 'we have ourselves a jolly interesting skeleton.' He looked up sharply, fixing his colleague with his surprisingly piercing blue eyes. 'It seems there's one thing about old George that we've overlooked until now.'

Mr Odell frowned. 'What would that be, sir?'

'We ought to be calling him Georgina,' quipped Mr Courtney. 'The bone structure analysis indicates it - here, look. As does the DNA extract from the tooth from the boffins at Oxford.' He tapped the clipboard, nodded sagely. 'Our Viking warrior is a *woman*, Mr Odell. No doubt about it.'

'How old, sir?' Mr Odell asked, stroking his beard. The monitor-screen next to him showed the skull, bathed in its reddish glow from the lamps. Mr Odell stared at it, deep in thought, and put out a hand to touch the image.

Mr Courtney shrugged. 'A thousand years, nine hundred at a pinch? You're the university bod, sunshine. You know when the Vikings poured through Northern Europe.'

'Actually, Mr Courtney,' said Mr Odell, smiling apologetically, 'I didn't mean that. I mean how old was the... lady?' He gestured at the screen. 'The age of the body when she was inhumed?'

'Oh, I, *harrumph*, see,' said Mr Courtney, clearing his throat to hide his embarrassment. 'Er, where are we now?... Yes, here. "Analysis of the tissue and the bone structures indicates that the subject would have been approximately thirty-five years old at time of burial."' He glanced up at Mr Odell. 'Got an idea, have you, lad? Eh?'

Mr Odell tapped a finger against his teeth thoughtfully. 'People didn't live so long back then, right? Thirty-five would have been, well, middle-aged - probably past the expected child-bearing age, yeah?... Now, I mean, those Viking guys had pretty traditional ideas about the role of women. Kept them in the kitchen, sir, as far as I recall.'

Mr Courtney frowned, tapped him on the chest with the clipboard. 'What are you getting at, lad, eh? Spell it out for me.'

'Well, we know it's bizarre for the tomb to be found under a Neolithic stone circle anyway. Not normal Viking burial methods either, right? They used to *cremate* their dead in a blazing boat. They'd put them in a jar and send the soul off to join Odin in Valhalla - their warriors' heaven - for a load of feasting and general revelry, yeah?... Well, quite apart from that, wouldn't you say it was pretty unusual for a woman in that time - a pretty affluent woman, to judge by the stuff they put in with her - not to be buried with her husband?'

'Pah! So, the filly didn't have a husband,' Mr Courtney blustered. 'Independent woman. Nothing wrong with that... Still, I see what you mean. Dashed unusual.'

'But what kind of person,' said Mr Odell softly, 'would be deliberately buried in a fashion outside the normal customs of the age? And on ground which would have been sacred not to the Vikings, but to an older religion?'

'You've been doing your homework, young man,' said Mr Courtney approvingly, and clapped him on the shoulder. They both turned as one to look at the fragmented skeleton in the blood-red light, then looked back towards each other again.

'I reckon,' murmured Mr Odell, 'that *they were scared of her.*' He heard himself say the words, and couldn't quite believe it.

Mr Courtney chewed the scraggy end of his moustache. 'So, what made the Vikings so frightened of this woman, eh - even in death?'

'I can only think of one possibility, Mr Courtney,' said Mr Odell. 'They were terrified she might come back.' He looked up and gazed into space, the red lights reflecting in the lenses of his glasses. 'Back from the dead.'

'Oh, yeah. She came back. No problem.'

Jess could hear Aunt Gabi on the phone. She was eating chocolates and watching a TV soap while having her regular weekly gossip with her friend Paula.

'She'd been out all night, though, the little madam,' she went on. 'With this new friend of hers, Emerald Greene.'

Paula's voice twittered in Gabi's ear.

'Well, I don't know *what* they were doing. Secret girls' things. I'm not going to ask... What? Oh, yeah, I screamed blue murder! Told her she was a stupid, irresponsible child. I must have yelled myself hoarse. End of the day, though, I was just relieved to get her back here in one piece. You know how it is.'

Paula jabbered away for another few seconds.

'Yeah, she's stubborn. Her father was always the same, you know. She gets it from him... Mmm, I was going to ground her for a week, but I haven't really got the heart... Oh, she's fine. Seems really happy. Back eating me out of house and home - '

Paula made another comment in a quizzical tone. Gabi cradled the phone under her chin as she started to unwrap a chocolate.

'Well, actually,' Gabi said, 'she's been spending *hours* on the Internet these past few days. It's for school, though, so I don't really mind. A local history project. Yeah, it sounds interesting, actually... Something to do with Meresbury's history of witchcraft...'

The Darkwater fizzed and bubbled. Mist steamed from the shining lake, drifted across the surface like phantoms.

A kingfisher came in to land with a bright flash of orange and sky-blue, churning the water. It splashed about uncertainly, looking this way and that for a few seconds, before flapping its wings in agitation and taking off in a state of some distress.

At least, it tried to take off. In mid-flight, about a metre above the lake, the kingfisher appeared to slow the beat of its wings, hanging in mid-air, defying gravity.

Its feathers drained of their orange and blue. The bird was, momentarily, a grey image of itself, like a picture on a monochrome screen. Its body turned in on itself, shrinking, until it was no more than a line of greyness - and then, with a fizzing, buzzing sound, the line shrank to a dot.

Rolling mist filled the blank space where the kingfisher had been.

Xanthë had seen the door to the Earthworld.

They knew, the other members of the Ten. They had nodded their twisted, warty heads as she flickered across the land, not quite in phase, conveying the news to them.

Xanthë sat on the steps of the moss-covered war memorial in the Black - the burned Green. She was a ragged grey figure, cradling the blue and orange bird in her arms. Although she had no real sense of touch, she could still imagine the smoothness of its plumage.

The bird was dead, of course - the shock of the phase transfer had killed it instantly. Their own bodies, she hoped, would be more resilient. The others, flickering like candles around her, nodded their agreement.

She looked around the village, tried to see if any were recognisable still. Martha's twisted form was there, at the door of the ale-house, her straggly white hair pulled tightly over her shrunken head. Over in the churchyard, shivering, leaning on her staff - could that, once, have been Róisín? And there, in the garden of a ruined cottage across the Black, there was the spindly, cracked body and skeletal face belonging to Bethan, who had been the most beautiful of them all.

Xanthë squinted through crusty, yellowing eyes at the place around her. A sign swung above the gawping, windowless wall of the ale-house. Down the street, tendrils embraced the church spire. All was decay, entropy.

The village was submerged under a hundred fathoms, but she and the others could visit here, slightly out of time-phase, for a limited period. The occasional glimpse of the Darkwater cracked through into the air here and there - ripples, weeds, fish poking themselves through the fragmenting reality, reminding them that this village lay beneath a lake in the real, physical world of the 21st Century.

Another figure flickered in front of her, and she sighed in exasperation. Here he was, plaguing them again, the one who had slipped through by accident - that fool of a scholar. Tall, male, white-haired, wearing a broad smile, dressed in some striped two-piece garb like that of a rich trader. He flickered in and out of phase, beaming at her.

'*Ull-Verr-Stone*,' she said, pronouncing each syllable of his name with transparent contempt. 'What do you want?'

'You're not still set on this absurd scheme, are you, my dear?' he asked. 'Passing through into the Earthworld again? You'll never do it. Why can't you just accept your spectral situation? After all, I have done.'

'You? You have accepted being a ghost?'

'Weeell, yes... I must admit I'm quite enjoying it, actually, frightening old ladies in tea-shops. Admit it, my dear ladies - your plan is ridiculous!'

'The plan is not ridiculous,' answered Xanthë patiently. 'We will survive.'

'Oh, come now. Look, what is there for you to go back to? I found myself pulled through to this dimension at the high-point of my life. Had I remained, I would have been rich - I would have been *adored*!' He pulled a face. 'I would have been the world-famous Professor Edwin Ulverston. But, no, it wasn't to be, and you know what? I've accepted that.'

'Will you cease your prattling and be gone, Ull-Verr-Stone?' she replied. 'You are not a witch. Please stop associating with us.'

He shrugged, began to fade. 'All right. But don't say I didn't warn you.' The echo of his words boomed around the Black after he had disappeared.

Before, she remembered, when they had been young and beautiful, they had lived in this abandoned village all the time, their bodies immune to that plague which ravaged the humans. It was the only place they had been allowed to live.

Hexbrook, the place was called.

The name stank of contempt and fear - but, given the choice of exile or death, they had each chosen exile, and they had lived here undisturbed for years. Undisturbed until the waters had come, flooding and drowning the only real home they had ever known.

But now they were to have another home.

Thanks to the foolish scholar Ulverston and his meddling, the power of the Fracture was growing. They had to muster their force, slip through when the psychic energy was at its height.

They knew that it was almost time for the Becoming.

6

In the Cathedral

'It is vital,' said Emerald, pacing up and down in Jess's room with her hands behind her back, 'that we maintain alertness. Sooner or later, the Enemy will try to break through the frayed threads of Time, and we must be alert.'

It was Saturday afternoon. People were hanging up their scarves for another week after seeing Meresbury Rovers draw 1-1 at home to York, or unpacking their shopping, or hauling pushchairs and picnic-hampers from their cars after days out with their families. The citizens of Meresbury brewed their pots of tea, toasted their crumpets and settled down in front of their televisions as the shadows grew longer and the day grew cooler.

Jess had been bursting with questions ever since the revelations in Rubicon House. But Emerald Greene knew how to be elusive. She would give answers which left Jess none the wiser, sometimes answers to different questions entirely. But facing Emerald now, up in her own bedroom at Chadwick Road, Jess got a sense of importance, of urgency. Emerald was going to tell them something.

Emerald paused by Jess's notice-board and for a second she peered at the picture which was pinned there next to the oddments. It was the one thirteen-year-old photo of her parents which Jessica kept out. Emerald gave a brief, curt nod at the photo, and Jess felt her face flush hot and red.

'Yes,' said Emerald again, 'we must be ready!' She whirled round, narrowing her eyes.

'We? You're taking us on as assistants, then?' Jess was being facetious to hide her discomfort and nervousness, but Emerald nodded, taking her seriously.

'Yes,' she said, 'if you like. You, for some unknown reason, appear to be slightly Time-intuitive. You can help me, Jessica Mathieson.' Emerald swung round to stare at Richie. 'And you,

Richard Fanshawe? Well, you seem to be of above average intelligence. We will find a way for you to help.'

'Thanks a bunch,' said Richie sardonically.

'You are welcome.' Emerald Greene gave a brief, formal nod of her head and (rather rudely, Jess thought) continued to prowl around her room, staring at the posters and photos on the wall.

'Back in Rubicon House,' Jess said tentatively, brushing crumbs off her skirt, 'you were talking about witches. Well, I've no idea what a witch should look like. And as for the ghost of a witch...'

'You will know when you see it,' said Emerald, swinging round from looking at Jess's framed swimming certificates.

Richie blinked. 'But they're not actually *there*, are they?' he said. 'These... ghosts?'

Emerald sighed. 'People see what they *want* to see, and disregard the rest!' she exclaimed. 'It is so easy to miss important points when you are *looking for the wrong thing.*'

There was silence in the bedroom. Outside, somewhere, a dog barked and one of Jess's neighbours revved a lawnmower.

Richie shook his head and pulled his fingers down over his eyes. 'If I'd only gone to King Ethelred's, none of this would be my problem,' he said gloomily.

'Now, please listen. Here, we may be safe. The enemy must have no inkling of our plans. For the moment you must carry on as normal - go to school, and pretend that you know nothing. Can you?'

Jess took a deep breath. 'I'll try,' she said.

Richie shrugged. 'It won't be difficult, will it? I don't have a clue anyway.'

'Good,' said Emerald Greene. 'You are both very brave.'

'So what next?' Jess asked. 'We take another look at the stones?'

'No! You will not get close, not with the authorities there,' said Emerald. 'But there is one place on the pattern we have not investigated. If we want to be ahead of the game, we should make sure we do so at the earliest opportunity.'

'Where's that?' Richie asked.

Emerald drew back the curtain of Jess's bedroom window and pointed down the valley into Meresbury. They followed her finger.

'The Cathedral!' exclaimed Jess, her eyes alighting on the tall, jagged tower.

'Yes. Perhaps you two could see if anything unusual is happening there? Meanwhile, I shall - '

There was a sudden scream from downstairs, and a sound of tins and bottles suddenly being dropped on the floor. Jess, who was off like a shot, got downstairs first, with Richie close behind. Emerald Greene hung back on the stairs, watching from a distance as usual.

In the kitchen, Aunt Gabi was backed up against the fridge, covering her beetroot-red face with her hands and breathing deeply.

As Jess ran into the kitchen, noticing the supermarket bags spilling their contents on to the floor, Aunt Gabi pointed with a wavering finger to the contented black cat which was perched on her pine dining table, licking the last remnants of milk from one of her bowls.

'What - is - *that* - doing here?' she gasped, and then let out a sneeze which made the crockery on the dresser vibrate. 'Aaah-CHOO!'

'Her allergy!' exclaimed Richie in dismay.

'I'm sorry,' Jess said, scooping up Anoushka in her arms and heading for the back door. 'I'll ask Emerald not to bring him again...' She opened the back door and let Anoushka out, murmuring softly in the cat's ear, '*Please* don't speak in front of Gabi - she'd never get over it.' Not waiting around for the cat to show his wounded dignity, Jess slammed the door shut and spun round to face Aunt Gabi with a contrite expression. 'Aunt Gabi,' she said, 'I'm really sorry!'

Gabi was simultaneously blowing her nose and wiping her eyes, so most of her face was obscured behind two large wads of tissues. She waved a hand, as if trying to say something, and sank slowly on to a chair. After a few seconds she regained her composure, and she looked up with watery eyes from a pink face. 'Don't do that to me, Jess,' she gasped. 'Please *don't* do that!' She reached instinctively for her cigarettes and was about to light one.

'*Not* in the house!' said Jessica sternly, plucking Gabi's lighter from her fingers and throwing it to Emerald in the doorway, who caught it instinctively.

'Fascinating,' said Emerald. 'A genuine allergic reaction! I have never seen that happen before.' She looked down at the lighter in her hands, doing a double take as if noticing it for the first time. 'What is *this*?' she demanded, holding it up with some distaste and clicking it on, her eyes widening as the flame leapt up. 'Astonishing! A simple flint mechanism, fuelled by...' She sniffed. 'Propane? No, butane! How quaintly primitive. What is it for?'

'Never you mind, madam,' said Gabi, and snatched it from her hand. She stared at her, blinking several times and dabbing at her eyes. 'So, you must be the famous Emerald Greene,' she said. 'Well, I'm pleased to meet you at last. Even if I wasn't so pleased to meet your cat.' They shook hands, awkwardly. 'You know,' Gabi added, 'I'd like to ask you a few things.'

Emerald cleared her throat and scooped up her school-books in one hand. 'Must go. Homework.' And with a nod, she had bolted out of the back door.

Gabi blinked again and shook her head. 'There's something very odd about that girl,' she murmured. 'Still, she seems polite enough.' She gathered her things together and headed for the stairs. 'I've got a college assignment to do. Supper's fish and chips, okay?'

Richie was still pensively looking out of the window, trying to see which way Emerald Greene had gone. 'You know what?' he muttered. 'I think she's just too smug for her own good.'

A tousled head of tomato-red hair popped back round the door, making Richie jump.

'By the way,' said Emerald, 'I forgot to add - I would draw your attention to the curious factor of Professor Ulverston's body.'

Richie and Jess exchanged puzzled glances.

'But... they never found Professor Ulverston's body,' said Jess slowly.

Emerald flashed a broad grin at them. 'Yes,' she said. 'That is the curious factor.'

And then she was gone.

'I wonder, sir,' said Mr Odell thoughtfully to Mr Courtney, as they sat in the parked Mercedes in a country lane just above Meresbury. 'About the potassium-argon test and the carbon-dating that the science guys did.'

'You wonder, do you?' said Mr Courtney. He peered inside his bread roll. 'Cheese and pickle. What have you got?'

'Ham and egg, sir.'

They looked at each other for a second, and then swapped sandwiches.

Mr Courtney chomped with enthusiasm into his. '*What mff you tthhff thtt thnnn?*' he asked indistinctly.

'Pardon, sir?'

'I said, what makes you think that, then?'

'Dunno, sir. Just a hunch, but I wonder whether we're dealing with what we *think* we're dealing with.'

'We very rarely are, Mr Odell. It's in the nature of the job. Remember the plague of frogs in Shepton Mallet last year?' Mr Courtney shook his head. 'Shocking business, that. Shocking.'

Mr Odell shuddered. He did indeed remember the incident of the plague of frogs, but was not prepared to dwell on it right now. 'And it's... just a feeling about Ulverston, too, sir. Like there's something we're missing.'

'Ulverston,' said Mr Courtney, nodding slowly and drumming his fingers on the dashboard. 'Professor Edwin Ulverston. I think our deceased Professor holds the key to this mystery, Mr Odell!'

'Yes, sir,' said Mr Odell. 'Look.' He flipped open the lid of his laptop and called up a 3-D digital image of the Professor. 'I've got everything about him from the Internet here,' he said, scrolling down the text.

Mr Courtney did a double-take. 'Have you got wireless fidelity on yours?' he asked enviously.

'Yes, sir.'

'Why have you got that and not me? I'm supposed to be in charge here!'

Mr Odell shrugged and smiled. 'Pays to be nice to the techie boys and girls, sir. Especially the girls,' he added, with a wistful look in his eye.

'Yes, well, never mind that. Is it all downloaded to the secure files back at base, too?' Mr Courtney asked.

'All done, sir.'

'What about his research papers? Did you get hold of those?'

'Yes, sir. The University authorities were very obliging.'

'And his Government file?'

Mr Odell folded his laptop shut and looked apologetic. 'Ah. Well, sir, it's all in a secure data-store. Top-level security, accessible only with restricted passwords, complex protocols... But we, um, had to change the access codes.'

Mr Courtney frowned. 'Why was that, Mr Odell?'

'A ten-year-old kid from Redditch hacked into it last week.'

'I see. I sometimes wonder, Mr Odell, if the Intelligence Corps should consider changing their name.'

'Yes, sir,' said Mr Odell with an indulgent smile.

'Tell me what you know, anyway.'

The shadows of the trees gathered around the black Mercedes as the two men carried on talking. Sometimes, the shadows almost looked like recognisable shapes, flitting in and out of the hedgerows. The wind passed through the trees, rustling the leaves like the voices of ghosts.

High above, a pale moon emerged like a watchful eye, and dusk gathered once again over the city of Meresbury.

'Splendid,' said Emerald Greene. 'Absolutely splendid.'

Rooks cawed in the trees beyond the Ten Sisters, their mocking *maaahk-maaahk* echoing across the shadowy plateau. High above Scratchcombe Edge, behind the meadow which led down to the stone circle, was a rickety five-bar gate. Emerald, in her duffel-coat, sat on the gate and squinted through the telescope.

Down in the gathering gloom by the Ten Sisters, the small team of Special Measures operatives laughed, chatted and smoked together. Their guns were holstered and their body-language was relaxed. The dish-shaped aerial on the black Transit van swept steadily back and forth.

'Obviously not expecting any trouble,' Emerald murmured. She collapsed the telescope and replaced it in the small rucksack she was carrying. 'Idiots.'

Anoushka, who was walking with perfect balance along the top bar of the gate, paused for a scratch. 'So why are we wasting our time here, Miss Emerald?'

'Just checking,' said Emerald Greene. 'I like to cover all eventualities.' Emerald rummaged in her rucksack and fished out a tangle of wiring and a small disc with a dial built into it.

'Don't tell me,' drawled Anoushka, who was sniffing around the bottom of the gate. 'Another device you haven't properly calibrated.'

'In an ideal world,' said Emerald Greene, frantically connecting wires around the outside of the dial, 'I would have had time to overhaul all of the equipment properly before we left. Such a thing was not possible. Now...' Emerald flicked a switch, pointed the device across the field at the stones and nodded grimly at the reading which the pointer gave. 'As I suspected.'

'You're certain?' Anoushka hissed, hopping on to her shoulder to verify the readings.

Emerald showed him the dial. 'I just hope the fools have not subjected the remains to any light from the non-visible spectrum.'

'Such as X-rays?' Anoushka suggested.

Emerald narrowed her eyes. 'Let us be honest. We are dealing with simple-minded imbeciles. I imagine their first act would have been to X-ray the Enemy.' Emerald shook her head, stuffing the dial and the wires back into her rucksack. 'Botheration! If *only* I could get in there.'

'They would have you arrested and impounded,' said Anoushka casually. 'And what good would that be?... Leave it to me.'

'Good advice, as ever, dear Anoushka.'

Anoushka leapt up on to her lap, and the two of them briefly touched foreheads. Then the cat jumped down from the gate into the bracken and was softly, swiftly heading for the stones.

Anoushka was a clever cat.

He wasn't sure who had given him the name Anoushka. It had not been Emerald. A previous owner, he supposed, some ignorant human who couldn't tell the difference between a boy kitten and a girl kitten.

Never mind - it was a striking, noble, exotic name and he was fond of it. He didn't answer to it as often as Emerald might like. He was a free spirit, and one with nine lives - and a bit of investigation of his own often proved more fruitful than anything Miss Greene might ask him to do.

The other thing, of course, was that people were used to cats.

They didn't, in general, try to keep them out of secure areas. Although he had been chased off a few gardens in Meresbury with the aid of a hosepipe, he was free to roam around private spaces in a way that humans just weren't.

The red-and-white tape barrier around the stone circle might as well not have been there for Anoushka. In the gloom, the patrolling Special Measures men didn't even see him. He could smell them all at a hundred yards, though; their scent was distinct, a mixture of synthetic clothes, normal human smell and cigarette smoke. For a hunter as seasoned as Anoushka, they might as well have been carrying big flashing beacons announcing their presence. He allowed himself a little purr of pleasure as he trotted over to the stones. *Foolish humans.* He wondered how they had ever become the dominant species on this planet.

He sniffed the earth beside one of the stones, and shrank back, hissing. Yes. As he had thought.

He trotted across the stone circle and hopped up the ramp through the tattered entrance of the tomb. The two guards on duty didn't even react.

Here, the soft red lights cast an unearthly hue over everything. Even Anoushka almost baulked; there was something in here which made his senses, more acute than those of a human, tingle in alertness. But he padded further inside.

The bones lay there, still half-submerged in the peaty soil, surrounded by soft red lights and electronic probes. A thin film of some plastic material had been laid over the top, but Anoushka could still make out the eye-sockets of the cracked skull and the neat, even bones of the ribcage.

And there was something else.

For Anoushka, who lived at a slight tangent to humanity, could sense things which human beings could not. And the aura around the bones was one which shot through several of his

senses; it had the smell of fear, the colour of blood, the taste of...
what? Old bones, old hollows and caves...the taste of death.

Anoushka shrank back with a growl, the hair rising on his
arching back, as he dug his claws deep into the peaty earth of the
burial chamber.

That feeling, wrapped around his head; he knew what it meant
as he had encountered it before. There was a presence there,
something to be sensed, something to be.... communicated with?
Anoushka could feel his heart beating. His whiskers twitched
in fear. He moved forward, and yes, there it was again, like a
forcefield of fire enclosing the skeleton. His mind sensed the
powerful intelligence immediately.

He lowered his head, blinked his green eyes and, digging his
claws in further still, Anoushka tried to tune his mind to the
other.

Something there.

Like... like a smell. Or a taste. The cat hissed as the sensations
flowed through his body. His fur stood up in menacing spikes
and his back arched as if he were about to pounce.

Earth. Mulchy, wet earth.

Longing. Deep, angry longing. A sense of containment,
something scrabbling for release, skittering like rats' claws in the
skirting.

Alone. So alone. Down there in the soil, in the dirt.

In the *dark.*

And now, Anoushka sensed, probing further, the longing had
a name. A murmured name, calling out like a whisper in a vault,
like a low sigh of anguish in the deepest of caverns.

'*Frey- gerrrrrrrrrd...*'

And now pain.

A crimson, *angry* pain, reaching out with a giant finger into
Anoushka's mind and -

With a sudden *skerrowl* of surprise, Anoushka jumped back,
breaking the connection, his claws scrabbling in the earth as he
attempted to find a foothold.

Hissing and baring his teeth, he backed out of the tomb
and ran, a bolt of blackness in the grey. Like a moving shadow,
he slipped across the dewy grass, darting between the feet of

the security men (who still didn't see him) before rejoining his mistress at the gate.

Anoushka jumped into Emerald's arms and, for a few moments only, pressed his head against her forehead once more, green eyes meeting green eyes.

Something passed between them.

Understanding. Information. Analysis.

'I see,' said Emerald Greene softly. 'Then it is more dangerous than I had feared. The children... Anoushka, you must go to the Cathedral - make sure they are protected. The cracks in the fabric of Time are growing. Things are starting to emerge. *They may not be safe.*'

Anoushka sprang down to the ground, and Emerald hopped from the gate and followed him.

The girl and her cat hurried along at a brisk pace. With dusk fading into night, they disappeared over the rise and melted into the shadows like ghosts.

Richie and Jess hurried through the darkening streets of Meresbury, trying to look nonchalant. In truth, nobody was around to see them, but Richie was still fearful that a passing police-car would stop and haul them up for breaking a curfew. He saw Jess pull her black-and-white checked cap lower over her face.

'I hope you realise what a favour I'm doing you,' Richie panted behind her. 'I don't abscond down the drainpipe for anyone.'

'Oh, shut up, Richie. Did you bring everything I asked you to?'

He patted his satchel. 'Phone, biscuits, water, candles, a stopwatch and an iPod.'

'I didn't ask you to bring an iPod.'

'I know. But I reckon it might be a long night.'

'Hmm. Let's hope we get the information Emerald wants.'

'Just one thing,' Richie whispered, as they came to a halt in front of the dark Cathedral.

'Yes?'

'Why did *he* have to come?'

Richie nodded down at the flagstones behind them, where the dark, sinuous form of Anoushka was licking his paws and preening himself.

Jess did a double take. 'Anoushka! You weren't there a second ago.'

'And now I am,' drawled the cat, prowling round them in a circle. 'You really have to stop thinking of Time in these terribly boring, linear terms, you know. Miss Emerald is *trying* to educate you.'

Jess and Richie looked at one another. Richie scowled and folded his arms, but Jess just shrugged.

'Emerald's orders, I expect,' she said. 'Someone to keep an eye on us.'

'Keep an... Jess, it's a *cat!*' Richie pointed accusingly at Anoushka. 'What's it going to do if a horrible demon from beyond the gates of Hell pops up breathing fire at us? Cough up a fur-ball at it?'

Anoushka looked up. 'That's right, just mock,' he said languidly. 'I'm used to it.'

With the cat trotting behind them, they hurried across the Cathedral Close, where soft lights still glowed in some of the imposing Edwardian houses. Jess wondered if the Bishop was ensconced in there, kept awake by coffee, hammering away at some evangelical treatise on his iMac. At the main Cathedral doors, they stopped. Jess tried the handle, and the door felt firmly locked. She tentatively pushed at the solid oak, but it didn't give.

'Okay,' said Richie in relief. 'Mission abandoned. Let's go home.' He turned around, only to find Jess yanking him back by the collar and lifting him up to her height with both hands.

'Listen, Fanshawe, I've not brought you along so you can chicken out, right? This could be the biggest thing to happen in Meresbury for yonks, and you want to go *home*?'

'Errk,' Richie suggested, pointing to his neck.

'Do you want me to tell everyone at Aggie's that I took you ghost-hunting and you acted like a total wimp? *Do you?*'

'Rrrrk?' Richie answered, which was about as much as he could manage with Jess's hands pressing against his windpipe. Jess let him go and he dropped, almost falling over but regaining his balance at the last moment. 'That wasn't fair,' he protested, rubbing his neck. 'You hurt me.'

'Well, you'll think twice before scuttling off, won't you? Honestly, I thought you'd want to stay here and protect me. Whatever happened to old-fashioned chivalry?'

'Errrr... I don't think you need protecting, Jess.' He nodded down at Anoushka, who was sniffing around the base of the Cathedral doors. 'What's *he* doing?'

As they watched, Anoushka braced himself, hissing and clawing at the ground. Then, the cat launched himself forward like a small missile of black fur, snarling and spitting as he headed straight for the Cathedral door.

Richie gulped and shut his eyes tightly, but the thud and squeal which he was expecting never came. He opened his eyes, just in time to see a black tail disappearing *through* the door - the surface seeming, just for a second, to become glutinous, fluid like treacle.

'How did he do that?' Richie asked in astonishment, his mouth hanging open.

'Maybe nobody told him he couldn't,' said Jess thoughtfully.

'Oh, come on. Laws of physics and all that.'

Jess shook her head. 'You know, Rich, something tells me that what's happening in Meresbury at the moment is going to rewrite the laws of physics.'

The door clicked, and with a long, low *creeeeeeeak*, it opened from the inside.

'What did I tell you?' said Jess with a smile. She gestured. 'After you.'

'Er, no. Ladies first.'

'Get in there,' she snapped, and pushed him through the doorway.

Inside, the cathedral was vast, cold, unwelcoming. Some candles flickered in alcoves, providing scant illumination and throwing wobbly shadows across the nave. Anoushka hopped down from the font, trotted along the back of the nearest pew and circled around their feet.

'The laws of physics, as you call them, Richard,' purred the cat, 'are merely interesting suggestions. People went along with

Newton because what he said seemed to fit the facts. Nobody ever came up with any more exciting ideas.'

'But all objects obey Newton's laws!' Richie protested. 'They have to!' His own voice echoed back at him from the high vaults, as if in mockery.

Anoushka gave a disparaging miaow. 'Objects obey them because they have no imagination. I prefer creativity.'

'Cat,' said Richie firmly, 'you *can't* pass through a solid object.'

'There is actually no such thing,' mewled the cat, scratching his ear and looking away dismissively. 'All objects are made up of protons, neutrons and electrons, constantly in a state of motion and flux. Nothing in the Universe is *solid*. Nothing is still. You just need to learn to move *with* it, rather than against it.' The cat's eyes narrowed. 'Do you not *learn* quantum physics in your schools?'

'We... don't really need it for GCSE,' said Richie apologetically. 'But I promise to Google it when I get home.'

The door slammed shut behind them.

They exchanged a nervous glance, and began to proceed cautiously. The dark, forbidding cathedral seemed to breathe a chill at them from its very stone.

Meresbury Cathedral was large for such a small town; the building had been founded in the 1400s by the auspices of a nearby abbey (which had long ago fallen into ruin) and so the city had been given a cathedral building as imposing as any of the greatest in England. Richie knew it was in a desperate condition, though, if you looked closely; the roof was constantly being patched and some of the stonework, both inside and out, had crumbled almost beyond repair.

'Never mind old moggy Einstein over there,' Jess said, flapping her arms to keep warm. 'This place has been here nearly six hundred years and it's hardly changed. I mean, Meresbury would have been like a little market-town when it was built. Which makes it the perfect place.'

'What for?' Richie asked with a scowl.

'Resonances. Echoes of the past. What was it Em called them?... *Temporo-psychic projections*. Otherwise known as ghosts.'

'I don't like it.' Richie took a biscuit from his satchel and bit into it for comfort. 'These kind of things aren't meant to be disturbed.'

'What are we looking for, Anoushka?' Jess asked, running her hands over the display of books and pamphlets at the back of the Cathedral.

'Anything unusual,' purred the cat. 'Anything which doesn't fit.' He sprang off suddenly into the shadows beyond the choir-stalls, disappearing out of sight. 'You'll know it. Like an apple in a basket of oranges.'

'What's all that about?' Richie asked, chewing his biscuit. 'Apples and oranges?'

Jess, hands on hips, was peering up at the carved stonework high on the Cathedral pillars. 'It's an analogy, Rich,' she said.

'What, like Gabi and cats?'

'No, you dork, not *an allergy*. An *analogy*. Like when you use one thing to illustrate something else. I got what he meant.'

Above the south transept, the stained glass rendition of Sir Gawain and the Green Knight looked disdainfully down on them.

Richie shivered. He was now convinced that he didn't want to be here at all. He could feel his teeth chattering, so hard that he was sure anyone or anything lurking in the shadows of the transept could have heard them clearly.

He watched as Jess took one of the small candles from the display and lit it from one of those already burning. He wrinkled his nose at the smell of hot wax. 'What's that for?' he asked.

Jess smiled nervously as the candle flickered.

'My mum and dad,' she said.

And Richie didn't know if it was his imagination, but he started to feel that the air in the cathedral had turned a couple of degrees colder.

Jessica, in truth, wasn't that keen to be here either.

She had never felt comfortable with religion, even though Gabi had tried her with it. Little Jess used to sit in the church, swinging her legs, muttering the prayers, thinking longingly of playing outside, of tender chicken and crunchy roast potatoes, of the Sunday-night ritual of the Top 40. And in Sunday school, she would test her teachers' patience with her continual questions. *Why* did Jesus raise Lazarus if being dead means you go to heaven? *Why* does God allow people to be tortured? She got a name for herself as a difficult one, for such questions were not welcome.

Today, the Cathedral managed to make her feel insignificant and guilty.

She stood and watched the small flame burning, and tried to picture their faces. Eternally youthful, caught forever in that snapshot of the time.

Their names were Christina LaForge and Mark Mathieson. In the pictures she had, they were a fashionable young couple: her dad with his flat-top haircut, bleached jeans and biker jacket, and her mum with her bottle-blonde perm, toothy smile, bangles and chunky gold belt. That just made her want to laugh. God, they wore awful clothes back then.

She sniffed, feeling the cold air loosening the mucus in her nose.

'I suppose you never really knew them?' Richie asked, as they stared into the heart of the burning flame.

'Nah. I was just a few months old.'

'It must be hard,' said Richie awkwardly. 'My mum and dad drive me up the wall, but I can't imagine them... not being there.'

'Miss Watson at Sunday school once told me not to be angry at God, you know? I'd never have thought of that, if she'd not said it.' Jessica pulled her jacket closely around her, aware that she was shivering a little. The Cathedral seemed to have become cold, and the shadows between the pillars and pews were growing darker and longer. 'And now I am,' she said softly. 'Angry at God, some days.'

They stood for a few minutes, watching the candles flickering against the dark stone.

'You always seem to make a joke of stuff,' said Richie after a while. 'I know it's easier that way. I know you don't talk about them. I've never really... felt I could ask.'

Jess nodded, smiled gratefully at him. 'That's okay.'

'Gabi must have told you what they were like?'

'Yeah... Gabi says my mum was great, you know? Really popular with everyone.' She blew her nose, sighed, folded her arms and gazed into the meaningless grey vaults above her. 'Some days I can almost see her in my head.'

Richie glanced at her. Jess looked over at him, angry at the way her eyes were blurring now.

'I've never asked you,' he said. 'How...?'

She smiled sadly. 'I'm not going to tell you unless you ask me properly.'

'How did it... well... what happened?'

'Richie, it's okay. You can say it.'

There was a long, cold silence in the Cathedral. Jess thought she heard something - pigeons, bats? - fluttering high up above them, but it could have been her imagination.

'How did they die?' Richie asked softly.

'That's better.' She blew a long breath. 'They were rock-climbers. Mad about it, they were. It's how they met. Chrissie, my mum, she hadn't been able to climb for nearly a year, while she was pregnant with me, of course. It was their big day, her first time back at Pendle Rocks. Gabi and my Grandma were looking after little baby me for the day.'

Richie nodded. He knew when he had to listen, and not speak.

'Anyway, Chrissie, she... she'd lost an earring, yeah? Aunt Gabi laughed at her, told her she didn't need earrings to go climbing. But she was fussing around, scrabbling behind the chairs and rummaging through bowls of pot-pourri, with one gold earring dangling from her ear. She was so desperate to find the other one, but in the end she had to go without it. So Gabi waved them off in their car. She was holding me. It was an old Renault they had. Bit of a scrap-heap. I've seen the photos. Gab was sure they'd have an accident in it, one day.' Jess paused, breathed hard through chattering teeth.

Richie's eyes widened. He nodded.

She shook her head. 'But no, the car was fine. It always had been.' Jess was staring up into the darkness of the vaulted ceiling, hugging herself.

'What happened?' Richie asked gently.

'They were late getting to the rock-face that day. All their friends had already arrived... I think some people were joking about them always being late.' She bit her lip, aware of the pain as the incisor marked the soft flesh. 'They just didn't check the line before they started to abseil. Someone else was meant to check, but they didn't. It was a moment, just a moment, when things came together like... like they shouldn't have done.'

The ghost-light above the altar was swinging gently in a current of air. The blue flame bent, almost imperceptibly.

'And the line gave.' Jess closed her eyes tightly. 'The line gave,' she repeated in a small, distant voice.

'That's terrible... I'm so sorry.'

She opened her eyes, let out a deep breath. When she spoke again, she heard her own words as if on a tape, as if spoken by someone else. Her voice was low, cracking with emotion.

'They... said afterwards that it would have been pretty instant, yeah? They both fell a hundred metres. They'd not have felt...' She shook her head again, stared at the floor, unable to find the words. 'It was quick,' she said.

Beside them, the flames of the two dozen or so candles were bending in the cold draught now.

Jess gave Richie a weak smile and shrugged. 'Sorry,' she said. 'Didn't bring you out to hear my family history.' She exhaled deeply.

'It's fine,' he said. 'Really.'

'After it had happened - weeks after - Gabi was cleaning the house and found her earring. It had got knocked under the sofa. She thought she'd looked there, but obviously she hadn't.' Jess gave a brief, sad smile. 'That's why Gabi wears it. The one earring. It used to be Mum's. That way, we can remember them every day.'

'I didn't want to ask about that,' he said.

'Nah, well. Some people do. Gab just tells them it's personal.'

'I thought it meant she was gay.'

'Oh, *Richie.*'

'Well, I'm sorry! It does for some people!' Richie protested. Jess gave him a mock-serious scowl, and he shrugged. 'Do you get sad?' he asked. 'I mean, about not having a mum and dad?'

'No, not really. That's just it, you see, it's not like I haven't *got* them. They still exist.' Jess tapped her forehead. 'In here.' She narrowed her eyes and gazed into the darkness. 'And out there. Somewhere. In places we can't see. I've always thought there was someone watching over me.'

'Right.' Richie sounded unsure. 'Do you... see them?' he asked.

She laughed. It sounded clear, open, incongruous in the cold and dim space. 'Oh, no.' She paused. 'Well, not really.'

'What do you mean?'

'Rich, you're a good mate. I don't want to freak you out.'

'Rrright. Jess, in the last couple of weeks we've heard people singing inside exploding computers. We've seen a bloke vanish into thin air in the middle of a thunderstorm. We've made friends with a girl who lives in an invisible house and met a talking cat who walks through solid objects. Trust me, the goalposts have been well and truly moved.'

She nodded, smiled. 'There have been times,' she said. 'About a year ago, yeah?... I was looking in the window of HMV in town. Bright summer's day, it was. Clear blue, not a cloud. I was trying to see when the new BigSky album was out. I could see the people rushing by, reflected in the window.' She paused, never quite sure how much of this she properly recalled. 'And then I... well, there was a gap in the crowd, just for a second, and I thought... I *thought* I saw the reflection of this woman across the street. She'd have been leaning against the window of WHSmith's. She looked about Gabi's age. And she looked a bit like Gabi, only her hair was different. Longer, fuller, more kind of frizzy. She was wearing a leopardskin coat and a long black skirt, and she was smoking. I saw, as clear as anything, the jet of smoke leave her mouth and fly into the air, and...'

Jess looked at Richie to check he was listening. He was wide-eyed, hanging on every word.

'You thought it was your mum?' he said cautiously.

'Well... of course it wasn't, was it? I mean, how could she be there? The age she'd be if she... if she was still alive? It was probably... I dunno, someone who looked a bit like her.'

'Did you turn round?' he asked.

'I turned round,' she said. 'Looked across the High Street. And she was gone.'

'What... just like that?'

'Yeah. There was nobody leaning against the window. Just the people rushing by, and the bright sunlight, and the street like it always was. Mums and toddlers, old couples, tourists with backpacks, the guy on the corner flogging his *Big Issue*. Whoever I'd seen - they'd gone. She frowned, looked up suddenly. 'And is it me, or is it getting a bit nippy in here?'

Richie moved to stand beside her, and they looked at one another, sharing a growing sense of unease.

It seemed to have grown dimmer within the Cathedral - indeed it was so dark now that Jess could not make out the south transept or the big stained-glass window above the doorway.

'Well, it's an old building,' Richie said slowly, trying to sound convinced. 'Missing tiles, all kinds of gaps all over the place. The wind gets in all the time, so they say.'

There was a sudden gust of wind inside the Cathedral, and it knifed right through them with a winter chill. As one, the candles beside them guttered and were snuffed out.

All around, lighted candles were being extinguished, as if invisible hands were pinching the wicks one by one.

Pop. Pop. Pop.

Out they went, eaten by invisible darkness, disappearing like bubbles on the wind. The last to be extinguished was the ghost-light above the altar.

Jess grabbed hold of Richie's sleeve. 'Okay. Now I'm not happy,' she muttered.

The Gothic arches and pilasters in the highest reaches of the Cathedral began to darken. The sound, now, was less like a wind and more like a low susurration, as if many voices were whispering urgently to one another.

And then, in the echoing space, the singing began again.

Mr Courtney chewed thoughtfully on a ballpoint pen as he stood and watched the sky darkening behind Scratchcombe Edge. He hadn't listened to any Verdi for a while, and the withdrawal symptoms were making him edgy.

'This worries me, lad,' Mr Courtney muttered. 'Does it worry you?'

Mr Odell nodded. 'Yes, sir.'

The portly technician, Strickland, scurried past the guards and out of the circle. He was puffing, panting and holding a clipboard.

'Well?' Mr Courtney snapped.

'I don't quite understand it, sir,' Strickland murmured, nervously polishing his glasses as he looked up at Mr Courtney. 'The spectrographic range from the skeleton should be diminishing, but instead it's growing steadily stronger!'

Mr Courtney snatched the clipboard from him. 'Let me see that!' He studied the figures for a fee seconds, then exclaimed, 'Pah!' and thrust the clipboard back in the face of the jittery technician.

Mr Odell frowned. 'What does that mean, exactly?' he asked.

'Well,' said Mr Courtney, clearing his throat, 'it, *harrumph*, means that... Well, you see, what it means is...' He poked Strickland in the ribs, making him jump. 'Come on, man! Tell him what it means!'

'It's not decaying,' said Strickland nervously. 'It seems to have been... *renewing* itself.'

Mr Odell looked worried. 'No sign of radioactivity, Strickland?'

'Above normal background radiation, sir, but only slightly. Not in the danger level.'

Mr Courtney stroked his moustache. 'But that... *thing*... was buried by the Vikings...'

'We *presume* by the Vikings,' said Mr Odell.

'Inside the stone circle to keep it at bay...'

'These days, sir,' said Mr Odell, 'we should maybe rely on better methods of protection.'

Mr Courtney looked up sharply. 'What did you have in mind, Mr Odell?'

'A barrier of lead sheeting, sir. If that thing is emitting any dangerous energy, we need to keep it contained.'

Mr Courtney nodded. 'Good idea. See to it, Strickland. And monitor it closely. Let me know if there are any sudden surges in the readings.'

Strickland nodded and hurried back to the van.

'Could I make a suggestion, sir?' said Mr Odell tentatively.

'Go ahead.'

'Those other strange energy readings they picked up earlier - at all those different locations. We should investigate their sources.'

Mr Courtney nodded. 'Good thinking, lad. Let's get on to it. Which one first?'

Mr Odell unfolded his copy of the Ordnance Survey Map. 'This one,' he said, consulting a piece of paper. 'Grid reference... 156787.'

'Which puts it...'

The two men followed the grid-lines on the map, Mr Odell tracing the vertical and Mr Courtney the horizontal. Their fingers met in the centre of the brownish blob that represented Meresbury - right over the symbol of the cross.

They looked up.

Mr Courtney gave a grim smile and nodded. 'I thought as much,' he said. 'The Cathedral!'

'Time to get out of here,' suggested Richie.

The dark voices of an invisible choir were echoing in the nave, curling like mist around the darkening pillars. Richie tried to move his legs, to break into a run, but for some reason his body would not obey his mind.

'Come on, come on!'

He looked in despair at Jess, who seemed equally rooted to the spot.

'Block it out, Richie. Block it out!'

She clamped her hands over her ears and he did the same, muffling the sounds of the singing. Finally, his right foot peeled itself from the floor of the cathedral, unsticking as if held there by glue. He dragged it along, feeling its leaden weight.

It was like a dream.

Like one of those dreams where you were running and couldn't get away.

Concentrate.

Anoushka suddenly seemed to leap from nowhere, landing on the floor between them. The cat arched his back, and began to hiss, his fur rising in sharp black spines.

Richie felt life return to his right leg, and then his left. He glanced at Jess, who also seemed to have picked up speed, and now they had grabbed each other's hands and were running full-tilt for the door. Or where they thought the door ought to be.

The singing voices seemed to pursue them, gathering momentum like a vast tidal wave of sound sweeping through the hollow nave.

Halfway down, they skidded to a halt.

Their way was blocked. In the nave, *something* had appeared. At first it seemed like another pillar; part of the architecture, but a part which was not properly tuned in.

Half-visible. Half-formed.

A shimmering column of greyish light, flickering in the darkness, like a giant, ghostly image of a candle.

Jess stumbled, almost falling over. '*What is it?*' she murmured.

'Technically, it isn't anything,' murmured Anoushka. 'It doesn't have form. It's what you'd call a spirit, a spectre.'

'Oh, great.' Richie realised he was shivering. 'That's all I need. Today of all days, I've got to start believing in ghosts.' He had a sudden thought. 'Waaaait a minute...' He pulled the satchel from his shoulder, undid it and started scrabbling inside.

'Let's... just try and be friendly about this.' Jess extended her hands in front of her in a calming motion. 'Ghosts don't hurt people, right?'

Richie swallowed hard and tried to stop himself from shaking. 'You're... quite sure about that?' he asked, still desperately searching through the satchel.

The shimmering blur coalesced, with a rush of cold air and a musty, damp smell like the carpet of an antique shop. A wizened face appeared, twisted like bark, and ancient limbs, and a frail, hunched body swathed in grey robes. Piercing, angry blue eyes fixed on them from behind a tangle of knotted white hair.

The figure grinned - or at least, its chipped, yellowing teeth twisted themselves into something resembling a grin - and it raised its gnarled finger to point at them.

Finally, Richie found what he was looking for - his phone. 'Right!' he said, pointing it straight at the intruder. 'Smile, please, spook. Lovely!'

Jess realised what he was doing. 'Get a few of those,' she said.

Richie was saving shot after shot on his phone. 'Don't worry, I will.'

Suddenly, he let out a yelp as something landed on his shoulder - but it was only Anoushka, arching his back and gripping on tightly to Richie with his sharp claws.

'We can get out through the crypt!' Jess yelled. 'This way, come on!'

They spun around - to find a second figure, taller and broader than the first, blocking their way. This one was hairless and toothless, and its lined face bore an expression of contempt.

They turned slowly to look at one another. Around them, the Cathedral became darker still, and the singing reverberated through the very stone.

They backed away.

'All right,' Richie said. 'Any more bright ideas?'

Anoushka was purring quietly, like a car engine turning over.

'One,' said Jess quietly.

She reached for the nearest pew and pulled out a leather-bound Bible, embossed in gold with the sign of the cross.

'You've got to be kidding!' said Richie nervously. 'You've been watching too many bad vampire films.'

'You may think so,' Anoushka murmured in his ear. 'But in folklore, it isn't the *symbol* that repels them, it's the essence. The impenetrable field of belief in a higher power that you set up around yourself. One of the ways to banish a witch is to create a barrier, one it can't cross.'

Jess lifted the Bible slowly, meeting the cold gaze of the creatures. 'Might be a good time to start having a little faith,' she murmured.

Richie swallowed hard. 'Listen, I went to Sunday school and didn't get it, right? I used to sit at the back and read comics.'

Holding the Bible up like a shield, Jess swung it round to face each of the witches in turn. They showed no sign of weakening or of slowing their advance.

'Not working, is it?' Richie muttered. Although they were almost in complete darkness now, he could see the concentration on Jess's face as she gripped the Bible intently, fingers turning bone-white. 'Well?' he said desperately.

Jess's eyes snapped open, and he could see the despair on her face. She shook her head. Her grip on the Bible was beginning to weaken. 'It's no good,' she whispered. 'I can't do it.'

'You can't? Why not?'

'Isn't it obvious?' Jess glared at the embossed gold cross on the front of the Bible. 'It doesn't mean anything to me. My faith isn't strong enough.'

The witches, crackling and glowing with energy, stepped forward, bony fingers reaching out to touch them.

'*Over here!*' shouted a strangely familiar voice.

They looked over to their right.

The doors had burst open and the dimness of the street-lighting was filtering in, along with flurries of autumn leaves which seemed to crackle as they touched the darkness. Standing in the doorway was a tall, white-haired figure in a pinstripe suit, beaming and beckoning them.

Jess's jaw dropped. 'Professor Ulverston!' she exclaimed. She and Richie exchanged a brief look of astonishment.

The witches, distracted, rounded on Ulverston with a synchronised hiss, their twisted faces white and cold and their yellow teeth bared in anger.

'Aha!' Ulverston exclaimed in amusement. 'You ladies really shouldn't intimidate people, you know. It won't help you to get a good name in the Earthworld!'

Richie and Jess retreated to the doorway.

Ulverston gripped the great brass handles firmly with both hands. Just as he began to pull on the doors, Jess turned and, with the action of a shot-putter, hurled the Bible straight at the nearest of the witches.

The book crackled with energy as it bounced off her grey body, and was held, twisting, in the air for a second. Then, it glowed icy-blue and began to strip away, layer by layer. First the leather cover, ripped from its binding, curled up and fell like a withered leaf to the dark floor. One page after another peeled off, the book turning banana-yellow and crumbling to dust in the aura around the witch.

Jess, rooted to the spot, stared in horror, but Richie pulled her away. They ran for the doors, hair whipped by the wind. Professor Ulverston gave one last heave on the doors and slammed them shut.

The sounds of singing, screaming and hissing from within the Cathedral suddenly cut off, as if someone had thrown a switch.

Richie, blinking, suddenly realised that they were standing in the cold drizzle outside. Cars swished by on the distant ringroad, headlights scattering in the sheets of water. He shivered, looking around for the Professor, but he was nowhere to be seen.

Jess, who was staring down at her empty hands as if she had just lost something of enormous value, slowly looked up at Richie.

'Was that,' Richie said, 'who I thought it was...?'

She swallowed hard and nodded. 'I... think so. Better not tell anyone about this one, eh?'

Both of them, instinctively, looked around for Anoushka - but the cat had disappeared into the darkness of the night, as quickly as he had come.

Richie patted his phone. 'Never mind. I'm looking forward to seeing what Facebook makes of these.' Jess raised her eyebrows at him. 'Joke?' he said. 'We're going to give them to Emerald, right?'

As they hurried away, Richie heard a rumble of thunder and saw the meanest, darkest clouds beginning to gather right above the Cathedral. For an instant, he thought he saw a pinstripe-suited figure reflected upside-down in one of the big puddles of rainwater, but it could have been a trick of the light.

And a sleek, black Mercedes, picking out the raindrops in the cone of its headlight-beam, emerged from the shadows of the Bishop's house and slowly followed them.

The moon was high over Meresbury.

An observer high on the moors would have seen humanity's influence slowly fade from the landscape as night grew deeper.

The glittering tower of the Cathedral stood proudly in its honey-golden floodlights until midnight precisely, when the lights went off and the edifice blinked out of sight as if swallowed by the darkness. Other yellow lights, evidence of pubs and restaurants, winked out, and the noise of music and cars diminished to just the odd passing whisper.

Further down the valley, the purple neon sign for the multi-screen cinema also went dark, as did the floodlights at the stadium. Only the orange specks of the streetlamps kept up their vigil, while winking dots of green and amber and red showed the endless loop of the traffic-lights.

It was silent and still on Scratchcombe Edge, where the Ten Sisters stood like eternal guardians in the moonlit mist.

It was silent and still within Meresbury Cathedral, where clusters of candles burned for the dead and the lost, and strange shadows still flickered high above the nave.

It was silent and still in St Agnes' School, where chairs were stacked on desks, the rafters sang in the wind and night-lights bathed the inert computers in a blood-red glow.

It was silent and still at the Darkwater, where the glassy lake showed only the gentlest of ripples and the pine-trees hissed softly in the lightest of breezes.

And at the edge of the lake, a slim figure in a green anorak, holding a small hand-held mp3-recorder, slipped out of the undergrowth and headed back up the path towards the forest.

Part Three
The Time Of Becoming

7

Nexus

'Absolutely *nothing*!' exclaimed Emerald Greene in frustration.

Jess, entering the dining-room with two steaming mugs of tea, stopped in her tracks. 'You must be joking! Richie took dozens of shots!'

Emerald held up Richie's phone disdainfully. 'Nothing in the memory,' she said. 'Not a single image.'

That afternoon, the house was pungent with paint fumes. Gabi, having decided that she wanted the Mint Seashell bathroom she'd seen on *Rooms For Life*, was upstairs on the stepladder, painting and singing happily along to an Abba CD.

'I don't get it,' Jess said faintly, as she sat down. 'He took pics of everything. The witches, Ulverston, the lot.'

'Do not be alarmed,' said Emerald cheerfully.

She had a sheet of newspaper spread on the table and was tinkering with odd bits of electrical equipment. Her glasses lay beside her and Jess could see her bright green eyes glowing like the jewel on her necklace as she prodded circuits with a screwdriver. Jess wasn't quite sure what she was doing, and didn't like to ask.

'It is often the case,' Emerald went on. 'Image resonancing can be blocked by bipolar frequency oscillation.'

'It can?' said Jess levelly.

'Oh, yes. Indeed. With digital data, the sub-etheric frequencies can cross-polarise and cause transitional interference, resulting in a null amplitude.'

'They... can?' *Worse than Science homework*, Jess thought grimly. She scrabbled around and tried to make sense of Emerald's techno-babbling. *Frequency. Blocked. Interference.* 'What you're saying is,' she ventured, 'our stuff got... zapped by their stuff?'

'Well... it is a little more complex than that.' Emerald pulled a face.

'But in a nutshell, that's it, yeah?' Jess persisted.

'I suppose so,' said Emerald Greene, perching her glasses back on her nose. 'Putting it crudely.'

Jess grinned. 'You just don't like the fact that I almost get you for once.'

Ignoring her, Emerald took out the Ordnance Survey map of the Meresbury area and spread it on the dining-room table. She pointed to the Darkwater, which was marked as a big patch of blue. 'This lake,' she said, 'you know what is so odd about it?'

Jess answered immediately. 'Yeah, it's artificial.'

'Very good, yes. But do you know what was there before?'

'A valley,' said Jess. 'Wasn't there a village there once?'

'Yes,' said Emerald softly, and she sat still for a second with her palms together.

Jess kept a respectful silence. It was difficult, because she could hear Gabi upstairs, belting out 'The Winner Takes It All' as she painted.

'Sorry,' Jess said eventually, 'are we praying?'

'What? Gracious, no. Just thinking.' Emerald leaned forward again. 'There was a village in that valley, called Hexbrook. That means Witches' Stream. And you know why it is called that?'

Jess shook her head. She could feel her fingertips beginning to tingle. She knew Richie still didn't trust Emerald Greene - but Jess herself was comfortable with her new friend now. She'd been proved right about Ulverston, hadn't she? And when Emerald Greene told you something, it was always important, and always relevant.

'It was a plague village in the 17th Century,' said Emerald. 'It had another name back then. Nobody seems to know what it was... But it was a village where every single inhabitant died of the Plague.'

'The Black Death,' said Jess, nodding. 'I know about that.'

'The place was abandoned afterwards. Nobody went near there. They called the village Hexbrook, because they thought witches had poisoned the stream to bring the Death to the village.'

'People believed... all sorts of stuff back then,' said Jess, shivering inside.

'Well, yes. But belief in witchcraft never really went away.'

The sunny afternoon outside seemed no longer to exist, and there were no sounds but Jessica's own steady breathing and Emerald's low, urgent voice.

'It's happened throughout history,' Emerald went on. 'A girl who was in any way unusual - say she had a birthmark, or she was prone to visions or talking to animals - could end up being accused of witchcraft... But Hexbrook was not an empty village for long. It became known, you see. Known as a village of death where nobody would go.'

She leaned slowly back, nodding.

Jess held her breath as Emerald added, so softly that she almost couldn't hear her:

'Nobody but the witches.'

Richie cracked his knuckles. 'Right,' he said. 'Time to test a theory.'

He was sitting in front of his computer, in his bedroom at home. He'd scanned in a picture of the Meresbury map, and zoomed in on the section he wanted.

Richie clicked the mouse a couple of times and fixed a small, glowing disc over one point. The lake, known as the Darkwater. Then he did the same thing again, this time putting a disc over the top of Meresbury Cathedral. And then, finally, he zoomed the pointer over the Ten Sisters at Scratchcombe Edge, the stone circle where, just days ago, Professor Edwin Ulverston had vanished into thin air.

Three discs. Three corners. A triangle.

One more click, and he had linked all three places with red lines, corresponding to the ley lines Emerald had told them about. That was easy enough. The three locations stood in a rough triangle - not quite an equilateral one, if he sized it up - which framed the city within its borders.

The red triangle over Meresbury sat there on Richie's screen, defying him to think.

He was missing something.

They were all missing something.

It had been nagging at the back of his mind ever since Emerald had shown him those lines on her original map, and he just couldn't think what it was.

'A village of witches?' whispered Jess.

Emerald's eyes opened wide and she smiled. 'Yes,' she said softly. 'Quite an unsettling thought, would you not say? Exiles, outcasts, all of them. They made their home in the village of death, because nobody else would.'

'Makes sense.'

'All kinds of things were said about Hexbrook. People said that they turned the church into a kind of parliament hall - full of runes, spells, pungent odours drifting up the church tower, and dark, ancient singing at moonrise. They would ring the bell at midnight. Just the tenor bell, long and slowly, to call the witches to council. It was said that they turned the altar into their own shrine, where they would summon Hecate, their goddess... Some people said they used to breed strange animals in the schoolhouse, misshapen halfbreeds which only came out to prowl at sunset and never lived more than a few weeks... And that they burned the Green one night, consumed it all with fire until the earth was ashes - and called it the Black from that day. Some said they put a barrier around Hexbrook, too, a kind of magic shield over the village so that nobody could enter or leave without the correct spell, and that anyone who tried to leave was frozen by the barrier, the blood and water in their bodies turning to ice.'

Jess had been listening, spellbound. 'Wow,' she said eventually.

Emerald shrugged, smiled. 'People fear what they do not understand. They fill the gaps in their knowledge with feverish imagination and stories.'

'But *you* believe,' she said softly.

'I believe in the truth of other realms,' said Emerald softly.

'So - Hexbrook,' Jess said. 'It's gone, yeah?'

'Not completely. It stayed unoccupied for years. People gave it a wide berth. People said the land for two miles around Hexbrook was a cursed place, and that no child was born even near to the village... Then - as far as I can tell from my research - in the 1930s, people started wanting to build dams and reservoirs, and that is when it happened. The authorities took the decision to flood the valley, creating an artificial lake. They flooded Hexbrook.' She nodded, slowly, leaning back in her chair. 'Hexbrook is still there, beneath the water. The church, the schoolhouse, the houses, the streets... all still there, submerged in the Darkwater. And you know what, Jess?'

'What?' asked Jess softly.

'You can hear it.'

This would have seemed laughable to her a few weeks ago. It would have seemed as silly as talking cats and eagle librarians, or a man disappearing in a blaze of light, or a girl from the future living in a house from the past. Now, it was almost normal.

'What can you hear, exactly?' she whispered.

'Restless, chattering voices, echoing through the night. Sometimes the church bell tolls, deep in the water - it is muffled by the lake, but it is the bell. And that singing.'

Emerald slid something across the table, and for a moment Jessica jumped. It was a recordable CD in a flat, square case.

'In case the authorities ask me questions,' she said, 'I want deniability. Please have it. Conceal it somewhere here. But do *not* attempt to play it on conventional equipment. You could do untold damage.'

Jess reached out. She hesitated.

What was it she had said? Not wholly good nor wholly evil? Emerald Greene, wherever and whenever she was from, had told her in no uncertain terms that witches were capable of evil. That they had to be defeated. Maybe something evil had been at work on that horrible day back when she was six months old. That terrible, black afternoon which had taken her mother and father away from her. Maybe this recording, whatever was on it, could help to keep evil out of the world. To banish it. And if she could help by doing as Emerald asked, then...

Jessica nodded, smiled. She took the CD and slipped it into her pocket.

Emerald smiled, seemed to relax. 'Thank you,' he said. 'I knew I could trust you.'

'Now, then,' said a voice from the door, 'am I gonna get any help from you girls this weekend, or what?'

It was Gabi, pointing a paint-soaked brush at them. Her denim shirt and trousers were flecked with white paint, and there was a patch of it on her nose as well. She looked as if she had got into a dispute with several seagulls.

Emerald Greene smiled nervously and gathered up her bits and bobs, frantically shoving them back into her satchel. 'I, er, have to go,' she said apologetically.

Jess saw Aunt Gabi staring at all the components Emerald was gathering up from the table. 'Physics homework,' Jess explained hastily.

'Right,' said Aunt Gabi doubtfully. 'It all looks a bit complicated. Hang on!' She strode over to the table and plucked something out of Emerald's hand. 'Is that *my* egg-timer?'

'Ah,' said Emerald. 'Um,' she added, looking at Jess for help.

'We needed something with a bell,' said Jess quickly. 'For the... circuit.'

'Hmm, well, okay... I suppose it's only an old one.'

'And it's not as if we eat boiled eggs a lot,' Jess added under her breath.

'Eggs!' exclaimed Gabi. 'You sure you won't stay for tea, Emerald?' She gestured with the brush. 'You'd be very welcome.'

'Very kind,' said Emerald. 'But I, ah... I need to feed my cat.' She hoisted her satchel on her shoulder and waved an awkward goodbye, scurrying for the door like a startled rabbit.

'Okay, I'm coming,' said Jess, pausing to giggle. 'Aunt Gabi, you look ridiculous.'

'Oh, a bit of hard work makes you look ridiculous, does it? Put some old clothes on, grab yourself a brush and get painting, girl! And we'll have you singing along to "Fernando", please. It's compulsory.'

Jess, aware that she still had Emerald's CD in her pocket, slipped it into her school-bag.

Just then, Emerald popped her head through the back door again, making her jump. 'One other thing,' she said. 'You have a... digital information network here?'

'The Internet?' Jess hazarded.

'Er, yes... that. See how much you can find out about Professor Ulverston. Oh, and *this.*' Emerald handed Jess a small piece of paper, a folded page from an exercise book.

'Right,' said Jess uncertainly. 'I'll try, Em.'

Emerald nodded, smiled, and was gone.

Jess unfolded the paper. Written on it in fountain pen, in Emerald's neat, clean hand was one word: FREYGERD.

Professor Ulverston was looking well - for a dead man.

The Professor, who had been flickering in and out of time-phase ever since the discharge of energy at the standing stones, strode through Meresbury with the confidence of a man who had become used to not being seen.

He shimmered through the streets under the gathering clouds, past people with their heads bowed as they hurried for buses, past the Big Issue seller on the corner, through the square to the Cathedral gate. His broad, knowing grin strangely looked more dazzling now that he was not fully corporeal.

At first, he did not see Xanthë. She was lounging in the shadows of the gateway, her eyes clear and blue in her wizened old-young face. She unpeeled herself from the recesses - a slice of shadow, a dark column which lightened and shimmered into her flowing, grey form.

Ulverston sighed, folded his arms. 'Ladies, ladies,' he said theatrically. 'We can't go on meeting like this!'

The buzz and chatter of Meresbury blurred behind him, as if the city had simply slipped into a lower level of reality. Xanthë lifted her proud, high-boned face and shook her head.

'It is the fool again,' she said. 'Ull-Verr-Stone. Does he not know when to leave us alone?'

'Ah,' said Ulverston, and rubbed his nose awkwardly, or tried to. 'Look, I was just passing through, and - well, to cut a long story short, I was looking for you.'

'You have something you wish to say to us?'

'Weeeeeellll... yes, actually. *Don't do it.*'

Xanthë laughed, her teeth shimmering. 'Is that all?' she said mockingly, and pointed her staff at the Professor. 'Begone!'

'Ah. That sort of stuff doesn't work with me, I'm afraid.' Ulverston clasped his hands behind his back and started to pace up and down in front of the Cathedral. 'So, you're drawing power from the residual energy of the fissure, eh? Breaking through into the real world so you can live again? Dangerous!' He held up a finger and wagged it at her. 'Very, very dangerous - for humanity.'

'We were abandoned by so-called *humanity*,' Xanthë snapped. 'Exiled. Sent to fester in the village of plague, then finally to drown there when they opened the rivers and filled the valley to make the Darkwater. Why should we care?'

'Mmmm, well, from a technical point of view I really wouldn't advise it. Nothing to focus the energy, you see. Could all disperse and fragment. Be terribly messy.' He looked up, sharply. 'I really wouldn't do it.'

'But then you are not like us,' said Xanthë coolly.

'Absolutely not. I'm a chap. A fellow. In fact I'm an Honorary Fellow, a very esteemed one of All Souls' College, Oxford.' He tried to tap his nose, missed several times and then shrugged, giving up. He hadn't totally adapted to this non-physical entity business, he reflected ruefully. 'And I have the Freedom of the City of Meresbury! Yes, they conferred that on me a while ago. People can be terribly nice, you know. Especially when one is a genius, like myself.'

Meresbury's landscape had faded into the background, molecules sizzling, pixellating and breaking up like a bad TV picture. Darkness gathered around Ulverston and Xanthë in their in-between world, and they circled each other like two predatory panthers.

'Genius or not, your prattling is worthless,' said Xanthë, staring past the Professor in contempt. 'The Becoming will go ahead as planned.'

'Ah, really? You know, I have learnt so much since being stranded in your little mid-world. I used to dismiss the supernatural as claptrap, do you know that?'

'I have no desire to know what you think.'

'Well, you should listen to me. I'm very clever,' said Ulverston, without a trace of modesty.

'You are an intelligent man, Ull-Verr-Stone,' Xanthë conceded, 'but you are still a fool.'

Ulverston ignored her. 'I still think a lot of it *is* claptrap,' he went on, 'but a lot of it is pure science, really, isn't it? It's just science beyond what we've already encountered. I find that fascinating.' His eyes narrowed and he lowered his voice, affecting a mock-serious, doom-laden tone. 'I also find it a little frightening, Xanthë - and so should you, hmm!' Ulverston's big, bulging eyes stared at her and he pointed accusingly at the witch. 'You are going to cause a dimensional anomaly of the most *terrible* order. Already minor rifts and instabilities are opening across the town... Who knows what you're going to let through? Mmm?'

'The Becoming will go ahead,' said Xanthë, but she gathered her robes around her haughtily and looked a little more perturbed than before.

'Listen to me, Xanthë,' said Ulverston, wagging his finger. 'I had my doubts about what I was doing at the dig, but I can see now that I unleashed something beyond our current understanding. The grave I opened was the resting-place of a legendary Norse sorceress called Freygerd - a terrible, restless soul of horrible form, one who took human shape. She was only slain by the combined efforts of the men from the Viking settlements. And after they killed her, they took the body and interred her in pagan ground, because it was a place they feared.'

Xanthë frowned. 'The Vikings feared nothing, Ull-Verr-Stone. They pillaged the ancient Britons' tombs, scrawled runes on them, looted without mercy...'

'Oh, but everyone fears something, my dear. They were a superstitious people. Beneath that contempt lay fear, believe me! They had long suspected that the ancient magic could exert great power over the land. And so they buried Freygerd in the centre of the ancient stone circle, and swore to tell no-one. Only someone must have broken their oath, because the secret was passed down through the generations - orally at first, then finally recorded in writing in some very interesting mediaeval documents.'

'And you found these records?'

'Of course,' said Ulverston smugly. 'I personally found them in the special, sealed vaults in the lowest level of the Bodleian Library in Oxford.'

Xanthë's eyes widened. 'The city of learning.'

'Well, quite. And to access these archives, you need a set of keys held by the Master of Chaucer College, given only to those in his closest circle of academic colleagues.' Ulverston beamed at the witch. 'I, of course, have just created the Edwin Ulverston Scholarship in Archaeology, and so my standing in the University is... respected, shall we say.'

'You gave the authorities a bribe,' said Xanthë coldly.

'Oooh, I would hesitate to call it that! And so I embarked upon my greatest ever dig, half-knowing and half-fearing what I would find... I told myself it was all mumbo-jumbo, naturally. Had to concentrate on the *scientific* approach. The only way.'

'And now you regret your actions?'

'Ahh, well, regret is a strong term. I would have approached the matter differently, in hindsight.' Ulverston spread his hands. 'All I can ask now is that you don't make it any *worse*. Think of it as a hole in a water-bottle, Xanthë. I made the hole, yes, for that I take responsibility. But you and your companions would be like water pouring through the hole and widening it! The very structure of Time could be in peril!'

Ulverston now noticed that he and Xanthë were not alone in the darkness, and despite himself he could not help feeling a slight shiver.

They appeared one by one in a circle around him, lit dimly in cobalt-blue, hoods masking all of their lined and wizened faces. One or two of them stooped, leaning on staffs. The air was full of an ancient, musty smell now, like damp old clothes.

'I take it the answer is no?' he murmured.

And then he heard their voices, singing together in harmony. He could make out no words, and yet the singing was - bewitching. That was the only word for it. The volume of their harmonies grew, echoing as if in a vault or a church. Deep, dark, inexpressibly beautiful, but somehow raw, the sound reminded Ulverston of the chants of Bulgarian folk-singers or the incantations of Tibetan monks, yet more musical and more intoxicating than either.

Above them, Xanthë's voice rang out loud and clear. 'Hear us, Ull-Verr-Stone. Hear our names. *Xanthë. Róisín. Bethan. Martha. Lizabeth. Anne. Kathleen. Yseult. Alice.*'

'Delighted, ladies,' Ulverston murmured. 'A pity it couldn't be in more pleasant circumstances.'

Another of the witches spoke: 'We have waited, biding our time, skulking for centuries in the darkness of these nowhere-lands.'

And then another: 'We have waited, growing weaker and more diseased as the winds of Time cut through our bodies.'

And then Xanthë again: 'We searched for a door that would lead us out of this living death; looking for even the most delicate fraying of the fabric. We found none, until now. And now we have found it, we will not wait again.'

Ulverston's white hair rippled in a gentle breeze as he stared into the bright, angry eyes of the witch. Eyes which were suddenly terrible, resolute, possibly even mad. Eyes he knew he could not argue with.

'Then it's over,' he said softly, 'and there's nothing I can do.'

Shaking his head in despair, Ulverston slipped away from the circle of nine witches as their singing grew in volume, echoing through the endless nothing-space of the Otherworld.

'Emerald!'

Richie, puffing and panting, abandoned his bike by the gate and scrambled up the field, heading for the woods by the Darkwater. He had caught up with Emerald Greene as she headed for the trees, her backpack on her back, and he wanted to catch her before she slipped through the barrier into Rubicon House.

'*Emerald!*' he yelled again, ignoring the muddy puddles he had to splash through.

Suddenly, Emerald was there in front of him. He almost collided with her as she emerged from behind a tree. Silent as a ghost.

She looked him up and down, green eyes and sharp and amused behind her blue spectacles. 'Richard Fanshawe. Have you dragged yourself through a hedge backwards?'

Richie, doubled up, his breath like fire in his lungs, struggled to speak. There was a tree-stump nearby and he sank gratefully down on to it, easing the pain in his legs.

'How... do you move... so fast?' he managed eventually.

'I merely keep myself in trim.' She prodded him in the stomach, almost making him lose his balance. 'You, on the other hand, should exercise more.'

Richie pulled a face. If there was one part of school he hated, it had to be Games. 'I don't... think...so...' he said, sitting down on the grass in front of her. 'You're going to... have to get yourself... a Blackberry,' he suggested.

Emerald made a dismissive noise. '*Phht*. Primitive devices. Might as well use a carrier pigeon.' She sat down beside him. 'Well? Did you have any information for me, or did you ride all the way out here merely to discuss methods of communication?'

Richie unfolded a piece of paper from his pocket.

It was a printout of a simple sketch done on the computer, showing the positions of the Cathedral in the centre of Meresbury, the Darkwater to its east and the Ten Sisters to the north-east, all linked by the ley lines:

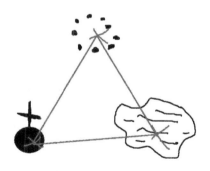

'Yes?' said Emerald Greene impatiently. 'And?'

Richie was becoming a little more animated now that he was getting his breath back. 'Here, ' he said, pointing to the triangle. 'I knew something rang a bell. I was reading about it only last week.'

Emerald held the map up to eye level. 'Enlighten me, Richard,' she said.

Richie grinned. 'You mean I know something you don't for once?'

Emerald turned and gave him a cold, green stare. 'Information is not a competition, Richard. It is a mutually beneficial system of sharing. *Expand.*'

Richie put the printout down on the tree-stump and took out a pen. 'Okay. Look. The triangle thing got me thinking... Come on, Em, you can do geometry. How do you take the exact centre of a triangle?'

Emerald Greene looked at him steadily for a few seconds, and then to his delight he saw her smiling, her green eyes widening behind the blue glasses. Then she drew back, exhaling a sharp breath, and produced a green felt-tip pen from behind her ear.

'The centre of this line,' Emerald murmured, estimating where it was and marking it with a cross, 'and the centre of this one... and the centre of this one.' Then she drew a line perpendicular to each of the sides of the triangle, and marked a ring around the point where they met:

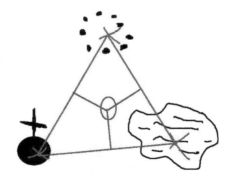

'Well?' Richie asked in excitement.

'Excellent, Richard Fanshawe. That shows you are thinking.'

'It does?'

'Yes. Your thoughts have mirrored the exact same ones I had twenty-four hours ago, when I first drew this model for myself.'

'Oh.' Richie looked crestfallen. 'You knew.'

'Yes, yes, but do not worry! It shows it is a logical deduction. Any force, whatever form it takes, is strongest when it takes the path of least resistance. What we have discovered here is the exact pattern leading to the nexus point - and all we need to do is plot this on to the map.'

'Which I suppose you've already done?' Richie asked gloomily.

Emerald beamed. 'Indeed!' she said delightedly, and pulled out the small-scale Ordnance Survey map of the city, shaking it flat with one deft twist of her hand. 'Look.'

Richie looked. Emerald had drawn the same diagram on a transparency, which she had stuck over the map. His eyes followed the green lines, and he saw the ring marking the nexus point.

He blinked.

He peered in to look more closely.

'It falls approximately halfway down Templegate Road,' said Emerald Greene, 'just outside the centre of Meresbury.'

'Templegate Road?' said Richie, looking up with a start.

Emerald stretched out one long finger and jabbed at the map. 'In fact, the nexus point is located somewhere we know very well.'

Richie leaned in even further to see exactly where she was pointing. His nose was a matter of millimetres from the map as he struggled to focus.

He read what was marked on the map.

After a few seconds, he looked up at Emerald.

'Oh,' he said.

'Em,' he added.

'Gee,' he finished.

And Emerald Greene just smiled.

At the kitchen sink, Jessica scrubbed the paint from her hands with pumice stone and white spirit, then rinsed them under the hot tap.

In the corner of the dining-room, the printer chugged away, churning out the information which Emerald had asked her to find. She gazed out across the garden at the lengthening shadows, deep in thought about the witches, the plague and Hexbrook.

Jess blinked. For a second, she thought she had seen a shadow move out there in the back garden, between the shed and the hydrangea.

She towelled her hands dry, quickly opened the back door and tiptoed out into the cooling evening air, narrowing her eyes as she scanned the flowerbeds for movement.

'*Over here,*' drawled a languid voice. 'No need to creep around like that.'

Jess sighed and straightened up, folding her arms, as she saw a familiar pair of yellow-green eyes staring at her from behind the herbs. 'Anoushka!' she hissed, squatting down to look at the cat. 'You're going to get me into trouble! Remember Gabi's allergy?'

'Only too well,' replied the cat. 'Why do you think I'm lurking out here like a common criminal?'

'I don't know,' Jess answered crossly. 'Come to think of it, why were you skulking about at this end of town when I first saw you?'

'I get around,' Anoushka muttered, lifting his nose haughtily as he settled down on the grass. 'Need to scout out the territory. Keep an eye on... things.'

'You've been watching me, haven't you?' Jess leaned forward, pointing a finger at the cat. 'You know what? Emerald and I may be friends, but I still don't quite trust you. And I don't think you fully trust me, either.'

'Keeping all options open,' answered Anoushka sulkily. 'Nothing wrong with that. If you were in our position - cut off across Time from your home, your people - you, too, would perhaps have a natural sense of mistrust.' The cat's ears twitched. 'We were betrayed, once before. Never again.'

Jess felt her body shaking with chilly excitement. 'And you're going to tell me, right? Exactly where you come from and how you got here? Because, to be honest, I'm getting a bit narked off with Emerald's evasiveness.'

'Absolutely not,' said Anoushka, and Jess could have sworn that he sniffed in disdain. 'Miss Emerald has the right to keep her secrets, and so do I.'

'Oh, great.' Jess scowled. 'You want my help and my information, but you won't trust me enough to tell me where you come from.'

'We are Displaced.'

'Yes, I know you're "Displaced",' said Jess sarcastically, and she drew the speech-marks in the air with her fingers. 'Change the record.'

Anoushka's whiskers twitched. 'The record?'

'You know - get a new line!'

Anoushka hissed at her, baring his teeth and arching his back.

For a second, Jess felt an irrational prickle of fear and she edged away. He's just a cat, she told herself. He can't do anything to hurt me.

'So you want me to tell you all about us, Jessica Mathieson?' Anoushka's tone was harsh and sardonic. 'Tell me this - are you as brave as you seem? Or as confident? As witty and intelligent? Probably not. Human beings are impressive at dissembling, putting on a show. You all wear a face to the world - one which reveals, at best, only part of the truth. Does this make you liars, schemers and villains? Or does it, on the contrary, merely make you *human*?' Anoushka spat the last word, leaping forward and burying his claws into the soft earth with a snarl.

Jess swallowed hard. It was, she admitted, difficult to answer that.

'Well,' said Jess, lifting her chin and sounding defiant, 'I have a theory about you.'

'Ohhh?' Anoushka sounded amused. He sat down and began feigning interest in the gathering midges, swatting them with his paws. 'Please, do tell.'

Jess felt her courage growing as she spoke. 'You're not just lost - you're... *fugitives!* That's the word, isn't it? Fugitives from another place. You ran away from something and ended up here.' Jess leaned back on her heels and smiled. 'I wonder why?'

'Always full of questions,' muttered the cat, and started chasing his own tail around in an attempt to look unconcerned. 'Quite bright, in your primitive way.'

Jess allowed herself a smile of satisfaction. 'So have you just come here to insult me, or did you have a message?'

Anoushka looked up. His eyes seemed to glow like little lamps in the gathering gloom. 'There are... movements in the psychic energy levels. Something is about to happen. There may be a nexus point forming... so take care.'

'Take care?' Jess felt her heart beating faster. 'How? What do I do?'

'*The school*,' Anoushka said. 'Take care in the school.'

'Jess?' Gabi's voice cut across the garden, and the back door creaked open. 'Who are you *talking* to out there?'

Jess scrunched her eyes shut in anger for a second, then scooped up Anoushka in her arms. 'It's okay, Aunt Gabi,' she called. 'It's just that... stray again. Hanging round the garden. I'll take it round to the path and let it go.'

'That blasted cat. Don't bring it near me!' Gabi called.

'Go,' she whispered.

Anoushka leapt from Jess's arms and darted back into the shadows. She saw him burrow under a gap in the fence, and then he was gone.

Jess slumped and sighed. 'None the wiser,' she muttered. 'And now I've got something else to worry about.'

She headed back into the house. The telephone was ringing when she got inside; Jess could hear Gabi splashing and singing in the bath upstairs, so she grabbed the receiver.

'Hello?'

'Jess, it's me.'

'Rich! How's it going, mate?'

'Listen, I've just been talking to Em. We've worked it out, Jess. Well, I worked it out and Em did it separately.'

'What are you talking about, Rich? Worked what out?'

'Jess, it's the school. It's Aggie's. That's where it's going to happen! Emerald thinks it might be as early as tomorrow.'

'What do you mean?'

'Look, if you plot the points where the witches have tried to break into the real world and then find their exact centre, that's where their power is going to be strongest. It's not going to happen at the stone circle, or the Cathedral, or the Darkwater. They're going to break through in the school!'

'Are you sure?' she asked, but she didn't really need to ask. She knew from the tone of his voice - and it made sense of Anoushka's warning.

'We've got to be ready, Jess. And we can't tell anyone that we know, or they'll just find out and change the nexus point.'

'Wow. So this is it, then?'

'Looks like it.'

'Meresbury won't know what's hit it.'

'That's for sure.'

'I'll see you tomorrow, then.'

'Yeah. Tomorrow.'

Jess put the receiver down.

For the rest of the evening, she was troubled by weird, unsettled sensations, and could not settle to reading her book or watching television.

And that night, only half-asleep, she had the oddest sensation. She imagined that she was looking down on her own sleeping form; the angle told her that she had to be the other side of her full-length mirror. She could see the room, oddly distorted; her posters, her dressing-table, her wardrobe, all of them blurred and shadowy as if viewed underwater.

The angle changed, now, as if she were approaching her own bed with a hand-held camera. She could see herself, sleeping soundly under her duvet, hair spread out in a dark fan on the pillow.

She swung round, approaching herself.

Above the bed was her small mirror, and she glimpsed a pair of crystal-blue eyes in a pale face... Her own? She could not tell, for her eyes felt heavy and crunchy with sleep as they always did in dreams.

And now, she saw a white hand reaching out to touch her cheek.

'*No!*'

Gasping, breathing heavily and raggedly, she sat bolt upright.

She was back in her own body, looking the right way, now. There was nothing in the mirror but her own reflection. Her heart was thudding away, so hard she could hear it pounding in her head.

Her alarm-clock was beeping.

It was still dark! Surely not? Jess picked the clock up, shook it angrily - but sure enough, it read 08:30.

No time for breakfast!

She swung herself off the bed, splashed water on her face, pulled on her school clothes as quickly as she could. She didn't have time to knot her tie; she shoved it in her pocket. Running out of the house, she was aware that books were spilling from her bag under the orange glow of the street-lamps, but she didn't care.

In slow motion, as if dragged back by Time itself, she ran for school.

'*Come on, girl! You're late again!*'

With the Head's voice ringing in her ears, Jess hurried up the steps. The bell was ringing for class, although for some reason the corridor was surging with pupils who were all heading in the opposite direction from her.

She found her seat in the Citizenship class - her usual seat? She wasn't sure. Mrs McSweeney, tall and graceful in her tartan dress, was already striding up and down the aisles, throwing exercise books on to their owners' desks.

'I am returning last Tuesday's homework,' Mrs McSweeney was booming, 'in which I asked you all to write a letter to an MP on an issue which you felt strongly about. In general, this was very well done.'

Last *Tuesday*? It seemed as if she'd done that homework ages ago. But hadn't it been in English, not Citizenship? She heard her own ragged breath echoing in her head, tried hard to concentrate.

Mrs McSweeney was striding up the aisle behind her. 'A number of you, however, are still getting *Yours sincerely* and *Yours faithfully* muddled up!'

Jess looked around, feeling faintly panicky, as if she had forgotten something. Could she, in fact, remember which way round they were meant to go? She wasn't sure. It didn't help that her eyes felt heavy-lidded and she couldn't focus properly on the blurred room.

Mrs McSweeney stopped right by Jessica's desk, held her exercise book out flat and dropped it. The book seemed to fall infinitely slowly, like an autumn leaf - and then hit the desk with a resounding SMACK which made her jump.

'Excellent work, Jessica!' said Mrs McSweeney delightedly. 'A well-researched, well-argued letter about blood sports in the Mere Valley. Well done.'

Jess blinked, and there on the page in front of her was a big, red A in a circle, with those same words, 'Well done,' scrawled next to it.

Jess grinned, feeling an enormous sense of relief washing over her. An A in Citizenship! All that extra work was paying off. Now, at last, she could -

She blinked. Mrs McSweeney was standing on the teacher's desk at the front of the room. Jess had not noticed her getting up - she was just suddenly there.

'In fact,' Mrs McSweeney was saying, 'I think Jess's letter was so good, that I'd like her to come out here and read it to us all.'

Jessica suddenly realised that everybody was standing on their desks and applauding her, including Mrs McSweeney - and, strangely, all her other teachers. For some reason, there was also a white rabbit on her desk, and it was contentedly munching away at what remained of her exercise book.

She looked Mrs McSweeney in the eye, suddenly finding herself dumbstruck with terror.

'Wait a minute!' she said suddenly, and folded her arms. The room had begun to pitch and toss like the deck of an ocean liner. 'I've rumbled you. This isn't a *dream*, by any chance?'

The rabbit sniggered. 'Of course it is, you silly girl,' it said in Mrs McSweeney's voice. 'You didn't think you'd really got an A in Citizenship, did you?'

Jess groaned and slumped into her chair. 'All right, all right! Let me out of here!'

And she was running.

She was racing through the school with her hockey-stick in both hands, and the corridors were full of smoke and screaming. Somehow, she knew that the smoke was only dry ice and the screaming was not real. In fact, it was on an iPod which she wore. Angrily, she ripped the white headphones off, stamped on them, watched the bits skitter across the floor and hit the walls.

'Control your childish impulses,' said the rabbit, which was somehow sitting on her shoulder.

Jess whirled around. She was in the school swimming-pool, and the surface of the water was blue, clear and still. She could smell the pungent odour of chlorine - no, of course not. She thought she *ought* to smell chlorine and so her subconscious created it. This was weird! She had never dreamed in such a knowing way before.

'Look who's here to *see* you!' said the rabbit in an oddly sweet, cloying voice - as it changed into a black cat and hopped down on to the side of the pool.

The water surged. As if pushed from beneath by a giant hand, it took form, shimmered with blueish light.

Jess gasped.

A face began to form in the water.

The face of a woman.

Crystal-blue eyes, white-blonde hair, pale skin, a kind expression.

Long, fluid arms reached out for Jess. The figure wanted her to take its hands, to join her in the water.

'Hello, darling,' the voice said. 'I've missed you.'

And then her body began to prickle with that horrible sensation; the thought that something was wrong, that things were not how they seemed, and she knew she had to deny this, to escape it.

'No!' she said. Then, again, louder: 'No! I am dreaming. I am *dreaming*!'

Gasping, she awoke.

Panting for breath.

She took a moment to assess the situation.

She opened her hands in front of her face, examined her palms. She reached out for the reassuring chunkiness of the digital alarm-clock - which was reading 01:22 - and listened for a moment, for sounds in the city far below. It was silent, as usual.

This was real. This was wakefulness. You knew it; you could feel it and smell it. Every sense was in place as it should be. It was nothing like the blurry reality of dreams, nothing like in the tricks your mind played on you.

Jess flopped back down on her pillow and closed her eyes.

She slept again, but that night her sleep was fitful and uncomfortable.

She could hardly believe any time had passed at all when the alarm bleeped at her, and the first grey light of day seeped in from the chink between the curtains.

8

An Incursion

A drizzly, grey Monday morning at St Agnes' School. As pupils streamed inside for registration, Emerald and Jessica met for a brief conference at the outdoor rubbish-bins.

'Have you seen anything?' said Emerald coldly.

Jess shook her head. 'Just the usual.' She took a wad of printed pages out of her satchel and gave it to Emerald. 'That's everything I've been able to find out. I don't really understand archaeology.'

Emerald leafed through the pages, tossing them casually over her shoulder into the bin. 'No... no... no....' She stopped. 'What is this?' she asked, her finger jabbing on one page.

'Oh, it's just a report from Oxford University. Sorry, it may not be relevant, but I did a search for everything containing his name. Do you know there's a Lake District town called Ulverston as well? Made it very diff- okay, so you're not listening.'

'I am not listening.' Emerald was scanning the paragraph, and Jess saw her pale fingers tighten their grip on the page. 'Meeting of the Grants Committee... recommends no further investment... findings not proven...' She smacked the page, making Jessica jump. 'This is it. This is it!'

'It's what?'

'The proof, Jessica!'

'Proof of *what*?'

'Professor Ulverston was about to have his research funding cut off. Look! The reports are all here!' Emerald waved the page under Jess's nose. 'Only the third full Viking tomb ever to be uncovered in the British Isles. An ideal addition to the country's heritage, you would have thought. *And yet the authorities did not want Ulverston to open it up.*'

Jess struggled to get her head round what Emerald was implying. 'So he went against them? Got private funding from somewhere?'

Emerald's eyes were sharp, intense and green. 'Ego and greed... Always remember, Jess, science is not pure. There is much about it that can be put to bad use, as well as good.' Her green eyes opened wide. 'You found the information on... the other?'

'That name? *Frey-gerd*?' Jess said it uncertainly. The name sounded cold, angry - evil. 'Yeah, got it here. Google's my best buddy.'

'Google?' Emerald looked quizzical.

'Okay, um, I'll show you another time... But once I'd eliminated all the stuff from online role-playing games, there wasn't very much.' She unrolled a second sheaf of pages from her pocket. 'Slight problem though. It's all in some foreign language.' Jess pointed to the characters on the page, which to her had looked more like gibberish when she printed them out. 'For a minute I thought my printer was on the blink.'

Emerald snatched the printout from Jess. 'Danish!' she exclaimed in delight.

'Thanks, but I've just had breakfast.'

'No, no, no, it is *written* in Danish!' Emerald breathed out and her fingers tightened with excitement on the page. 'Freygerd, a Viking warrior queen with fearsome magical powers... thought to be slain by her enemies in the 11th Century...' Emerald looked up slowly and then turned to look at Jess.

'Some sort of legendary Viking woman? Is that what you were after?' Jess wrinkled her nose. 'Can you *read* it?' she added, once more in awe of her strange friend.

Emerald shrugged modestly. 'I have picked up a smattering here and there.'

'Where did you find out the name?' Jess asked.

'Anoushka. He... reached out to that thing in the tomb.'

'Reached out? What are you on about?'

'Trust me, Jess, I do not have time to explain everything to you right now.'

Jess whistled. 'So where does this leave us?'

Emerald tapped the side of her nose. 'Empowered,' she said. 'With information.'

'So what do we do?'

'We wait for it to happen.' Emerald gave one of her rare, broad grins. 'Exciting, is it not?'

'Exciting?' Jess shivered, remembering the thing in the Cathedral. 'Em, I don't know if you've ever heard this, but there's an old Chinese curse. It goes, "May you live in interesting times". Have a think about that. It worries me. Doesn't it worry you?'

'Oh, very well.' Emerald shoved the papers into her satchel, folded her arms and scowled. 'I sometimes wonder why I bother. No doubt you would prefer your life to be filled with vacuous electronic music, cheap cosmetics and beans on toast. How *exciting* that would be for you.'

'Oh, Em... I didn't mean...'

'You have a *chance* here,' said Emerald, and she rounded on Jess, her eyes gleaming behind her blue glasses. 'A real chance to *see* what binds this reality together, rather than just accepting everything at face value like those mindless children, all those *sheep* in there.' Emerald pointed a long, white finger in the direction of the school. 'But if you are not bothered, well, forget it all. Forget that Emerald Greene ever existed. I will disappear, quietly, and leave you all to sort the mess out for yourselves.'

'Okay. Okay... Look, I'm sorry. I do want to know what's going on. Really I do.'

Emerald grinned. 'You have an enquiring mind, Jessica Mathieson. I like you.'

'Well, I try.' She smiled, shrugged. 'So what now?'

Emerald hoisted her satchel on to her shoulder. 'Registration!' she announced firmly. 'Let us go and act like sheep for now... and wait for the Enemy to show its hand.'

The day went on as normal.

Mr Stone told Leeann Brooks to get her feet off the desk and confiscated her phone for about the tenth time that term. In Assembly, Miss Pinsley groaned at the Lower School's rendition of the Harvest hymn. 'No, no, no. You girls have no *idea*! And you boys are even worse,' she exclaimed, striding up and down the stage and waving her stick. 'What does "We plough the fields and scatter" mean? It doesn't mean *anything*!' She sighed in exasperation and stared out at the puzzled Lower School. 'It is

"We plough the fields and scatter the good seed on the land"...
You do *not* take a breath!... Now, let's try it again. And this time -
no breathing!'

Later on, Suzie Chang was arguing in the corridor with Mr
Kenworthy about her nose-stud. He reminded her loudly that the
school had a policy: nose-studs were allowed only 'for cultural
reasons'. Suzie's reply was, 'What about youth culture, sir? That
should count, surely?' There was a loud guffaw from Ollie Church
and some of the other boys, who were leaning against the wall
nearby and enjoying the show. 'It is for cultural reasons, sir,'
offered Ollie. 'She's growing bacteria in her nostril.'

A normal day, then, at St Agnes' School.

It was about to become a day like no other.

Jessica was sitting by the window when it happened.

She was in Maths - a subject for which Emerald, thanks to
her abilities, had joined the Year 11 class at the other end of the
school. Jess had just managed to solve her last equation when she
glanced out at the window at the grey expanse of the playground.
She was sure she glimpsed a shape out of the corner of her eye.

She frowned. She looked again and there was nothing - just
a weak September sun and the grey shadows of the mobile
classrooms and the netball hoops. But something, now, made a
sound in her head - a twittering, buzzing noise, like something
trying to tune itself to the right frequency.

Jess, biting her lip, glanced across the room. Ms James was
busy helping Leeann Brooks with her equations. Jess stood up,
pressed her hands against the glass and concentrated on the
sunlit playground.

The sound began to coalesce in her mind. A twitching,
twittering, scratching noise, interspersed with fragments of -
voices - yes, the voices again, those stone-ancient, hollow singing
voices full of approaching menace. Her heart beat faster and the
sunlight seemed to scorch her eyes; she felt them watering, but
she dared not blink for fear of losing concentration. Fixing her
eyes on the centre of the playground, she pressed her face up hard
against the window, smelt the odour of warm glass -

And she saw it.

The pilot concentrated as she brought the helicopter in low over the city of Meresbury.

Mr Odell leaned out at an alarming angle, zooming his binoculars in on the Cathedral precincts. Mr Courtney, meanwhile, was in the back seat of the helicopter, leafing through some notes. Both men and the pilot were wearing black headphones with radio-mike attachments.

'On your right, beautiful Meresbury,' said Mr Courtney softly. 'Home to a 13th-Century Cathedral, one of the oldest city walls in England, and forty thousand inhabitants... What are you hiding, beautiful Meresbury? What are you hiding?... Well?'

Mr Odell shook his head. 'Just over there,' he shouted over the noise of the rotors, pointing beyond the Cathedral.

'Saint Agnes' School...' said Mr Courtney, tapping a finger against his moustache. 'Saint Agnes?' he repeated, more loudly, towards the front of the cockpit this time.

Mr Odell leaned back. 'Patron saint of girls, betrothed couples and gardeners,' he called over his shoulder. When the older man raised his bushy eyebrows in surprise, Mr Odell shrugged and looked sheepish. 'I had a Catholic education, sir.'

'I see,' said Mr Courtney. 'Let us hope it serves you well, Mr Odell.' He tapped the pilot on the shoulder. 'All right, Lieutenant. Take us in!'

She nodded and gave him the thumbs-up. The helicopter banked steeply and started its descent.

In the Transit van at Scratchcombe Edge, all was quiet, except for the gentle hum which indicated that the equipment was still running. Two white-coated technicians monitored readouts - Strickland, the nervous scientist, and his colleague Arossi, a tall and wiry Australian girl.

On the bank of screens, the bones were glowing under the red lights in the tomb. For a second, the interior of the tomb seemed to pulse, scarlet becoming crimson, then a bright orange for a fraction of a second, before dying away again.

Strickland looked up from his instrument panel, glancing over his shoulder at his colleagues. 'Did you register that?' he asked worriedly, chewing a fingernail.

Arossi shook her head. 'Nothing on my readouts, mate. What did you get?'

'A surge in the energy supply. As if...' He turned, stared up at the screens. 'As if something was drawing strength from here.'

Arossi clapped a hand on his shoulder. 'Have you been drinking, Strickland?'

He shook his head. 'No way.'

She took a flask from the inside pocket of her white coat. 'Then maybe you oughta start.' She waved it at him. 'Here, settle your nerves.'

Strickland took the flask unwillingly, sniffed the brandy but did not sip. 'You're not taking me seriously, are you?'

Arossi sighed. 'Look, you know as well as I do that this equipment is state-of-the-art. Cutting edge. It does all sorts of things that even Mr C doesn't understand. So if you get the odd glitch on the readout, don't let it freak you, mate.' She shrugged. 'I certainly won't. I want an easy life, me.'

There was a noise, like a throbbing pulse right through the van. This time, the screens glowed orange for a full two seconds before the light died away.

Arossi grabbed the brandy back from her colleague. 'On second thoughts,' she said, turning pale and gripping her chair, 'maybe I'm getting freaked after all.'

'You - you see?' Strickland licked his lips and began polishing his glasses on the sleeve of his coat. 'I didn't imagine it. Now what's happening?'

'The dead stay dead, don't they?' Arossi's tone didn't sound convincing, though, and she took a swig of brandy, narrowing her eyes at the glowing screens. 'Vikings go to Valhalla... I thought they had to stay there.'

'All the same,' said Strickland, his voice shaking with fear, 'it wouldn't do any harm to run some tests. And I think we should call Mr C.'

Arossi sighed, and placed a friendly arm around the little man's shoulders. 'Strickland, how long have you been with Special Measures?'

'A few months,' he admitted. 'I was in academic research before that.'

'And why are you here? Why are we both here?' Arossi persisted. She leaned down, so that her pale blue eyes were on a level with her colleague's nervous, bespectacled face. 'We're supposed to be people who know how to use our initiative, right? And running back to bug the boss-man every time some little thing gives us the jitters is *not* good initiative. For all we know, this could be one of those - whatsit - test things they throw at us every so often.'

'You think we're being tested?' Strickland hadn't thought of that.

'Hey, I'm just saying it's a possibility, right?' She tapped him on the nose. 'So what d'you say we run those checks, and see what's going on? Try and work it out for ourselves.'

'All right,' said Strickland, but he didn't sound convinced.

He turned back to his instrument panel, glancing at the screens again. As Strickland's fingers flickered over his keyboard, his hands were shaking. It had always made him nervous, this mysterious Viking taken from her grave. Now, it terrified him.

Jess's heart missed a beat. She looked again.

Something was moving slowly and purposefully across the middle of the playground. It flickered, like a poorly-tuned image on a TV - and it seemed, as she watched, to change in colour, from blue to grey to black. It was shrouded in a dark cloak with a hood, and moved in a humpbacked crouch, arms outstretched as if feeling the way.

For a second, Jess stood there, paralysed with fear, and then the image began to cloud over with grey - her own breath, misting the window. She leapt back, hearing herself gasping now, aware that she was trembling, backing away from the window with her hand over her mouth.

'Jessica?' Ms James was hurrying over. 'Is everything all right?'

Jess grabbed Ms James' sleeve. 'Miss, which room's the GCSE Maths class in?'

'What?' Ms James looked utterly bewildered. Everyone was staring.

'*Please, Miss, which room?*'

'Room 21, but - Jessica Mathieson, *wait!*'

Ms James' voice, useless and distant, rang in Jess's ears as she ran from the classroom and bounded down the stairs three at a time, almost tripping over.

At the bottom, she ran past the lockers, then stopped, thought for a moment. She turned back, tugged her locker door and - ignoring the cascade of books, magazines and oddments - yanked out her hockey-stick and hefted its comforting weight in both hands. For all she knew it might be useless against witches, but it made her feel better.

Now she was running again. The blood was pounding in her temples and she could hear her own breath, ragged and desperate, above the pounding of her heart.

Down, down, down, and along the corridor she ran, classrooms and their lessons whizzing by as she glimpsed details - flasks of copper sulphate, *je suis allé en ville*, "Imagine You Are Wat Tyler", a film about India - and teachers looking up in alarm as Jess ran, ran, ran.

Where was the classroom? Where was Emerald?

Room 19, Room 20, Room 21. *There.*

Pause.

Breath.

She burst into the classroom, hockey-stick first, without knocking - not even looking to see which teacher was at the front of the class. It wasn't important.

Year 11 pupils turned and stared at her. She spotted Emerald's bright red hair, and saw her friend turn, turn, turn towards her... standing up as if in slow motion.

Their eyes met.

Emerald nodded, and Jess nodded back.

'They're here,' Jess said. '*I've seen them.*'

The teacher, Mrs Barnes, dropped her book in astonishment with a loud THUMP on the desk. '*What do you girls mean by disrupting my lesson?*' she demanded in booming tones.

Emerald Greene, ignoring her, bounded over three desks, knocking books and papers flying as she joined Jess in the corridor. 'You're sure?' Emerald asked, sounding calm.

Jess, who had no breath left to speak, nodded fervently.

Emerald cocked her head on one side as if listening hard. She seemed to turn a shade paler, as if she had somehow confirmed what Jess had just told her.

'We need to get everybody out of the school,' said Emerald.

'But Em, the thing's out in the playground!'

Mrs Barnes was there in the doorway - stout, furious and red-faced, hands on hips. 'What do you two girls think you are *playing* at?' she demanded.

Emerald completely ignored her. 'They will want the school,' Emerald said to Jess, and her eyes held utter conviction. 'We must clear the area in case they damage anyone.'

'Did you two hear what I just said?' Mrs Barnes squawked indignantly. 'Emerald Greene, being a genius does not allow you to be arrogant! Get *back* into your classroom *immediately!*'

Jess glanced down the corridor. Her eyes zoomed in on the small, red box of the fire alarm. 'We could - ' she began.

'Do it,' said Emerald.

'But we shouldn't, it's just for fires...'

'It is for emergencies, is it not?' demanded Emerald. Jess nodded. 'Fine,' Emerald said. 'This, I feel, is an Grade One emergency. *Hit the button.'*

'You, girl!' Mrs Barnes exclaimed in utter horror. 'Where on earth do you think you're going with that hockey-stick?' She grabbed Jessica's arm and halted her in her tracks, holding her there with surprising force as she squealed and wriggled.

'Mrs Barnes,' said Emerald Greene, turning towards her for the first time and lifting a hand, 'please, do not excite yourself. The very fabric of the Time-Space continuum is under threat, and shouting is not going to help.'

'I don't care what games you girls are playing! What I think, young lady, is that you are being disruptive and rude!'

Emerald Greene sighed, hands on hips, and tilted her head to one side. 'Mrs Barnes, if you do not let us hit that alarm, then you, like the rest of the school, could well be reduced to a puff of smoke within the next few minutes. So with all due respect, your opinion is most *spectacularly* irrelevant.'

For the first time in her life, Mrs Barnes stood with her mouth gaping open and was utterly speechless.

Jess took her opportunity to break free as Mrs Barnes slackened her grip. She skidded to a halt, feet slightly apart, in front of the fire alarm. She lifted her hockey-stick back over her shoulder, then swung it hard and smashed the glass.

An instant later, bedlam began.

From every fire-exit, excited girls and boys streamed - not quite running, but not quite walking either. They headed out on to the field, shepherded by anxious teachers waving their clipboards. The blaring klaxon of the alarm resounded through every room of the building, echoed out on to the playground and the school field.

Something else happened, though, as the pupils began arranging themselves into straggly lines in register order. The sky above them was filled with a mechanical clattering sound, and several hundred faces gawped skywards as a dark helicopter swooped in over the red-brick gables of the school like a giant, black bird.

It cast an undulating shadow across the masses below. It bore no markings, and yet it somehow managed to convey power and authority. And then behind it, there was another helicopter, exactly the same, and yet another.

The first helicopter, keeping a steady vertical path, came in to land on the school playground, right on top of the centre circle of the netball court. The other two held back and settled over the field, descending slowly and rippling the grass like water. The anxious teachers - commanded by a brusque, stick-wielding Miss Pinsley - shepherded the excited, waving children out of the way.

Mr Courtney and Mr Odell, tall and powerful in their black coats, alighted from the first helicopter, followed by young, black-uniformed men and women with low-slung machine pistols.

They strode across the playground as if they owned the place. Mr Courtney signalled to the operatives to spread out, and they did so gradually, black uniforms forming a semicircle advancing on the school entrance.

Richie had seen it all from his vantage-point.

He'd slipped away from his class when the fire bell sounded and watched, aghast, at the upstairs window of the Physics lab, from where he had a grandstand view across the grounds of Aggie's. He had given a start as he recognised the men he'd seen on the stairs that time.

The incessant blaring of the fire alarm cut off, leaving an eerie silence. Richie couldn't help noticing that it seemed to have grown unnaturally dark inside the school. Corners, crevices and alcoves seemed to have gained new shadows; classrooms stood empty, the desks cold and stark like rows of graves. Richie shuddered - he had to get out.

He headed for the stairs and almost ran into Emerald Greene and Jess, who hurrying upwards.

'Where are you going?' Richie gasped.

Emerald held up a slim, wand-like device with a dial on the end. 'Witch-hunting,' she said.

Richie looked anxiously at Jess, who shrugged and hefted her hockey-stick. Richie started to wish he had brought something to carry.

'They will be heading for the temporal nexus point,' said Emerald, 'to attempt to break through into the Earthworld. Come on!'

They hurried after her.

'Emerald, do you know what those helicopters are?' Jess asked, running to keep up with Emerald's long strides.

'Oh, yes.' Emerald threw the contemptuous comment over her shoulder. 'Those imbeciles from your Government's special division, I expect... Officials pretend in public that the Otherworld does not exist. When they try and deal with it in their bumbling fashion, they usually make things worse.' Emerald clicked her tongue in despair, then stopped dead as they came to a T-junction. She waved her wand-like device, appeared to do a quick 'eeny-meeny-miney-mo' and pointed left. 'This way, I think,' she said.

Richie and Jess followed Emerald's index finger. A second later, Emerald tilted her head, said, 'Mmmm,' turned about-face and set off in the opposite direction, leaving Jess and Richie to skid round in a half-circle and hurry after her.

They raced across the deserted quadrangle. The school seemed eerie with nobody in it, Richie thought, as if it was waiting for something.

Expecting something.

'Em, what exactly is that device of yours?' asked Jess..

'A detector for disturbances of temporo-psychic energy,' Emerald muttered, casting her gaze up and down the quadrangle. 'Left here,' she added.

'When was it left here?' Richie asked, confused.

'No - left *here*,' Emerald repeated, and kicked open the door to the Assembly Hall. She swooped inside, sweeping her detector in a wide arc.

Jess and Richie followed, at a more hesitant pace.

The Hall, with its wooden panelling, dusty parquet floor and rows of plastic chairs, was shrouded in shadow. It seemed darker than ever today; only the feeblest of grey light peeped through its high windows. Their footsteps echoed as they stepped forward, Richie and Jess keeping a couple of paces behind Emerald with her detector.

At that moment, the device began to make an alarming warbling noise and to flash with a bright orange light.

'A disturbance of temporo-whatsit energy?' Jess suggested.

'Or just a flat battery?' Richie asked.

She suddenly rounded on Richie, making him jump. 'Richard Fanshawe! Tell me again what you saw that time in the computer centre!'

Richie licked his lips, a little frightened now by Emerald's manner. 'Just a machine exploding. It hit the wall in pieces.'

'Anything else?' asked Emerald, pointing the detector in his face.

'I - heard singing,' said Richie. 'Sort of... old singing, like it was coming from deep in the earth. And there was an odd smell. Like... damp. Mustiness.'

Emerald Greene drew breath sharply. 'My goodness,' she said.

'What?' Jess asked urgently, tugging at her sleeve.

Emerald shook her head. 'Visual manifestations are commonplace, even instances of sound projection... but things are very grave when the subject breaks through into the olfactory range.'

'Sorry, the what?' Jess asked, baffled.

'She means smell,' said Richie smugly, pleased that Emerald had used a word he could explain for once. 'Sense of smell. Olfactory.'

Emerald nodded. 'Yes, yes... Only a step away from the tactile - and that would really be serious.'

She swung her detector around the Hall. There was the main stage, quiet and still and dusty. There were several exits: to the quadrangle, the car-park and the Science Block. Emerald tried every direction, and when she pointed the device towards the Science Block, it started bleeping, the needle on its dial oscillating wildly.

'Does that mean it's cooked?' Richie joked nervously.

'*You kids!*'

They spun around. Standing on the Hall stage were the two black-coated men. The older one with the moustache had his hands behind his back and was smiling benignly at them, while the young black man had his arms folded across his chest and looked stern. They were flanked by a pair of black-clad soldiers, a young man and a woman, who were levelling small, lethal machine-pistols.

'Unless you get out of here right now,' said a stern voice, 'you're going to be in very serious trouble.'

Jess sighed. 'Wouldn't you know it?' she said to the world in general. 'Just when things are getting interesting, the adults come along and spoil it all.'

9

Enemy Interference

Strickland looked up from his computer with an expression of alarm and beckoned his younger colleague. 'Arossi? You'd better come and look at this.'

She sauntered over, wearing a gently mocking smile. 'Hey, what is it now? You worry too much.'

'Yes, and you drink too much. Look!' Strickland jabbed at the readouts. 'I don't like this one bit. Argon emissions are up fifteen percent. Temperature is eight hundred Kelvin and rising. Do you want me to go on?'

Arossi peered at the monitor screen. 'Are you sure that machine's accurate?' she murmured sleepily.

Strickland shrugged. He stared transfixed at the softly pulsing screens, his hands gripping the rail so tightly that his knuckles went bone-white. 'I don't like this. Look at that... thing! It's playing with us!' Beads of sweat glistened on his forehead and he dabbed them with a spotted handkerchief from his pocket.

'That thing, Strickland, is a pile of old bones.' Arossi folded her arms and looked at him sternly. 'Listen, if you don't get a grip, I'm going to have to - '

'What's that noise?' Strickland interrupted her.

There was a sound, now, echoing in the tomb chamber and relayed to them in the van through the speakers... A low, sonorous sound like the harmonies of voices.

Strickland looked up at Arossi in panic. 'You hear that? Can you *hear* that?'

She went over to the nearest control desk and grabbed the headset, listening intently at one ear. 'Pulse fluctuation... Amplitude and frequency inconsistent with any standards...' She looked over at Strickland, and for the first time, her normally impassive face bore signs of concern. 'There's no central source to the transmission.'

'What do you mean?'

'It's wide-banding, looped throughout the immediate area. As if it's tuned into the whole of Meresbury, using the city as one giant transmitter!'

Strickland, sweat gathering in rivulets on his forehead, grabbed the phone. 'I'm calling the boss,' he said. He grabbed his coat. 'And then I'm getting out of here. And if you know what's good for you - so will you!'

Jessica had no idea how the new arrivals had managed to get in unheard. She knew one thing, though - they thought they were in control.

She tried the usual approach - if in doubt, be flippant.

'Off on your holidays?' she asked, nodding at Mr Odell's sunglasses. 'I hear the South of France is good at this time of year.'

The older man stepped forward. 'My name is Courtney, Special Measures Division. This is my colleague, Mr Odell.' The two men briefly held up small, silver ID cards, so quickly that they could have been anything. 'But you youngsters can call me Sir,' Mr Courtney added with a superior smile. Jess took an instant dislike to him, and from Richie's expression she could tell he felt the same. 'This school is now under the authority of the Special Measures Division - and that, kiddies, means *we're in charge*. So just do as you're told and everybody's happy.'

'You think this can be sorted out with the usual military blustering?' said Emerald Greene sharply.

'We're not military,' murmured Mr Odell with a languid smile.

'And, yes, don't think we don't know about *you*,' added Mr Courtney sternly, pointing at Emerald. 'You shouldn't be here at all, madam! Don't worry, hmm, we'll deal with you in good time.' He swung round suddenly to face Jessica. 'Now - you, young lady.'

'Me?' she said, alarmed. She looked over her shoulder, as if in the hope that he was addressing someone else.

'Yes,' said Mr Courtney sternly. He strolled over to stand beside her and bent down so that he was looking her in the eye, so close that she could see the individual grey hairs of his bushy moustache and the red, blotchy skin of his face. 'You have something which it isn't safe for you to have,' he murmured. He held out his hand. 'The compact disc, please.'

Jess put her head on one side. 'Phhhhww. Dunno what you're talking about,' she bluffed.

'Oh, dear me,' said Mr Courtney, shaking his head. 'Young lady, don't play around. I am a gentleman of the world. I've been lied to by more deceitful young women than you've had hot dinners.'

'That's not that many, actually. My aunt's a lousy cook.'

'The CD,' said Mr Courtney, raising his hand so that it was level with her face. 'I shall count to five.'

'Really?' Jess wrinkled her nose. 'You're sure? Not three?'

'One,' said Mr Courtney, unblinking.

'Two comes next,' Jess offered with a smile.

'Two,' Mr Courtney continued, unruffled. 'Three.'

'Three-and-a-half?' offered Jess, backing away. She collided with a wall behind her, and knew she couldn't go any further.

'Four.' Mr Courtney straightened up. 'Five.' He nodded to the two impassive operatives. 'Mr Braxton, Miss Hicks - search her.'

Jess held up her hands as if in surrender. 'All right, all right. No need for any of that.' She put her hand in her blazer pocket and drew out the plastic CD case.

Mr Courtney smiled and reached for it.

'Ooops, butterfingers!' Jess yelled, as she fumbled the CD and pretended to drop it. 'Richie, catch!'

She lobbed the CD to her friend, who caught it neatly. *Blimey, Richie*, she thought, *that must be your first ever clean piece of fielding.*

'Give me that!' Mr Courtney snarled, rounding on Richie.

'Why?' Richie snarled. 'Why should we trust you?'

'Because we have a serious investigation in progress, and you... *children* are likely to get in the way,' said Mr Courtney sternly. 'Now that disc is very important evidence. Give it to me, please!'

Mr Courtney lunged at Richie, making a grab for the CD - but with a cry of, 'Here!' Richie skimmed it back to Jess like a Frisbee, and she caught it neatly between both palms.

'Better be careful, Mr C,' Jess said. 'Don't want to risk breaking it, do we?'

Out of the corner of her eye - just too late - Jess saw the woman operative, Hicks, lunge for her. She tried to skim the CD back to

Richie, but too late. The young woman grabbed her arms, pinning them behind her back, and twisted the CD from her grasp.

Jess gave a yelp of pain. 'All right, all right! You've made your point!'

Mr Courtney snatched it and nodded in satisfaction, and nodded to his underling to let Jess go. 'Thank you for being sensible,' he said. 'And now - '

Suddenly, the lights flickered and went off, and then a low, crackling noise began, a sound like static electricity magnified several hundred times. Richie gasped, grabbing Jessica's arm. She shrugged him off, irritably. A second later, the school's emergency lighting kicked in, a dim reddish glow from the ceiling.

Mr Courtney pointed at Emerald, Jess and Richie. 'You lot, get out on the field with the rest of them. You're getting in the way. Mr Odell, check those doors.'

Richie and Jess backed away, but Emerald Greene silently stood her ground.

The Special Measures team advanced down the corridor, through the swing doors to the Science Block.

Mr Odell kicked open the doors to the Chemistry lab.

They swung back with a creak and a thud, and the smells of metal, bleach and gas wafted out. Mr Odell marched boldly in. They saw him through the glass, marching up and down the silent benches and gas-taps, appearing to sniff the air. He opened cupboards, prodded the various items of equipment - retort-stands, circuit boards, solenoids and resistors.

He lifted up a glass globe with a smaller ball contained within it - Jess recognised it as the plasma-ball Mr Gretton used to demonstrate electrical discharge - and hefted it in both hands. Mr Odell looked back out at Mr Courtney and shook his head.

'Listen to me,' snarled Emerald Greene, and Jess was shocked by how angry she appeared. 'The thing that is loose inside this school is here for a reason. Evil *cannot* be shot at and it *cannot* be arrested. If I am right about what they want, there is only one way to stop them!'

The crackling noise was growing steadily louder.

'Out of the way - *now*,' said Mr Courtney, and he actually moved to brush Emerald Greene aside.

Uh-oh, thought Jessica. *I wouldn't do that.*

One moment, Mr Courtney's arm was reaching out to grab Emerald's sleeve. The next, his arm flipped upside-down, spinning his whole body through a circle. He yelled in astonishment, loose change falling from his pockets along with a compass and a hip-flask, and a moment later he gave a dull 'Oooof!' as he was flipped on to his back on the floor of the corridor.

Just then, there was a shout from within the lab. They all turned as one, to see Mr Odell cautiously backing away from the plasma-ball. The glass globe was alive with flickering crimson light, the tendrils straining at the transparent glass. As they watched, the crackling ball lifted itself up into the air without any visible support and began to float through the air towards Mr Odell.

Mr Courtney was on his feet in a second, dusting himself down. 'Here they come,' he murmured.

The dim light in the corridors flared brighter for a second, then the lights began to flicker and buzz alarmingly. Jess clung instinctively to Emerald. 'What's going on?' she asked, staring as if mesmerised into the red lightning.

'The wraiths are using electrical impulses to break through the thin reality into the real world,' Emerald muttered. 'We are at the Nexus.'

Before either of them could stop her, Jess had run into the science lab and was pulling Mr Odell back by his sleeve. 'You've got to get out of here! Come on!' She brandished her hockey-stick at the globe, just to make herself feel braver.

'Get back!' Mr Odell snapped, and levelled his revolver at the globe.

'Do not be a fool!' shouted Emerald Greene. 'You think *bullets* can stop it?'

Ignoring her, Mr Odell fired once, twice, three times into the heart of the globe. There were three cracking, popping sounds, like nutshells in an open fire, but apart from that there appeared to be no effect.

Jess, horrified, stared at the globe of light, unable to take her eyes off it.

Then the globe flared suddenly, for an instant as bright as burning magnesium. There was a powerful gust of wind which ripped the posters from the wall of the lab. The tattered fragments, pulled into the heart of a mini-tornado, whirled in the air like hideous birds of prey before burning up in showers of incandescent red light.

Mr Odell holstered his revolver and grabbed Jess's arm. 'Come on,' he ordered, 'let's get - '

His lips froze in mid-sentence. Jess blinked, did a double-take. Mr Odell appeared to have stopped talking and moving. He stood at her side, as still as a waxwork dummy, his fingers immobile on her arm.

Time stood still.

Jess, drawn to the light, felt strangely detached from her own body, although she could see her arms and legs shaking. She heard the energy crackling, the sound like the crunching of crêpe paper amplified a hundred times.

The room darkened around her, and suddenly she was in a dark, open arena, cold and empty. It had to be the size of a football pitch - no, surely several football pitches. In fact, she could not see any boundaries to it at all.

There was now a dot in front of her, shimmering with cobalt-blue; and as it grew in size, coming closer, she realised she was looking at a blue, human-shaped hole in the blackness. It came closer still, then shimmered, forming a shape not unlike the one she had seen in the playground. She could smell the damp, vegetable odour again.

Jess swallowed hard and tried to control her shaking limbs. Features formed on the shape. It was a woman, her face wizened but her eyes clear and bright. She leaned on her staff and moved jerkily, leaving traces behind her like photo negatives.

'Girl,' said the witch's voice. It had the resonance of a church bell, and seemed to come from everywhere and nowhere at once. 'Girl! Can you hear me?'

'I hear you.' Jess, without realising it, had thought the words and not spoken them out loud. She shivered, not daring to move, nor to wonder where she might be. 'What are you doing in the school?'

The voice murmured inside her head now - secret, soft and calming, like a soundtrack on headphones. 'An interface, that is all. As we grow towards our Becoming.'

'So you're the ones who've been causing all the weirdness,' Jess said, narrowing her eyes. 'What do you want?'

'My name is Xanthë. We do not wish you any harm. Yes, we are outcasts - yes, witches, if you like. But all we desire, all we need, is to regain form. Can you not understand that - Jessica?'

She shivered inside at the witch's use of her name, but did not let it show outwardly. 'What do you mean, regain form? You're ghosts, aren't you? Ghosts are always ghosts...'

'Are they?' said Xanthë softly. She lowered her eyes, quivered as she leaned on her staff. 'Sometimes, girl, I feel I am only a fragment, only a molecule away from living fully again. And then it drifts away, out of reach, and I realise that the molecule might as well be a thousand light years, for it is equally impenetrable... I remember the sunsets, yes, the sunsets... the moorland dripping with honey-light as the chimney-smoke drifts up into the clear blue evening. And the villages burning, fire painting the night sky vermilion, the sparks lifting up on the wind and then falling, softly, like shooting stars... I remember the *idea* of smell, but I have forgotten the old aromas; I cannot remember when I last smelt the scent of the herbs and flowers in the forest. They are just names - wolfsbane, hemlock, foxglove... All these things are gone, now... gone, like teardrops in rain.'

'I'm sorry,' said Jess, and there was a catch in her voice as she felt her eyes prickling with tears. 'I'm so sorry for you. But it's over. You have to accept that.'

'And I remember a man, a young man with hopeless loss in his eyes as I was sent from the village, sent to the other place whose name could not be spoken. The place down in the valley.' She looked up, and there was an angry light in her eyes. 'All we want is to return. To have another chance. The dead can live again, Jessica. Surely you realise this is true? Have you not thought and wished this, keeping it at the back of your mind, for your whole life?'

Jess felt herself shaking with a mixture of emotions, but she was determined to show nothing.

'You understand, do you not?' Xanthë went on. 'You have experienced death and loss. So unusual in one so young. That is why I reach out to you. *To ask you to understand us.*'

Jess held her hands up. 'Please. Don't get me involved. I'm sympathetic, honestly... But I trust Emerald, and she thinks it's wrong.'

'But just think, Jessica.' The witch stretched out a spindly hand, and despite the translucent blueness surrounding it, it seemed somehow solid and real. Jessica stared at the hooked yellow fingernails, the brown liver-spots on papery skin, the knotted blue veins. 'Imagine if you had the chance to see your parents. Would you not take that chance?' Her mouth formed a misshapen, toothless grin.

'No. No!...' She backed away. 'What's done is done. They can never come back. Never! It's wrong to think like that.'

'Jessica...' said the witch softly, and then her voice changed. It became a voice she thought she had heard before - a voice she knew, and yet... 'Look at me, Jessica.'

She opened her eyes and looked.

Instead of the witch, a young woman stood there. Tall, blonde, in a long black dress. Light shone through her mane of golden hair, illuminated her pale skin. She wore two hooped gold earrings, and her mouth was red and full and kind, smiling down at Jess. She held out a hand with its fingernails painted blue and silver, a loving hand for Jess to hold.

'Hello, darling,' she said. 'I've missed you.'

Jess's heart was pounding against her ribs. She suddenly felt the sense of knowing something, someone that she had never truly known before. A love she had never experienced was rushing into her life like the waters of a swollen river, sparkling and full of sunlight and life.

No! said a dissenting part of her brain, *it's a trick! It's a witches' illusion!*

But surely it was her?

She drew nearer.

It was just like that time in the High Street, when she had seen the woman's reflection in the shop window, and had turned to find nothing there.

She felt her right palm moving towards her mother's, closer and closer. (*No, no!*) Their hands clasped.

Jess's palm tingled. There was a harsh, electric coldness against her fingers. *No!* Something made her pull her hand away.

'Jessica?' said the woman quizzically, hands on hips. 'Don't you recognise me?'

What would Emerald Greene say if she was here in this strange realm with her? She would tell her that it was all a devious deception, something designed to gain her confidence. She gnawed a fingernail and backed away, shaking her head. 'It's not you,' she said softly. 'Stop this! My mother and father are dead!'

'Darling,' she said, folding her arms and looking down at her with quizzical kindness. 'I'm not dead. Whatever are you talking about? I'm here!' She held out a hand again, the nails glittering blue and silver. 'Jess. Come here, love.'

Jessica closed her eyes, screwing them up so hard that she saw hot, red shapes, and she clenched her fists until they hurt. 'I've visited their grave and I've put flowers on it. Every year on November the first, we light a candle to remember them... That's how it is! You can't change the past! You can't!'

The figure shimmered and flickered for an instant, like a poor picture on a TV screen.

'I deny your illusion!' shouted Jess triumphantly. 'Chrissie LaForge is dead! *She's dead!*'

And she opened her eyes and looked unflinchingly at the figure in front of her. It was warping, changing back into Xanthë again.

The witch spoke once more, and this time her voice was metallic and cold. '*Go, then, girl! Go, and be like all the rest!*'

And suddenly, without warning, she was back in the school lab again.

Mr Odell, instantly unfrozen at her side, finished his sentence:
' - out of here, now!'

The ball sprouted tendrils of light, like guy-ropes whipped by the wind. They lashed across the science lab, searing workbenches and smashing flasks in their crackling wake, with a noise like tortured screaming. The lab was filled with a chemical stench and the odour of burning wood. Windows cracked like icing-sugar, the popping and splintering of glass punctuating the tortured screams like gunshots.

Just for an instant, before Mr Odell pulled her away to safety, Jess saw a tall, grey figure forming around the globe, holding it in both hands as the light coruscated around the room. Its face was twisted, enraged, a mask of pure hatred.

And then the door slammed shut, blocking it from her view.

Part Four

Alarums and Excursions

10

Witchcraft

A storm was gathering above Meresbury.

Clouds clashed like gods in the steely sky. They loomed above the Cathedral, vast and black. When the thunder rolled, it was like a stentorian voice from down the centuries, bellowing into the valley. At the centre, the Darkwater pulsed, shimmering with a gentle light which caught the raindrops and froze them for a millisecond at a time. Wraithlike clouds of steam billowed from the surface of the lake, twisted upwards into unearthly patterns.

Things were changing.

'Those clouds don't look normal,' said Richie.

They were thick, black, evil-looking clouds, he thought, edged with a crackling energy. The air hissed, as if full of static electricity.

'The witches are mad,' said Jess, shivering. Outside, one of the operatives had thrown a quilted foil blanket around her shoulders, and she wrapped herself in it like a successful marathon-runner. She didn't seem to have heard Richie.

'We have enraged them, yes,' Emerald agreed. 'But that may be to our advantage.'

'No, Em, I mean *mad*,' said Jess. 'Bonkers. Barmy. Nutcases.'

'Oh, I see,' said Emerald. 'Mentally unstable? No, no. They are logical and sane. And that makes them a most fearsome adversary.'

Every window in the school was pulsing with a spectral, bluish light. It reflected in the puddles, broken into sparkling dots by the rain. Everyone had retreated to the school field, where the helicopters had been joined by black cars, including Mr Courtney's Mercedes; nobody seemed bothered about keeping Jess, Richie and Emerald away, so they had just followed.

Richie counted about thirty Special Measures men and women spreading out to encircle the school, little black dots against the green. It occurred to him to wonder why they carried those mean-looking machine-pistols, as he didn't imagine they were all that effective against spectral beings from another dimension. Maybe they were just showing off?

He glanced at Jess. 'You okay?'

She nodded, tried to smile. But she looked pale and shaken, and she kept glancing anxiously back towards the school - as if she had lost something, Richie thought.

The rain was turning the field into a quagmire. Emerald Greene produced a small, pen-shaped object, which blossomed into a giant golden umbrella. Richie only had a second to be impressed before he saw Mr Courtney and Mr Odell bearing down on them.

'Look out,' said Richie. 'Here come the Chuckle Brothers.'

Mr Courtney folded his arms and glowered at the two girls and Richie. 'You lot have got some explaining to do. Especially *you*,' he added, pointing at Emerald. 'You knew this was going to happen, didn't you?'

Emerald shrugged, smiled. 'I did try to warn you.'

The warble of Mr Odell's phone cut through the conversation. He flicked it on. 'Odell, Special Measures?... Oh, I see... Yes... yes, just one moment, Madam.' He winced and held the phone at arm's length. 'Sir?'

'What now?' Mr Courtney snapped, turning on him.

'It's... the Prime Minister, sir. Wants to know what the latest is.'

Mr Courtney hesitated only for a second. 'Ah, I see. *Harrumph.* Err... well, summarise the situation, Odell.' He waved a hand. 'Key salient points, and all that.'

'Me, sir?'

'Yes, you, lad! Didn't you go on a course last month?'

'That was just about problem-solving, sir.'

'Well... just do your best! This is a problem. Solve it!'

'Sir,' said Mr Odell resignedly. He retreated to a discreet distance and began murmuring into the phone, occasionally nodding.

Mr Courtney turned back towards the children, to find Emerald Greene looking at him slightly pityingly.

'Please understand,' Emerald Greene said, 'I do know rather more than you about what we are dealing with.'

'And so what *are* we dealing with, you young madam?' growled Mr Courtney.

'The wraiths will attempt to manifest themselves at different access points on the ley-line,' Emerald said, beginning to pace up and down in her cone of dryness.

'They will?' Mr Courtney folded his arms and glared at her.

'They must be prevented,' she said firmly, 'otherwise the... entity will draw power from their breakthrough and emerge through the access points. Now - there is a way we *can* contain them. You have the equipment to set up a strong magnetic field?'

'Magnetic field?' Mr Courtney tutted. 'What is this, school Science Week?'

Mr Odell finished his conversation and hurried over, snapping his phone shut. 'The PM gives us full Situation X approval, sir. The decision is in your hands.'

'What does that mean?' asked Richie, looking from one to the other.

Mr Courtney sighed. 'Situation X,' he said, 'is the PM's way of saying nobody at Westminster has got a clue what's going on here, and can we please sort it out without anybody having to know about it. Least of all the Government.'

Mr Odell stood with his hands behind his back. 'Elegantly put, sir, if I do say so myself.'

'Thank you, lad.' He shot a look at Mr Odell. 'The PM *definitely* said Situation X?'

'Yessir. She did.'

'Right. Just checking.'

Emerald directed a look at Mr Courtney, one which Richie knew well by now, and whose impact he could almost feel himself. 'Well?' she said coldly. 'Do you wish to listen, or not?'

Mr Courtney shook his head and gave a sigh of frustration. 'Have I got time to listen to prattling schoolgirls? We've got a serious situation here!'

'Wait, sir,' said Mr Odell. 'Let the girl speak.'

Emerald smiled her thanks at him. 'You need a few hundred metres of cable and a wire mesh,' she said. 'And some junction boxes, and a transformer.'

Mr Courtney's moustache bristled. 'And that's all, is it? Are you trying to tell me how to do my job, young lady, hmm?'

'Allow me to spell it out to you.' She squared up to Mr Courtney, rain streaming off the shiny surface of her umbrella. Richie, despite the cold rain and his concern for Jess, watched the exchange in fascination. 'There are two ways you can contain a wraith in the Otherworld. *One*, a psychic barrier - which means controlling your own belief in something equally strong. Or *two*, a physical barrier - which means containing it within the medium it has chosen to manifest itself through. These wraiths have chosen electricity.'

'So?' Mr Courtney muttered, folding his arms.

'So hit them with a dose of magnetic force and it will scramble them like eggs. Or you could try putting up your psychic defences. What do you believe in, Mr Courtney? Anything strong enough? Guns, perhaps?' She stood close to him, nose-to-nose. 'You like guns, do you not? Your operatives seem to brandish them menacingly enough, despite the fact that they are utterly useless. Or did you think we had not noticed that?'

Mr Courtney's nostrils flared. Emerald Greene stood her ground, her red hair fluttering in the wind. The few seconds in which they stared at one another seemed to last forever.

'We've tried your way, Mr Courtney,' said Emerald, 'and it was spectacularly useless. So why don't we try mine?' She raised her eyebrows impudently.

Richie held his breath, and out of the corner of his eye he thought he saw Mr Odell give a little half-smile.

Then, to Richie's delight, Mr Courtney - nodding slowly and resignedly as he maintained eye contact with Emerald Greene - lifted his radio. 'I'll get my specialist in,' he said, and thumbed the call button. 'Mr Vance? Going to need some equipment. Get over here and make it snappy.'

'*Very good, sir,*' said an efficient-sounding voice.

Mr Courtney clicked the radio off. 'This had better work,' he snarled.

'Oh, it will,' said Emerald Greene. She pulled a notepad and pencil out of her pocket and scribbled a brief diagram in less than five seconds. 'Provided you set it up like this.' She tore the page off and handed it to a bemused Mr Courtney.

'Right,' he said, staring at the piece of paper for a moment or two. He nodded. 'That's actually... quite clever,' he admitted through gritted teeth. He lifted the radio again. 'Vance? Cable, wire mesh, junction-boxes, heavy-duty transformers. Got that?'

'*Wilco, sir. The truck's on its way.*'

To Richie's delight, Emerald Greene gave a dazzling smile. 'Well done, Mr Courtney. You may just have saved your career.'

'You okay?' Richie asked Jess.

She nodded, smiled weakly. 'Yes,' she said. 'Fine.'

Emerald strode over to them. 'There is no time to waste,' she snapped. 'I have a plan, and I need to put it into action.'

'Oh, good,' muttered Richie. 'I'd hate to think you were just improvising.'

Emerald peered at them over her blue glasses. 'I need someone to come back to Rubicon House with me.' She produced a coin. 'No prestidigitation, agreed? A straightforward flip?'

Richie peered at the coin. 'Right.'

'Richie, you call.'

'Tails!' said Richie firmly.

Emerald flicked the coin and caught it smartly on the back of her hand. She lifted her hand. It was heads. She shrugged, flipped the coin at Richie, who caught it instinctively. 'My apologies,' she muttered. 'Must be your unlucky day... Still, the universe is essentially a random construct.' Emerald nodded to Jess, and they started to hurry off, but Emerald turned as she remembered something. 'Oh, Mr Courtney? One other thing. Get your people at the stone circle to switch off *all* their equipment.'

'What, everything?' Mr Courtney scoffed.

'Yes, *everything!* You do realise any emission of energy is a potential source of power for this thing? So turn it all off! Come on, Jessica.'

The girls hurried away, heading for the car-park.

Richie realised he was clasping the coin so tightly that it had left a red mark and a metallic odour on his palm. He flipped it over and realised he was still staring at the Queen's head. Puzzled, he flipped it back again. Still heads.

'Wait a minute!' he exclaimed.

But the girls had already disappeared.

'Mr Odell,' said Mr Courtney through gritted teeth.

'Sir?'

'Radio to Arossi, get her to close down all equipment at the stone circle.'

'Yes, sir.'

'But tell her to leave the radio channel open,' Mr Courtney added, wagging a finger. 'I don't want anybody left isolated,' he muttered under his breath.

'Good afternoon - I'm Mike Devenish, coming to you live at County TV with a special news report. Freak weather conditions in the Mere Valley have resulted in what the Met Office this afternoon called "strange phenomena". Torrential rain, flooding and strong winds have been reported, while observers report seeing "unusual" lightning in various parts of the city.

'At 15:05 hours this afternoon, the Met Office issued a special warning, advising people in the area to stay indoors unless their journey is absolutely vital. The Meresbury Transport Executive has also given a statement, informing us that all bus and train services in the area are subject to severe disruption. Emergency services will attempt to run as normal, although we understand that flash flooding is making some roads difficult to pass.

'Stay tuned to County TV - your only TV station for the very latest live updates! For the moment, though, we return you to Win It Or Bin It.'

An early dusk fell. On the darkening horizon, fork lightning with a vermilion glow played across the valley.

Richie was observing the Special Measures team encircling the school in a ring of wire mesh. It looked like a gigantic doughnut of closely-knit wire, and formed a fence around the school at a distance of about fifty metres from the walls. It went round into the car-park and back again. He watched as two of the team, under Mr Odell's direction, started connecting the wire with heavy cables to a couple of insulated black boxes.

He polished his glasses and squared up to Mr Courtney's ample waistline. 'So, you're going with Emerald's idea. Better make sure she gets the credit, hadn't you?'

Mr Courtney turned, pointed his radio at Richie with a thoughtful expression on his face. 'Listen, sonny.' He squatted down so that their faces were level. 'I don't know where your young friend's gone, but you seem to know enough about her.' Mr Courtney narrowed his eyes. 'So you're staying right beside me!'

'Sure,' said Richie. 'But only because I don't want to miss anything.'

Shivering, he stared into the rain with growing unease. The wind was getting up as well, twisting his hair and pushing it into his eyes, and his glasses were steaming over again.

A few feet away, the Special Measures crew hovered, black uniforms glistening in the rain.

Something crackled inside Mr Courtney's coat, and everyone turned to look at him. He frowned. 'Get me my indigestion pills,' he snarled at the nearest of his operatives.

'Er, I think it was your radio,' Richie offered politely.

'Harrumph! Of course it was.' Mr Courtney fished his two-way radio out of his inside pocket. 'Courtney! Go ahead?'

'*It's Arossi, sir. We've got a big problem with the specimen. It... still seems to be gathering energy, sir. Looks like it's about to break out!*'

'Where's Strickland?' snarled Mr Courtney.

'*He's... gone, sir.*'

'Gone? What do you mean, gone?'

'*Vamoosed, sir. Absconded. Disappeared off into the sunset. Said he wasn't paid to risk life and limb.*'

Mr Courtney gritted his teeth. 'Why, the little... All right, Arossi, I need you to power down, d'you hear me? Switch everything off, disconnect the power and get out of there!'

'*I can't, sir! It's all going into overload! I've tried polarising the neutron interface, but it just has no effect!*'

'Sir!' someone yelled over to the right. 'Something happening!'

'Hang on, Arossi,' snapped Mr Courtney. 'We've got our own problems here.'

Richie saw it at the same time. The main arched window of the Hall, glowing with a blue fire, appeared to be bulging outwards, expanding like a balloon.

Crack!

The window burst, scattering a shower of molten glass like glutinous raindrops. They hung in the air for a second, defying gravity, as if an iridescent flower of glass had bloomed from the side of the school. And then the droplets fell, as one, with a hiss of steam, solidifying on the grass about thirty metres away from the ring of Special Measures operatives.

And from the hole came the witches.

It had to happen. Two of the youngest operatives, jittery and frightened, reacted instinctively, firing upon the spectral, grey-blue figures as they flowed from the gap.

Richie put his fingers in his ears and ducked behind the bonnet of Mr Courtney's car. *No way is this like the films*, he thought grimly. The sound of bullets was unbelievably *loud*, like fireworks going off right beside him, and their pungent smell, wafting on the wind, made him sneeze.

'Hold your fire!' Mr Courtney was shouting furiously. '*Hold your fire!*'

But more Special Measures operatives were firing now, some dropping to one knee, others standing. The guns chugged and coughed and spluttered, belching hot lead, carving out brick dust and glass from the school building, scorching and searing it, smashing windows, ripping drainpipes from their housing and splintering doors.

The witch-wraiths strode on, through the fire, unheeding.

Finally, the firing stopped.

'What the *hell?...*' Richie heard Mr Courtney mutter.

He lifted his head above the bonnet, risked a look.

They were whitish-blue pillars of radiance - he counted nine of them. But if he squinted through the driving rain, he could see their form: tall, young, beautiful women with long limbs, graceful movements, hair which flowed like coils of pure light, wrapping around the drenched air and crackling with energy. And beneath the cowled hoods, he could make out features; beautiful faces suffused with light, and bright eyes of gold, shining like halogen bulbs.

Standing there. Waiting.

Richie looked away. They hurt his eyes. Something told him he ought not to look at them for too long.

He scurried over to Mr Courtney. 'I don't think you can just shoot them,' he said angrily. 'That's just stupid. I mean, it's like shooting light. Or air. They're not *like* that.'

'So we use your friend's plan,' said Mr Courtney, eyes narrowing.

With a shower of mud and a skittering sound, Mr Odell scrambled over to join them.

'Ready to activate, sir!' he snapped. Two operatives were backing away from the wire fence, unfurling cable as they went. Mr Odell held up a small black box sporting a silver switch and two dials - no more advanced than something from the school physics lab, Richie noted wryly.

Mr Courtney nodded. 'Go!'

As one, they saw the shimmering forms of the witches advancing towards them.

Mr Odell flicked the switch on the box.

The effect was astonishing.

One second the spiral of wire fence was there between them and the ghosts, and the next it was replaced by a thrashing, bright barrier of blue energy. Like a living thing made out of lightning it crackled, scorching the school field - Richie, taking cover behind Mr Courtney's car, could smell the burnt mud and grass.

The witch-wraiths, as one, held their hands to their ears and screeched. The sound was unearthly - Richie thought it sounded like a discordant choir of voices, mixed with a noise like the rending of sheet metal and the screams of animals being tortured. He winced, scrunching up his face in physical discomfort as the noise attacked his ears.

'The dials, man!' shouted Mr Courtney, making a twiddling gesture towards Mr Odell.

Mr Odell twisted the controls on the box, and the keening noise subsided, replaced with a low, buzzing hum like that made by strip-lighting. The crackling barrier settled down too, coalescing and forming softer-edged shapes which ducked and dived like will-o'-the-wisps caught in a cage of wire.

A strong, harsh odour of burning drifted towards them through the rain. It reminded Richie of the smell of sparklers on Bonfire Night.

Richie straightened up. He hardly dared speak to Mr Courtney. 'Holding them?' he said.

The Special Measures man's eyes narrowed as he nodded. 'For now,' he grunted. He swung round towards Richie. 'So, lad. We'd better start hoping your friend Miss Greene is right about all this - hadn't we?'

Rain hammered on the Dormobile's windscreen as it cut through the mud of the forest. It juddered and skidded, Emerald Greene stepping hard on the accelerator.

'Will I be all right?' Jess asked, her teeth chattering.

'I cannot say. You let one of them touch you. Anything is possible.' Emerald's tone was shockingly casual.

There was an expression of intense concentration on Emerald's face as she steered the shaking van through the forest towards the chronostatic barrier. Mud sprayed up on all sides, splattering the windows.

'Don't worry,' purred Anoushka, fixing Jess with a hard stare. 'You'll be fine. If the witches had intended to harm you, they could have done so far more seriously.'

'Oh, thanks,' said Jess bitterly. 'That's really reassuring.'

'I think,' Anoushka drawled, 'that they just wanted to let you know they were there.'

Jess frowned. 'So what makes you an expert, moggy?'

Anoushka twitched his whiskers and looked away, his emerald eyes flicking upwards towards his young mistress for a second. Jess didn't see what passed between them. 'I have enough experience to speak with confidence,' the cat muttered. 'Let's just say that.'

A second later, the van slammed to a sudden halt. Jess would have been jolted from her seat in the back if she hadn't been hanging on.

The engine slowed to a purr. They had reached the clearing.

'Let's go!' Emerald yelled, and the van leapt forward.

Jess felt, for a moment, as if her body had left her stomach behind. She was aware of the Dormobile surging forward, churning up the ground. Onward they pounded, the engine roaring, the van shaking, the rain flaying the windows like a thousand lashing whips. She shivered as a sudden chill passed over them, and for an instant she stared at the rear window, sure that she had seen something terrible scraping at the glass and trying to get in. Anoushka leapt on to the back of Emerald's chair, fur standing on end, arching his back and hissing like a mad-thing. Jess thought, for a second, that she heard a terrible, unearthly screaming noise.

And then it was gone, and there was just the rain and the buckling trees and the darkening sky rushing by outside.

A second later, they hit the Chronostatic Barrier.

11

The Last Gathering

Mr Courtney and Richie leaned against the Mercedes and watched the glowing line of witches.

'You know,' Mr Courtney said thoughtfully, 'you remind me of my two boys.'

'Really?' said Richie nervously.

'Oh, yes. Intelligent. Inquisitive. Never willing to take the easy answer.' He nodded to himself. 'I like that,' he said. 'I like enquiring minds.'

Richie blinked. 'What do your sons do now?' he asked tentatively.

Mr Courtney looked down at him, and for a moment his face creased into a kindly smile. 'William's a sheep farmer in the Australian bush,' he said, 'and Lewis is an accountant.'

'Wow,' said Richie. 'Bit of a difference.'

'I know,' said Mr Courtney with a heartfelt sigh. 'Only to be expected, though. Lewis was always the strange one.'

Richie folded his arms and stared at the glowing forms of the witches. 'I wonder what they're waiting for?' he murmured, almost to himself.

Mr Odell strode over to join them.

'I was wondering that myself.' Mr Odell stood with his feet apart and his hands behind his back, and stared pensively at the glowing forms of the witches.

'If I was them,' said Richie, 'I'd have broken through that barrier by now. Which suggests they can't. Yet.'

Mr Odell and Mr Courtney looked at one another, then down at Richie.

'Well, think about it,' said Richie, who had been. 'They broke out of the school easily enough. So the field's keeping them at bay. What would *you* do? You'd think, wouldn't you? You'd work out that you're contained there. So you've got to do something else.

Either find another medium, or...' He looked up at the two men. 'What's the other option?'

'More power,' said Mr Odell softly. 'I'd be waiting for more power.'

The radio hissed again. Mr Courtney snatched it up. 'Arossi? What's going on?'

The crackling of the radio grew louder, then disintegrated into static.

Mr Courtney growled angrily and shook the radio, whacking it with one big, meaty hand. 'Arossi, come in, please!' He shook his head and looked up at Mr Odell in despair. 'Nothing. Any way we can boost the signal? *I need to know what's happening down there!*'

Rubicon House was pale and fragile beneath the full moon, its marble statues like watching ghosts. The white façade of the house was suddenly picked out in the arc of the Dormobile's headlights, as the van screeched to a halt outside the main doors.

Jess shivered again. It was not normal cold, she told herself - it was spreading from within, working outwards from her numbed, hardened fingers.

Emerald flung open the sliding door, which made a crunching, squeaking sound. She threw something at Jess, who caught it instinctively. Looking down, she saw she was holding a packet of smoky bacon crisps.

'Salt, protein, glucose,' Emerald reminded her. 'You need extra unless your body has become accustomed to the Barrier.'

'Right. Um... I'm not that keen on this flavour.'

Emerald threw her hands up in agitation. 'The barriers of reality are threatened with destruction, and you are quibbling over food additives!' She grabbed the crisps from a startled Jess, tore open the packet and thrust them at her. 'Eat them! Eat!'

'All right, all right,' Jess muttered, chewing uneasily.

Emerald consulted her watch. 'Now, then,' she said, her eyes shining, 'I would estimate we only have about thirty minutes. Come on.'

Jess hopped out on to the gravel. She was pale and shivering, but still felt a thrill of excitement when she gazed at Rubicon

House. 'This place is still amazing,' she murmured, popping crisps in her mouth as fast as she dared.

'Really?' Anoushka purred, jumping down behind them. 'I find it a little ostentatious myself. I'd hoped for something rather more modern. Still, one can't pick and choose when one is an exile, can one?'

Emerald fumbled with the great, iron key to the front door. 'I just hope the Librarian is still up,' she murmured.

'I still don't really get it,' Jess said, munching, staring back down the gardens as if trying to detect the point at which they had entered the barrier. 'How can it be dark here? And not raining?'

Emerald sighed, turned round with her hands on her hips and stared at her. She peered over her glasses, and for a second, Jess thought her eyes actually glowed. 'It is a different dimension,' Emerald explained impatiently. 'Why are you people always so full of questions?'

'Sign of intelligence,' protested Jess, as the door creaked open.

'Right,' said Emerald. 'In, now!'

They ran through the labyrinth of corridors and rooms, lit by flickering candlelight. Still shivering, even with her foil blanket around her, Jess found herself wondering whether the internal alignment of Rubicon House had somehow adjusted itself since her last visit.

At last, Emerald stopped, spinning round on one heel in front of a pair of oak doors with wrought-iron handles. 'Here,' she said. She grasped the handles firmly and flung the doors open.

The Library yawned in front of them, vast, cold and high-vaulted. The towers of ancient books were now lit, Jess noticed, by lanterns hanging from the ends of some of the shelves. The light was uneasy, painting thick shadows in the furthest recesses. The vaulted room smelt of dust and damp, and Jess was sure she could hear skittering noises like a dozen mice running for cover. She looked around for Anoushka, but the cat seemed once again to have disappeared when he was needed.

Emerald, her footsteps echoing off endless books, marched to the centre of the nearest aisle. She climbed on to the big wooden desk, kicking over a SILENCE notice as she did so.

'Lesson for you, Jessica Mathieson,' said Emerald grimly, staring up into the highest reaches of the Library. 'Some rules were made to be broken.' And to Jess's astonishment - and delight - Emerald put her fingers to her mouth and let out a piercing, echoing whistle.

For a moment, there was silence. The girls held their breath.

Then, there was a movement in the air, and a leathery, fluttering sound. Down came a great, cold shadow from the uppermost heights, descending towards them at an astonishing rate. Even though Jess knew what to expect this time, she still felt her heart beating a little faster.

The eagle settled on the table, hooked its claws on to the silver globe as before, and surveyed the girls with its beady eyes.

'*Who calls the guardian of the books -* ' it began.

'No, no,' Emerald exclaimed, waving her hands in agitation. 'Please, Librarian, just this once, can we forgo the poetry? Time is of the essence.'

'Hmmm,' said the Librarian in obvious disapproval. 'Time always of essence, hmm? Humans need a little perspective, mmm.'

'Do you have the book for me?' Emerald persisted.

'Oh, book is it you are wanting? Thought perhaps was something, ah, *urgent*, mm, for which you were disturbing my sleep.' The eagle shook his great head, rummaged inside his plumage and pulled out the leather-bound book which Jess and Emerald had looked at, offering it to them in his beak. Emerald reached for it gratefully, but the Librarian snatched it back. 'Well?' he said indistinctly. 'Is urgent?'

'Librarian,' Emerald said in her most adult and serious voice, 'a dimensional anomaly is spreading across Meresbury, one which threatens to disrupt the very fabric of the continuum. It could release into this world a host of spectral creatures who have no business here. It would mean...' Emerald's eyes gleamed. 'It would mean chaos!' she cried.

'They might even get in here,' said Jess, 'and mess up the order of your books.'

The eagle's beak fell open another couple of millimetres. 'Urgent,' he agreed.

Loosened, the book fell, turning slowly as it dropped towards the table. Emerald caught it, slamming the leather covers between her palms in a cloud of ancient dust.

'Thank you,' she said, looking up.

'Return by date stamped,' said the eagle haughtily, and, spreading his wings, he lifted off the ground and rose slowly, slowly, disappearing back to his eyrie high among the topmost shelves.

Jess shrugged off her foil blanket and looked expectantly at Emerald. 'Now what?' she demanded.

Emerald leafed frantically through the book. 'I need to find the right information,' she muttered.

'Emerald, it's a tome full of ancient ley-lines! Maps of chalk horses and drawings of garlic pentagrams! How exactly is it going to help us?'

Emerald fixed her with a cold gaze. 'It contains *information*,' she said with unnerving calmness. 'Certainly, it needs to be interpreted in a different form - translated, if you like - but the building blocks of a scientific solution are here.'

'And can you... translate it?'

Emerald held the book open on the nearest desk, pulled one of the lanterns close and skimmed through the book's pages - a little less calmly now, it seemed to Jess.

'Well?' Jess demanded, slamming her palms down on the desk and wincing at the pain.

'I do not know,' Emerald Greene admitted.

'Emerald, you have no idea what you're looking for, have you?'

'Very well!' Emerald's eyes shone with a cold, green light. 'You and Richie always look to me for the answers, for the explanations of all that is outside your experience. Do you think I have ever had such explanations? Someone to stand over me, to hold my hand, to tell me how all the strangeness of the universe works? *No!* I have had to use my *intelligence!*'

Jess took a step back and found herself pressed against the nearest of the immense bookshelves. She was sure she had never seen Emerald Greene so angry. 'Calm down, Em,' she muttered.

Emerald scowled and tapped her forehead. 'I am not a genius. I have had to work the mysteries out for myself. I watch for the invisible threads that bind this fragile life together, and sometimes, just sometimes, I see when they fray and break. *That is all!*' Narrowing her eyes, she hefted the book in both hands. 'So, do you want to try, if you think you are so clever?'

'Em, be careful with that - '

Emerald lobbed the book at her. 'Catch!'

Jess caught it.

Her right hand - the one which had touched the wraith - was seared with a harsh, burning cold unlike anything she had ever felt before. It ripped through the veins of her hand like liquid ice. As Jess stared in horror, she was sure she saw her hand draining of blood, turning alabaster-white as it reacted to whatever force was contained in the book.

Emerald snatched the book back, and the pain began to recede.

Shuddering, Jess rubbed her hand with her other sleeve, stared accusingly at her friend. 'You knew that was going to happen!'

'Yes!' Emerald's face was triumphant. 'So, do you doubt the book's power now?'

'No... no, I suppose not.'

'And what about me? You doubt me?'

'I...' Jess heard her dry throat croaking, aware that no words were coming out. 'I know you're not perfect.'

Emerald's face broke into a broad grin. 'Excellent!' she exclaimed. 'Anyway...' She glanced at the book. 'I think I have the basis of the proper realignment spectrum. It's just a matter of calibrating the interface... should be possible.'

'What should be possible?'

'Sealing the door to the Otherworld,' said Emerald grimly, 'and sending them all back where they came from.'

Even from here, Richie could feel the intense heat. A pungent smell permeated the air, hot and metallic.

There was a sudden bleeping noise from Mr Courtney's wristwatch. He frowned, stared at it for a second.

'But I set that to sound if...' His eyes widened in horror. 'Get down! *Down!*'

Richie ducked behind the car door, feeling his knees squelch on the wet ground. An instant later, there was a booming, screeching noise like the eruption of a thousand fireworks. The smell of burning earth filled Richie's nostrils. He peeked out from behind his hands, and his eyes widened in horror at what he saw.

The wire barrier was starting to fragment.

It burned like cotton-wool. A hole was appearing in it, glowing whitish-blue as if some kind of cutting equipment were slicing its way through the barrier. Richie could feel the heat, and after a second or two the brightness was too much to look at.

'Sir!' called Mr Odell in desperation.

Mr Courtney was already there. 'I can see it, Mr Odell. Any suggestions?'

'Power's up to max, sir.'

Richie looked from one to the other, and over to the two operatives squatting by the junction-boxes. 'Well, tell Max to whack it up a bit, whichever one he is.'

'Max-*imum*,' said Mr Odell long-sufferingly. 'Are you still here?' he added. 'Not got a home to go to?'

'Come on,' said Richie. 'You think I'm going home to tea and *Blue Peter* while this is happening?'

The screeching noise grew steadily in volume, as if the sounds of some animal in pain were on a looped tape. It echoed around and above them, like a whirlpool of sound.

'Where's it getting the extra energy from?' Mr Courtney growled. 'And where's your friend, eh? Vamoosed and left us in the lurch, like that spineless cretin Strickland!'

'Emerald wouldn't do that!' Richie exclaimed angrily, and to his own astonishment he actually gave Mr Courtney a hard shove.

Instantly, two operatives had their hands on his shoulders and were pulling him back through the mud, and Richie realised he might just have gone a little too far this time. He was dumped unceremoniously in the back of one of the cars, and peeped over the head-rest to see the bright, burning disc of blue flame had almost destroyed the structure of the wire-mesh fence.

'Come on, Emerald,' he murmured. 'Whatever you're doing, it had better be good...'

Jess felt a twinge in her hand again. She stared down at its whiteness, felt the cold grip her bones. She was thinking about Xanthë and her memories of the lost scents of woodland flowers, of distant sunsets and of old love.

She looked up, and met Emerald's cool, hard gaze.

'Tell me about Freygerd,' she said.

Emerald, consulting maps and charts, raised her eyebrows. 'She was an ancient Norse witch. A sorceress of terrible power, some would say inhuman power. When she was finally defeated in England, the Viking men did not dare give her a traditional funeral. They laid her in the ground. In an ancient, pagan place. Somewhere from thousands of years before.'

Jess's eyes widened. 'The stone circle.' She tutted. 'Em, how did you find all this out? I mean, I suppose some of it was in that Danish stuff? I spent about three hours on the Internet and that was all I got.'

Emerald smiled, and waved a hand at the stacks of books around them. 'Sometimes,' she said, 'the old ways are the best. Books, Jessica! Pamphlets, papers, journals, arcane writings, parish records and books!' She snorted. '*Internet*, indeed... And yes, she would have been fine in that hallowed ground for thousands more years, had it not been for the interfering Professor and his desire for fame.'

'But... look, she's dead? Right?'

Emerald Greene looked up, and in the dim light of the Library her pale, chiselled face was serious, almost frightening. Her green eyes, hard like gemstones, shone with mischief. 'Oh, you think so? What *is* death? We understand so little about it. Some say it is not the opposite of life, but just a passing to the other side of a very thin door, one which divides the two existences. A door which can be very easily broken. The Professor made the hole. Xanthë and the others, who are at best misguided and at worst malicious, almost enlarged it. And Freygerd, believe me, will come through it. Ready to unleash a terrible revenge on the world which killed her.'

Jess laughed, then folded her arms when she realised how hollow and false it sounded in the vaults of the Library. 'Em, you're not seriously talking about a Viking witch who's been dead for over a thousand years coming back to life and... killing people?'

Emerald Greene folded the map shut. 'Yes,' she said casually. 'Is that a problem?'

If Jess had ever doubted that Emerald was deadly serious, any doubt was cast aside now. 'And... and what you were saying about sending them all back where they came from. You mean like... casting a spell?'

'Of course not,' Emerald snapped. 'The application of an advanced, arcane branch of science, that is all...' She began pacing up and down and muttering. 'Evidently, they are using a wide-band sound transmission to stimulate the frequencies...' She looked up at Jess, raising her eyebrows. 'The singing, you see? It serves a purpose.' She tapped a fingernail against her teeth. 'I can distract them, but it would make it easier if I had a way of *jamming* the signal. Something oscillating on the same frequency.'

Jess seized on the first words she understood properly. 'Same frequency?' she repeated excitedly, her heart skipping a beat. The dark library seemed to fall utterly silent, as if even the skittering mice and insects and whatever other creatures lived here were holding their breath to listen. For a second, even the numbing pain in her hand was forgotten. 'So a recording of their voices would work? Like the one you made at the Darkwater?'

'Yes, well, that *would* have been ideal,' said Emerald Greene, scowling and folding her arms.

A slow, cunning smile spread across Jessica's face. She rummaged inside her coat pocket for a moment and pulled out a matt-black CD case, which she waved gleefully at Emerald Greene.

Emerald's astonishment was plain to see. She took the CD from Jess, flipped open the case and stared at the silver disc inside. 'Jessica Mathieson,' she murmured, 'it seems I under-estimated you.'

Jess shrugged. 'Yeah. You could say that.'

'So... what, if you do not mind my asking, did you give to our friend Mr Courtney?'

Jess grinned. '*Abba Gold*,' she said. 'All their greatest hits on one fabulous album.' She wrinkled her nose. 'I hope he's a fan,' she added as an afterthought.

'Jessica, you are *brilliant*! Now we have everything!' Emerald, her eyes shining, pocketed the CD, tucked the book under her arm and marched towards the great oak doors of the Library. She stopped, turned round when she realised Jess was not following. 'Well, come on!'

'Where?' Jess asked, confused.

'Back outside, of course!'

'But we're safe in here!' Jess wailed.

'Safe? Your *thinking* is too safe, Jessica Mathieson!' Emerald wagged a finger. 'Here, we are protected - but also powerless! Even I do not know how to make *this*,' Emerald hefted the book, 'work across the Chronostatic Barrier. Now, come on - we must go!'

Like a fountain of liquid light in slow motion, the blob of light grew - five, ten, twenty metres above the field, towering over them all. It was now a great, formless mass of swirling iridescence, swivelling this way and that as if searching for something to latch on to.

Richie got out of the car to take a closer look, opening his mouth in an O of wonderment.

The screeching grew louder still - it still sounded to Richie like the screams of a trapped, wounded animal, but now mixed with the sound of shearing metal. A hot wind howled, tearing Richie's glasses from his face and pulling his hair back. He clung on to the door of the car. On the other side, Mr Courtney was doing the same. Richie shot him a desperate look.

'Hang on, boy! *Hang on!*' Mr Courtney mouthed at him, struggling to get a hold on his radio.

The towering *thing* of light was growing bigger and bigger by the second, thrashing like a cat in a bag, crackling with raw energy. Richie was certain he could hear singing, now, the dark choir he had heard before. And it was getting louder.

'*What is it?*' Richie mouthed, scrabbling for his glasses. He found them hanging from his sleeve and replaced them on his nose.

Mr Courtney was issuing instructions into his radio. 'All units, fall back! Repeat, fall back!' He shot a quick glance at Richie.

Mr Odell was on the radio beside him. 'The Professor's Viking! Arossi says it's disappeared from the tomb!'

Richie stared open-mouthed at the thrashing tower of light. He tilted his head back to look at it, and his lenses reflected the luminescence.

And then he felt a hand on his shoulder.

Richie spun round, and his feet squelched in the mud.

It was Emerald Greene, sensibly clad in a cagoule and wellingtons. Anoushka was curled around her neck, his claws hanging on to her waterproof hood. Emerald was staring, transfixed, into the heart of the red maelstrom, and the ruby light gave her face an unearthly sheen.

'How did you get past my men?' Mr Courtney bellowed above the tumult.

She shot him a withering look. 'Easily. They see what they want to see.' Anoushka, meanwhile, arched his back and hissed at Mr Courtney, making him recoil. 'But I fear I may have miscalculated the parameters a little,' said Emerald worriedly, shading her eyes and looking up at the thrashing vortex of light.

'Mis-*what*?' Richie asked. 'You mean you got it wrong?'

'It has been drawing energy *from* the barrier,' said Emerald. 'I had not expected it to manifest itself so soon.' She took a deep breath. 'Never mind. Here goes, as I believe you say.'

She pulled out her blue glasses and put them on, and as Richie watched, they darkened from azure to aquamarine to a deep, velvety blue which was almost opaque.

Jess hurried forward, squelching in the mud. 'You all right?' she asked Richie.

'Yes, I'm fine - Jess, does Emerald know what she's doing?'

'I'm not entirely sure,' Jess admitted.

Emerald was looking past them, up and into the heart of the shining spectre, her high-cheekboned face pale and translucent, as if she was a ghost herself.

And she was walking forward, into the heart of the tumult.

Her unruly red hair streamed backwards in the hot wind, revealing her high forehead, where Richie could see a prominent blue vein throbbing as she frowned in concentration. She was holding an old book open in front of her, he noticed, the pages fluttering in the harsh gale.

Mr Courtney grabbed Jess and Richie by the shoulders and bundled them towards the cover of the undergrowth. 'Less of the touching reunions, kids - that *thing* is growing by the second!'

Richie twisted angrily and broke free. Jess gave Mr Courtney an angry push, and he overbalanced into the mud with a bellow of rage.

'Emerald!' Richie shouted, and tried to run back to help her - but he was stuck firmly in the muddy ground.

Emerald Greene, still with Anoushka clinging on to her neck, was holding the book in one hand and had the other hand out in front of her, palm flat. She was muttering some incomprehensible words. Richie wondered for a moment how he could hear the sounds above the bedlam, and then he realised that they were echoing in his head.

He looked fearfully around for Jess - yes, she was there. For some reason she seemed to be rubbing her right hand, furiously, as if it was chafing with cold.

And her eyes seemed strange - distant and unfocused.

'Oh, no,' he murmured. 'Jess...'

'Xanthë.'

Jess waded through darkness visible, running in slow-motion as she called the witch's name. Her feet felt as if they were dragging through treacle, just like in her dreams when she was running from unimaginable fiends.

'Xanthë, are you there?'

Nine columns of blue light blazed into being, forming a perfect circle around her. Nine witches, no longer leaning on their staffs, but holding them firmly like weapons.

They were young, unblemished and beautiful. They had lissom, unbroken limbs and flowing hair - of raven-black, of spun gold, of auburn. Xanthë stood there, tall and proud, her blue eyes glowing triumphantly. She looked to Jessica like a young woman of twenty-five or thirty. Her hair, so brilliantly gold it was almost alabaster-white, streamed behind her like coronas of the sun, framing high cheekbones and flawless skin, while her mouth was bright and broad, a stripe of lurid red across her face. Xanthë and all the witches around her seemed to glow from within, incandescent with new power and new energy.

'We are Becoming,' Xanthë said, as if in answer to an unspoken question from Jess. Her mouth did not move in time with the words - instead, it just hung open and a tongue of light blazed from between her red lips. Her eyes, too, shone like dazzling searchlights.

Jess held up a hand to shade her own eyes, not daring to look directly at the witch. 'You don't know what you're doing!' she snapped. 'This other force - the one you know as the Viking - it's using your powers for itself! It will just discard you when it's finished breaking through into the physical world!'

'Nonsense, Jessica. Together, we are magnificently powerful!'

'If you say so. I'm just trying to warn you, that's all!'

'Look at my face,' Xanthë commanded.

'No, it's wrong. I can't!'

'Jessica... Remember your mother.'

'My mother is dead!' Jess screamed angrily. '*My mother is dead!*'

'What barrier is death to an existence of eternity, beyond life, beyond death? To a life that transcends worlds now that the door has been opened?' Xanthë hissed in delight, and the sound was echoed around her by the other witches. 'I can *be* mother to you, child. I can be sister, companion or guardian angel. All you need is to join hands with us. Complete the circle.'

Xanthë's hand extended towards Jess. It was the same gesture as before, only this time the hand was slender and milky-white rather than blotched with the ravages of Time.

Jess felt the pain in her own hand growing stronger again. She suddenly realised that this pain was there because the hand was unlike the rest of her body, out of tune with it. She only had to join with Xanthë, complete what they had started, and it would be good, be whole again -

No! What was she thinking? Jess pulled her hand back as if she had been burnt. 'I won't do it!' she shouted, cowering in the centre of the circle. 'I won't!'

Xanthë towered over her. '*Give me your hand, child!*'

Jess sat up, still not daring to meet the gaze of the witch. She could feel the diamond-hard eyes searching her, trying to compel her to look up. She wrapped her cold hand tightly in the sleeve of her coat and shook her head.

'No,' she said. 'No! And I've just realised something. You *need* me, don't you? You always needed me - or someone like me. You need a tangible link to the Earthworld, otherwise you can't be sure your crossover will be stable!'

Xanthë hissed in anger.

The witches raised their staffs above their heads.

Nine towering, fearfully beautiful figures glowed in rage around the cowering form of Jessica Mathieson. Their mouths streamed with light and with their ancient song, now, which echoed its fearsome beauty through the invisible vaults of the Otherworld.

'That's why you had to break through into the school!' Jess shouted, covering her eyes. 'You were looking... searching for someone to use as a handle, a lever!'

And then, with a sudden snarl of rage, Xanthë grabbed Jessica's hand and hauled her upwards.

For an instant, their eyes locked and Jess stared deep into a face of fathomless, ancient and terrible beauty. The face was a composite of them all - of Xanthë, Róisín, Bethan, Martha, Lizabeth, Anne, Kathleen, Yseult, Alice.

And deep within the eyes, far beyond, dark and twisted with anger, was the face of another, a thing with the blackest hair and yellowing teeth and red-rimmed eyes, framed in the light of flickering candles.

Jessica's hand grew horribly, unbearably ice-cold.

'*Now, Emerald!*' she screamed. '*Now!*'

Richie heard Jess scream, '*Now, Emerald, now!*' and then he saw her collapse on to the muddy field, clutching her hand in pain.

'Jess! Jess, are you okay?' Richie ran to her, grabbed her arms and held her up.

The snarling maelstrom sizzled with power, lifting above the school, high into the night sky like a gigantic fountain of light. Richie was sure that he could see a twisted, angry face - the face of an enraged woman - flickering in the flames. All around them, rain was sizzling as it turned into steam.

The nine witches strode forward, their glowing staffs upraised in triumph.

In the dim light, Richie could only vaguely make out Emerald Greene. She appeared, to his astonishment, to be crawling across the front seats of Mr Courtney's Mercedes, trying to slide a CD into the car stereo.

A second later, a shockingly loud eruption of beautiful, terrifying music shook the car, the field around them and, Richie thought, his very bones as well. He suddenly realised what the sound was - the singing of the witches, amplified a hundredfold by the power of octophonic stereo. It sounded like a choir of a hundred, of a thousand, harmonious and yet discordant at the same time, the sound echoing off the wall of the school building and bouncing back at them. Louder than cars, then helicopters, than thunder, it made Richie's teeth shake and forced him and Jess to their knees, clamping their hands over their ears.

The effect was electrifying. The sounds slammed together above the school with an audible crunching noise, pushing and straining against one another like two huge wrestlers.

For what seemed like an eternity, a storm of light and sound raged above the school, like two titanic giants fighting for possession of the sky.

The ground shook. The school building was shaking, vibrating, its turrets shedding tiles like autumn leaves from trees, the remaining windows popping one by one like firecrackers, twisted showers of glass bursting out into the darkening sky.

Blue, strobing light flashed in the darkness. Richie, shading his eyes, thought he could see shapes again, like the flickering images in fire; half a face, the hint of a hand, a flash of a screaming mouth.

Jess and Richie clung to each other, watching in astonishment.

And then, slowly, the giant, thrashing mass of light began to shrink.

Professor Ulverston, running in darkness, knew he would only have the slimmest of windows to escape through.

There, ahead of him, he could see the circle of blue lights, like a child's bead bracelet cast adrift upon a dark stream. Ulverston gathered the last resolves of his energy. He loosened his tie, wiped the sweat from his brow and headed towards it.

Bigger and bigger the circle grew, until he could make out the nine individual points of light which formed it, eight of them swarming around the central one. As he glided closer the points became globes, and now he could see the shimmering figure of a witch trapped inside each one, all of them thrashing and screaming frantically.

All bar one. Alone, still and silent at the centre, Xanthë stood, her face impassive, her arms spread-eagled as if to embrace her fate.

'Things not going to plan, dear ladies?' he murmured. 'Don't say I didn't warn you!'

Then, he saw the gap. He hadn't known what he was looking for, but there it was - a slice of artificial light just beyond the circle, light which obviously came from elsewhere, cutting into the Otherworld like a sharp knife.

Light from the physical world.

Ulverston steadied himself, peering towards Xanthë's globe. He looked into her eyes and saw that they were dull, now, and that her skin was yellowing and drying. Wrinkles cut across her face. Her gold tresses were drying up like old flowers, crinkling and withering to strands of white.

She reached out a hand, and her aching, desperate eyes seemed to recognise him.

'*Ulllll -* '

He shook his head. 'I'm sorry,' he said.

He leapt for the gap, which was already starting to close. On the brink, feeling his body tugging as he was pulled back through, back into the world where he belonged, Professor Ulverston managed to turn back in slow-motion and to look.

' - *veeerrrrr* - '

Xanthë's hand brushed his. Tantalisingly close. The gap was closing around him now, pulling him through. He was sinking into the hole between the dimensions, disappearing into it like quicksand.

If he touched her hand again, he knew he could possibly have lost his chance for ever. She was screaming his name, and the syllables became stretched, warped through Time.

'- *stooooooooonnnnnnnnnne!*'

And Ulverston felt himself sinking rapidly now, as if through soft and enveloping water. The portal closed around him and his eyes were filled with darkness.

'I'm sorry,' he whispered, 'I belong back there, and you don't.'

The scream which echoed through the winds of Time was agonised, seemingly endless. Nine incandescent globes fell as if into an endless abyss, dwindling to nine points of light which shrank, shrank, shrank into the darkness until they were no more.

Down and down, the maelstrom dwindled.

Richie glimpsed Emerald standing right underneath the thing, pointing at it as she read from the book. An enraged bellowing and screeching, like the sound of an animal being put to death, echoed out across the field and through the Mere valley, up into the cloudy night sky. Jets of fire - one, two, three - sizzled like stray fireworks across the school field, cutting flaming furrows, turning rain into steam and exploding in showers of sparks. Fountains of earth shot upwards, and there was a horrible, pungent odour of burning earth and hot metal. Everyone ducked behind cars, helicopters and bushes.

One sizzling bolt of fire smashed straight into the windscreen of Mr Courtney's car, turning the glass to liquid in seconds, splattering the molten residue across the bonnet.

And still Emerald held her position, her hand held high, her red hair streaming out from behind her, as the amplified bedlam of the singing reached a crescendo -

And stopped.

There came a sound like a popping balloon, and then a great, echoing gurgle. The maelstrom gave one last, angry surge and then was sucked in on itself. It shrank like water down a plughole, swirling back into nothingness.

Then nothing. Stillness and silence, apart from the gentle fizz of the rain.

A second later, the axles snapped on Mr Courtney's Mercedes.

The car's chassis crashed down into the mud and the remaining windows burst, breaking into tiny cubes of glass which spewed out on to the mud like an avalanche of ice-crystals.

There was a loud, firm *thump* as Emerald Greene slammed shut the leather-bound copy of *Lore of Albion Guiding the Fullest History, Taming and Containment of Witches*. Then, she turned back to face her friends and let out a long, deep breath. As Jess and Richie watched, she lifted her finger, licked it once and chalked up an invisible mark in the air.

'*Yesssss!*' Richie exclaimed, punching the air.

Jess smiled weakly.

As the rain gently continued to hiss around them, Richie saw Jess pull her sleeve back, exposing her hand again. She gave her fingers an experimental flex and nodded to herself, as if happy.

Mr Courtney lifted his head from the mud, uncovered his ears and slowly picked himself up. He was staring in horror at the shattered husk which had once been his Government-issue black Mercedes.

'Mr Odell,' he said faintly.

'Yes, sir?' His right-hand man, re-adjusting his glasses and brushing himself down, appeared from the shelter of one of the other cars.

'Get the PM on the line. Tell her Situation X has been contained, and she'll have my full report in the morning.'

Mr Odell nodded, gave a grim smile. 'Right away, sir.'

'And Mr Odell?'

Mr Odell paused with the phone halfway to his ear. 'Yes, sir?'

'Please tell me,' said Mr Courtney, pointing shakily towards the wrecked Mercedes, 'that we had up-to-date insurance cover on that?'

Professor Ulverston awoke with a jolt, flat on his back in the dark.

He became aware that a light drizzle was falling on him, and a slow smile of recognition spread across his face. He was cold and hungry and he had a splitting headache, but he knew the taste of that rain all right - it was real rain, and more to the point, it was good old British rain.

Ulverston sat up and looked around, his wide and staring eyes getting used to the darkness. He blinked - and glimpsed on his retina an imprint of the witch as she spiralled away, away, down into the depths of despair. Calling his name.

He pulled a face and shook his head, trying to clear it of the image. 'Charming filly,' he muttered. 'But it would never have worked out.'

Grunting with the effort, he hauled himself to his feet. His limbs ached and his suit was spattered with rainwater. Blinking, he realised in astonishment that he had been deposited back beside the shore of the Darkwater. Just a few metres from him, a gentle drizzle spattered on the lake's surface, and water lapped gently against pebbles.

'Well, I never,' said the Professor, and he allowed himself a broad, satisfied grin. Stretching his aching limbs, he reached up to embrace the autumnal drizzle. 'I'm back,' he said, and then, spinning round with his arms held aloft, he threw back his head and laughed, shouting up at the stars. '*Professor Edwin Ulverston is back!*' he bellowed in delight. Then he took a deep breath, shook his aching head and cleared his throat. 'Time for a cup of tea,' he added, and, straightening his tie, he set off back towards Meresbury.

12

Resonances

'Hello, I'm Mike Devenish with Mike's Open Mike *on County TV, presented in association with* Chox *bars, the chewier and more chocolatey snack.*

'Well, before we go on, a little bit about tomorrow's programme. I'm afraid to say that tomorrow is the last in the present series of Mike's Open Mike. *We'll be, er, taking a break, to make way for the new interactive game-show* King of the Castle, *hosted by the lovely Vanessa Shaughnessy. Don't forget, though, that you'll still be able to catch me at 1.30 am, with the, ah, late news update. Mmm.*

'However, as it's our last show tomorrow - aaaaaah! - it will be a very special one indeed. I shall be talking to the Dean of Meresbury Cathedral, the Right Reverend Toby Walmsley, about supernatural phenomena - and I'll be welcoming back the famous Professor Edwin Ulverston. Yes, the famed archaeologist was, just a few weeks ago, missing and presumed dead - but, ah, the rumours of his death have been greatly exaggerated, haha. He is now, I understand, promoting his new series of lecture tours. A former sceptic of the paranormal, Professor Ulverston will be talking about the importance of understanding myths and legends when excavating the past. I'll look forward to that, I have to say...

'And we'll have music from It-Girl, *who'll be in the studio performing their new single* Boy, You Wind Me Up. *Smashing. Can't wait.'*

It was a clear November afternoon, and pale sunlight filtered through the stark trees. At Beeches Point, above the Darkwater, shadows lengthened on the forest paths and small animals scuttled for shelter.

Jess Mathieson was hurrying along the woodland path, crunching dried leaves underfoot and pausing to pick the occasional blackberry. She was dressed sensibly in a black woollen coat, roll-neck sweater, jeans and Caterpillar boots, and she was struggling to keep up with the long strides of Emerald Greene, who was marching ahead in her eternally-uncool cagoule and wellies.

'So,' Emerald said over her shoulder, 'Richie could not be here?'

'He's being kept in to finish his half-term project,' Jess said, indistinctly. 'I think his mum isn't very pleased at the moment. She sees me as a bad influence. Honestly - me, a bad influence! Aunt Gabi would love that. She thinks I'm so square you could put shelves up with me.' She chewed and swallowed the last of her blackberry.

'And how is your aunt?' Emerald asked.

'Oh, fine... she got over her nasty experience. Thanks for the pasta, by the way. I think she'd like to employ you!'

'A pleasure,' said Emerald.

Emerald, at Jess's request, had shown Gabi her culinary skills the previous evening. She had produced a beautiful Capricci Formaggio with a tomato and basil sauce and home-baked ciabatta bread, the success of which had made Gabi wonder about taking some cookery lessons. 'Honestly,' Gabi had said, 'you kids are so cosmopolitan. When I was your age, tinned ravioli was exotic.'

Jess caught up with her friend in the clearing. She took a deep breath of the peaty, ferny forest air. It was cold, refreshing and made her lips numb, but it reminded her she was alive.

Emerald, hands clasped behind her back, was patiently waiting, her eyes unblinking behind the blue lenses of her glasses. 'It sounds,' she said quietly, 'as if everything is more or less back to normal in Meresbury.'

'Yeah, you could say that. Well, what passes for normal round here.'

'That is good.' Emerald sighed, shook her head. 'I fear I almost made a terminal error in letting the Viking draw power from the barrier. Still, all is well. Freygerd showed her hand, and was defeated.'

Jess nodded. 'Look, Em... I've been meaning to say this before, but with everything else... We've really got to do something about the way you talk, you know.'

'There is something amiss with my accent?' Emerald Greene demanded.

'Not your accent, no, but...' How could she put it? Jess sat cross-legged on the forest floor and smiled up at her friend. 'Look, maybe you just need to chill out a bit.'

'Chill... out?' repeated Emerald Greene doubtfully.

'Mm. Chill out,' said Jessica. She put her thumbs and forefingers together and extended her arms, palms upward; then she tilted her head back and closed her eyes. 'Like this, twice a day. It's relaxation. Gabi taught me it.'

'I... need to learn this?' said Emerald Greene, peering down at her in consternation.

'Well, yeah!' Jess opened her eyes, let her arms fall by her sides and sighed. 'You do if you're going to settle in around here, Em.'

'Oh. I see,' said Emerald Greene, and for a second she looked away, guiltily.

'I remember the first time I came to this clearing,' Jess went on, leaning back and gazing up at the trees with their twisted branches and their fragments of yellowing leaves. 'It seemed so weird, seeing you vanish through the Barrier. Now, though...' She shook her head, smiling ruefully. 'Can you get used to weirdness?'

Emerald tilted her head on one side, in that way she had of appearing to listen for the answer. 'The definitions change,' she said quietly. 'The strange becomes normal. It is all part of being... attuned to the right wavelengths.'

'Well... thanks for tuning me in.' Jess tapped her forehead. 'I think I'm beginning to understand... Em, we did defeat them, didn't we?'

Emerald laughed, shrugged. She put her hands in the pockets of her cagoule and began to pace up and down, kicking the leaves up into flurries. 'We saw a fracture in the threads of Time and mended it,' she murmured. 'But Time is an ancient garment which easily becomes worn.' She swung round, and her eyes were wide and urgent. 'Eternal vigilance is the price you pay. You must always think, now. Think twice, three times.' She began walking round her in a circle. 'Whenever you see a grey shape out of the corner of your eye, or hear a sound that seems out of place, or hear a song you think you have heard somewhere before... all those unsettling experiences will start to take on new meaning.'

'Because...' Jess paused. What was the expression Emerald had used? 'Because I'm... Time-intuitive, right?'

'Of course. That is part of it.' Emerald stopped circling. 'How is the hand?' she asked.

Jess noticed that she sounded merely curious, rather than concerned. 'Um... still stings a bit,' she admitted, rubbing the back of her right hand. 'Aunt Gabi's worried. She thinks I might have rheumatism.'

'Tell her from me not to worry. It is not... *rheumatism*.' Emerald said the word almost with amusement. She squatted on her heels, faced her friend. 'Experiences change us, Jessica Mathieson. These past few weeks have seen unimaginable forces awakened in the Mere Valley - changes and disturbances not seen in this realm for centuries or more.'

Jess tried not to let herself be frightened by the chill in Emerald's voice. 'I know,' she said.

'We are all older now,' said Emerald Greene. 'Remember that.'

Jess, as usual, wasn't sure if she was meant to understand. 'Look, umm...' She stood up, brushing the leaves off her, and gestured towards the centre of the clearing. 'Are we going through the Barrier? Only you said you'd show me the swimming-pool, remember? I need to practise my backstroke. And I'd like to see the Librarian again to thank him for the book - oh, and Anoushka, if he can be dragged away from his mice.' Jess grinned. 'Yeah, I even miss the miserable moggy.'

Something, though, was wrong.

Emerald Greene straightened up, not looking her in the eye.

'I've... brought my own snacks,' Jess added hopefully, holding up a packet of dry roasted peanuts and a small bottle of Sprite. 'Salt, protein and glucose? For the... other side...' She let her voice tail off, words falling dead into the clearing like the crackling leaves around her feet. She swallowed hard, her throat suddenly tight and dry.

'Jessica,' said Emerald Greene, biting her lip and swivelling on one foot, 'please understand. I am not of this time, or of this place. My work is done here.'

'Done?' Jess felt her heart gripped by a strange, unexpected coldness. 'What do you mean, done?'

'I do not belong here,' said Emerald, with an apologetic shrug of her shoulders.

'But you can stay... Surely you can stay?'

'It is already decided. This morning, I programmed the Barrier to a delayed setting.' Emerald paused. 'In fifteen minutes, the link will automatically disconnect. This gateway will be gone forever, and I shall go with it.'

Jess opened her mouth and no sound came out.

She remembered how, years ago, Gabi had sat her down and told her - because she was old enough now to understand - what had actually happened to her mother and father. She had listened to the story, her mind reeling as detail after detail became clear, as image after image took shape in her mind. The story took on the pictures and the sounds it was to have for the next decade, for the rest of her life to come. Echoing down the years. And when Gabi had finished, Jess felt physically shattered, her every limb aching, as if the energy had been drained from her body in preparation for a new phase of her life.

She felt like that now. Her legs were giving way beneath her, the forest was blurring. All the new certainties in her life had suddenly been pulled away and replaced with a great, yawning chasm.

Eventually, Jess murmured, 'You brought me up here just to say goodbye.'

'Yes. I am afraid so.'

'You can't be going,' she whispered, her voice fracturing. 'You can't! I'm only just starting to understand the things you tell me!'

'I am sorry,' said Emerald. 'It is... better this way.'

'How?' Jessica demanded angrily. 'How is it better?'

'It was never intended that I should stay here. My presence in your school is already provoking... difficult questions. It is difficult to maintain a low profile while doing the research I need - '

'But you said you were... *displaced*? I thought that meant you'd washed up here and you were... well, stuck here?'

'I am Displaced, that is true. I cannot return down the path I came from. The Barrier has some flexibility, though. Anoushka has been experimenting. And I need to explore its capacity myself.' Emerald tilted her head on one side, in what Jess now saw as her oh-so-annoying way of looking mildly curious. 'My apologies. I thought you realised. I did not know you would be so upset.'

This couldn't be happening, Jess thought angrily. It just wasn't true. 'Damn it, Emerald, you're my friend!' She lowered her voice to a cracked whisper. 'You can't go.'

'I am... sorry?'

Jess bit her lip. She couldn't look at Emerald. She felt the hot, angry lump in her throat and knew that she was probably going to cry at any minute. 'I'll miss you,' Jess said.

Emerald Greene appeared to think for a moment, and then she smiled, as if she had realised something. 'I shall also miss you,' she said, nodding, and her voice carried an unexpected note of sadness.

Jess shook her head in incomprehension, flapped her arms as if unsure what to do with them. 'So... did you ever finish reading the *Encyclopaedia Britannica*?' she asked, her voice cracking.

'Yes!' said Emerald brightly. 'The final volume was especially interesting. Did you know that Zürich was the fifth member state to join the Swiss Confederation in 1351, but was expelled in 1440?' Emerald sighed. 'But X was a little thin. I got through that in about half an hour.'

Jess smiled sadly. 'You see, this is the kind of thing you say... It's just you. And I'm going to miss it. This can't be, Em... I thought we were going to be friends forever.'

Emerald Greene looked at her, smiled ruefully. 'Jessica,' she whispered. 'Nothing lasts forever.'

They hugged, briefly, under the grey autumn skies. Jess could not help herself now, and she felt the warm, dissolving sensation in her eyes and nose and mouth.

'Please don't go, Emerald,' she heard herself saying. '*Please don't go!*'

'I must,' said Emerald sadly, drawing back from her. 'Do not try to follow me.'

Then Emerald Greene turned, hiding her face, and walked away, across the leafy clearing towards the barrier, her slim shape blending into the forest so that she seemed almost like a ghost.

At the barrier, Emerald turned, lifted her hand.

Jess's eyes were awash, stinging. She could only raise her own hand in farewell as the cold, dark feeling of loss swept through her body.

There was a breeze, and a rustling of the leaves. When Jess blinked and looked again, her friend was gone, carried like distant birdsong on the wind, with no trace of her in the clearing to show that she had ever existed. And then it was over, and Jess had to turn away as the world dissolved in a hot stream of tears.

'Goodbye, Emerald,' she said softly.

She waited a full minute in the stillness of the clearing before she turned to go.

She was halfway down the hill to the bus-stop when she put her hand into her pocket, and encountered the cold, hard feeling of an object that should not have been there.

And when she drew her hand out of her pocket, she found it was grasping a silver omega-chain pendant, sparkling with the green of a single, inlaid emerald.

13

Echoes

'*Meresbury!*' said the authoritative voice of Mr Quentin Lancelot Courtney, commander of the Special Measures Division.

In a secret bunker somewhere beneath Charing Cross Station in central London, a group of about a hundred government officials sat in the dim orange light of a lecture hall, watching the screen in front of them. It showed the cobbled streets and gabled houses of a picturesque English city basking in the afternoon sunlight.

Mr Courtney strolled into the light of the picture and his dark suit was wrapped in the image for a second or two as he passed from one side to the other.

'Meresbury. A place to keep an eye on, ladies and gentlemen.'

Mr Courtney was holding a hand-held switch, and he punctuated his talk by clicking the button. He gave a brief history of the City of Meresbury, remarking on its medieval status as a confluence of trade routes and its tenacious survival during the Black Death. He outlined its key role in the English Civil War, its Victorian prosperity, and the recent battle to preserve its character in the heart of the country. Paintings, old maps and even a page of the Domesday Book were flashed up on the screen to illustrate his points. Having survived both World Wars and the modern town planners, he enthused, Meresbury was now an oasis of beauty in an England full of multiplying road-schemes and housing estates.

And then - just as the audience was beginning to grow slightly restless from the history lesson - Mr Courtney hit them with the ghost photograph.

It showed the precincts of Meresbury Cathedral at sunset. Long, black shadows lay on the paved Cathedral Close.

'Observe, ' he declaimed, 'this amateur photograph, taken at approximately 19:15 hours in the city centre. A warm autumn evening, the streets still full of people heading to pubs, restaurants and the theatre.'

He pressed the button again and the slide was replaced with a tighter close-up of the same image. The picture zoomed in on a blue car parked in front of the Cathedral doors.

'Luckily,' said Mr Courtney, 'we have been able to enhance and magnify the picture with the aid of the latest imaging software.'

He clicked the button again, and the frame had closed in on something else which could now be seen clearly hovering behind the car.

There were murmurs, now, from the seated company, and Mr Courtney allowed himself a brief smirk of triumph.

'We have, of course, had this photograph verified by independent expert sources,' Mr Courtney went on. 'All of them attest that it is genuine, and has not been tampered with in any way, shape or form.'

He gazed proudly at the picture. The shape hovering behind the car, and which was causing such interested murmurs among his audience, was ragged-edged and slightly blurred. It was, though, unmistakably that of a pretty, wide-eyed girl with light-brown hair, wearing a plain white dress and clutching a posy of flowers. Her clothes and hairstyle were Victorian in appearance and she was, at a guess, about fourteen or fifteen years old. She appeared to be staring directly out of the picture with a troubled gaze.

'A haunting?' said Mr Courtney carefully. 'An image resonance? Psychic disturbance? Call it what you will, but Meresbury is rich in them. In fact, it seems to have more incidents per square mile than previous English record-holders like the city of York, for example.' He smiled out at his audience. 'Interpret them how you will. The evidence is clearly there.'

The murmuring began again in the audience, and one or two people cleared their throats, perhaps in disapproval. Mr Courtney held up a hand for silence.

'Why, you may wonder,' he went on, 'should I be bothered about this one particular shot, taken one day in Meresbury, when I could furnish you with a dozen other, probably more impressive pictures of ghosts? I shall tell you why.' Mr Courtney paused for dramatic effect, swivelling on the spot as he surveyed his orange-lit audience. 'The reason, ladies and gentlemen, is that *I have seen this young woman before.*'

He clicked again. The screen now showed a group of present-day children gossiping at their school gates at the end of the afternoon.

Mr Courtney took an electronic pen from his lapel and used it to draw a white circle of light on the screen around the face of one of the pupils - a slim, pretty girl of around thirteen, with brownish hair and bright eyes.

It was her. A little younger, but unmistakably the same. She was the spectral girl from the previous slide.

There were subdued mutterings in the audience, which rapidly rose in volume to become an excited, inquisitive babble. Once again, Mr Courtney had to quell them with a raised hand.

'This picture,' he said, 'was taken during a recent incident which I and my colleague Mr Odell dealt with. A psychic disturbance, focused partially around a Meresbury secondary school.'

He pressed the button again and the slide was replaced by a close-up of the girl. Obviously unaware that she was being photographed, she was smiling. Her hair was blowing a little in the breeze and her eyes were narrowing slightly against the sunlight as she chatted with her friends.

'The girl exists - today, in this century,' said Mr Courtney quietly. 'And I have, as yet, no explanation for this particular confluence. I can only conclude that it is the resonance of a catastrophic event which has yet to occur.' He turned back towards the screen. 'This is why we will be keeping a close eye - a *very* close eye - on Miss Jessica Mathieson.'

On the screen, Jessica's face stared out into the lecture theatre, caught forever in that moment, blue eyes looking out with the carefree gaze of a girl who had no idea that she was being watched.

Watched for the past, and watched for the future.

Jessica's Diary

Christmas Day

Haven't written in this for a while. Thought I'd better update things.

Didn't really feel very Christmassy today. We went to church with our faces tingling and our breath cutting jets through the air, and I sat and listened to the words - shepherds abiding in the fields and angels from on high and people walking in darkness and seeing a great light, and all that - and I thought it all rang hollow. It's a good story, but it's just a story.

Some of it might be true, I don't know. If I can believe in witches and demons and sorceresses, then surely I could believe in angels and the Christchild? All part of the same thing. All a big, ongoing story that never ends, I told myself.

But then, as someone said once, nothing lasts forever.

Aunt Gabi is saying how next year is going to be good for us. She'll have finished her course and she'll get a proper job, and I'll have decided on my options and I'll be well on the way to GCSEs.

I suppose she's right. I need to get back to the real world.

Richie and I are still mates, but we don't really talk as much as we did. He seems a bit embarrassed to be seen around me and the other girls. I'm not sure why.

One thing worries me a bit - my hand has been hurting again, just a little. My palm tingles and I keep having to rub it. It's as if I've been handling a frozen leg of lamb, or crunching snow into a ball with my bare hands. It doesn't always feel like that, but sometimes it just bites, as if trying to remind me of something - and then goes away. It's like it's trying to speak to me.

Meresbury seems to have got back to normal. The stones are still roped off and nobody can go near them. As for the school, they claimed it had been a gas leak, and everybody swallowed the story. I can't believe how gullible people can be.

Oh, there was a wild fuss about old Ulverston returning, obviously. He appeared on County TV again and explained it all away by saying he'd been in a private hospital in France recovering from his injuries and didn't want anyone to know.

Apart from that, you'd think people walked around with their eyes shut, given how little the media have made of things. It's almost as if someone had silenced the TV and the papers. What's that Government thing - a D-notice? They can put one on almost any news item to suppress it.

The Special Measures guys packed up and left as soon as it was all over. I know that much. I saw them rolling up the cable outside the school and packing their equipment into plain white vans. Mr Courtney and Mr Odell were watching from a distance, but they didn't acknowledge me.

I'm sure I saw one of their cars pass along at the end of our street one morning, just before the end of term, but the windows were tinted and I couldn't see who was in it. They moved off pretty sharply when they saw me coming, anyway.

If I close my eyes, I can see her now. So clearly.

It's sunset in the forest. The sun is low behind the trees, swollen and orange and spreading its thick light as it sinks behind the hills. She's standing at the Chronostatic Barrier and she's looking back towards me. She seems troubled, as if there's something she has forgotten to say.

She turns, slightly, raises a hand. And then, a second later, she slips silently through, and there is one less shadow in the forest.

It is colder, now.

The sun has set, and I am alone.

While I've been writing, it's been getting darker outside and a few flakes of snow have been falling. They're gathering pace, now, flurries settling and coating the grass and the roofs.

People have retreated inside their houses and they've drawn the curtains. I can see Christmas lights twinkling in people's windows, and in the distance I can just make out the floodlit Cathedral, tall and proud beneath the snow.

Somewhere, there is no snow. Somewhere, just out of reach, there is a place called Rubicon House, a place where it is always summer and hot coffee is on the table.

And inside, there is a strange girl called Emerald Greene, a girl who sees the holes in reality and mends them, a girl who knows far more than she ever lets on - a girl who trusted me to be her friend.

The weather reports have been saying we're in for a hard winter.
Is this where it begins?

Lightning Source UK Ltd.
Milton Keynes UK
UKOW04f0449090118
315768UK00001B/14/P